MW00901881

Born Under Fire

RINA Z. NEIMAN

Copyright © 2018 Rina Z. Neiman

All rights reserved.

ISBN: 1986349144

ISBN-13: 978-1986349147

DEDICATION

To my mother, Shulamit Dubno Neiman (1928-1975)

CONTENTS

Chapter 1   1

Chapter 2   22

Chapter 3   39

Chapter 4   63

Chapter 5   84

Chapter 6   102

Chapter 7   127

Chapter 8   146

Chapter 9   155

Chapter 10   167

Chapter 11   183

Chapter 12   210

Chapter 13   224

Acknowledgments

This is a work of fiction. Names, characters, businesses, places, events, locales, and incidents are either the products of the author's imagination or used in a fictitious manner. Any resemblance to actual persons, living or dead, or actual events is purely coincidental.

This book features QR codes attached to certain audio and/or video clips to illustrate the music or historical content referenced. Their use is only intended to deepen the experience for the reader, if they choose. Links do not constitute endorsement by the author of the content or content provider.

To view the study guide, additional research sources, historical photos, and documentation visit the Born Under Fire website: https://www.bornunderfire.com/

Or scan here:

Chapter 1

Nazareth, British Mandate Palestine

February 1934

Shula stares into the rectangular iris of the baby goat's ice-blue eye. She is close; close enough to see the soft, white hairs that surround its pink nose. Watching it balance on the edge of the village well, she envies its grace. The animal nibbles on the vegetation springing out from between the bone-colored limestone. Scraping her knees on the rough surface, Shula grips the ledge tighter and inches forward.

She would show them. If her friend Mahmud could take care of a goat at age six, why couldn't she? They were the same age, same size and had the same curly brown hair. Her heart burst with love for this animal. She would care for it so well her mother would come crying to her with apologies when she saw what a good caretaker she would be.

"Shula! No! Get down!" Avraham yells. Flicking her eyes up she catches her older brother running down the hill, his white shirt flapping in the breeze. She turns back and, hand over hand, moves ahead. Her concentration focused, she no longer smells the scent of livestock and produce mixed with earth, nor can she hear the sounds surrounding her: men and women talking, laughing and arguing about the news of the village and the world beyond; British military trucks rumbling by, manned by soldiers under scarlet berets; and animals neighing, braying and grunting, their tin bells clinking and clanking as they wait their turn to quench their thirst.

"*Yallah*," she whispers. "Come on, *motek*. Please?" She scans the crowd, searching for her brother's white shirt among women dressed in indigo, large clay pots balanced atop their scarf-covered heads, and men, their long white *keffiyeh* billowing out behind them, leading camels, donkeys or goats in for a drink. No sign of him. She still has time.

Inching forward she twirls her fingers around a few blades of grass growing out from between the stones, and pulls. Bracing herself with one hand, she reaches forward with the other, holding the grass between the tips of her fingers. *Come on,* she thinks, *just one snuggle.*

The goat bleats, bows its head and edges towards her. Reaching out further to touch it, Shula loses her balance and falls.

She gasps. Icy water swallows her, enveloping her in darkness. Cold liquid enters her nose and fills her mouth. Her lungs burn, her pulse races. Light filters down from above.

She must take a breath.

Heart pumping, chest bursting, she pushes herself up towards the surface but her toes and fingers slip on the slick, green moss that covers the ancient stones encircling her. Looking down she sees no end to the blackness and tilts her face back up. She hears the muffled cries of the women surrounding the well.

I have to get up.

I have to get up!

Wavy fingers reach out to her from the light and grasp her shoulders. Suddenly, she is out of the water sputtering and choking, trying to get air back into her lungs. A hand delivers six hard slaps to her back. Liquid spurts from her mouth onto the dry ground below. Her throat and nostrils burn. She coughs, then finds her voice.

"EEMA!!" She cries for her mother as hot tears burn paths down her frozen cheeks. It seems as if the whole population of Nazareth surrounds her but she can't find her mother in the sea of worried faces. She jerks her head around one way, then the other, her short brown curls spraying water this way and that. She smells the familiar scent of sumac as she brushes her cheek against the rough embroidery on the *thawb* worn by the woman holding her.

"Shula!"

Her brother and mother push through the crowd toward her. Rachel's soft brown hair falls out of a loose bun, fear on her face. Shula has never seen her mother look frightened.

"Eema!"

Shula falls into her mother's arms, shivering despite the heat. Squeezing her tight, Rachel kisses her daughter's wet cheeks, nose and forehead. She grasps the other woman's hand.

"*Shukran*," she says, thanking her. Shula looks at her savior and recognizes Mahmud's mother. Her dress is soaking wet. As she adjusts the striped *keffiyeh* surrounding her face, her worried look turns to relief.

"*Alhamdu Lilah!*" she clasps her hands and looks at the sky while saying the familiar prayer of gratitude.

"*Alhamdu Lilah!*" answer several onlookers. Shula peeks over at the crowd gathered around them — the concern on their faces replaced with smiles of relief or curiosity. She shuts her eyes and wraps her legs tight around her mother's waist.

"*Na'am.* Thanks be to God," Rachel replies. Shula feels a tug on her sleeve. She looks down to see Mahmud and the little white goat. He holds it out, and his mother motions for her to stroke its fur. She shrinks back and turns away. The mothers laugh. She closes her eyes. The overwhelming urge to hold that goat is gone.

"Patch!" Shula shouts as she slaps her hand on the tile floor of the house. She flicks her palm up towards the ceiling as five small mosaic stones land in her hand. "Ha!" she says, giving Avraham an insincere smile. "I win!" He sticks out his hand.

3

"Let's play again."

"I guess someone is feeling better," Rachel says as she sets the dinner table for four. "Put the Five Stones away and let me see your hands." The children run over and hold out their hands for her to examine. "Hmm. Did you clean those pieces after you dug them out of the ground?" Shula looks at her brother. He shrugs. "Your father will be home any minute. Go wash your hands. And after dinner, clean those rocks!"

Shula holds her hands out over the sink. Avraham scoops a ladle full of water from a bucket, pouring it over her hands. "They're not 'rocks,' Eema," she says. "They're ancient mosaic tesserae."

"Tesserae? Where did you learn that word?"

"The Monsignor, at the church. He yelled at us to stop digging up the tesserae." Rachel looks at Avraham with concern.

"Is that true?"

"Yes, Eema." he says, looking down at the ground.

"No taking rocks from the church! Do you hear me?" she admonishes them both, as the front door opens.

"*Erev Tov*, good evening!" With just his voice, her father's warmth fills the room.

"Abba!" Shula yells running into his open arms. She breathes in the mixture of tar and sweat that permeates him. Up close, she can see the dirt that fills the lines on his high forehead, outlines his long thin nose and makes his hazel eyes look brighter than usual.

"Guess what happened to me today?" Shula asks wriggling out of his embrace.

"What happened, *motek*? Tell me. Please," he says, untying his dust-covered boots.

"I almost died!" she says, folding her arms across her chest and shaking her head like her idol, Shirley Temple. She wishes her curls were longer.

4

"What?" her father looks over at Rachel, who bursts into tears. He crosses the small stone room in four strides and wraps his wife in his arms. "What happened, Rachel?" She wipes her eyes with a tea towel.

"She was playing on the edge of the well and fell in!" Avraham blurts out. "But Mahmud's mother saved her. She reached right into the water and pulled her out." He laughs and points at Shula. "She looked like a wet cat!"

"I did not look like a wet cat, and I wasn't playing! I was trying to give Mahmud's goat a piece of grass so I could hold it!" Shula says, realizing for the first time that she might be in trouble for breaking the rules. Yaakov kisses his wife's forehead and walks back over to Shula. He gets down on his knees, taking her hands in his own.

"Shulamit. You know the rules about playing near the well." The seriousness in his voice reflects the look in his eyes. She tries to free her hands to no avail. The heat from her cheek rises.

"Yes, Abba. I'm sorry." His frown turns to a smile and he envelops her in a hug. Taking in her father's smell — the dust, the tar, and the sweat — she squeezes him tight.

"Besides, the King of England doesn't like to lose pretty subjects like you." He picks her up and carries her to the sink.

"I am no king's subject," Rachel says, stirring the pot on the single burner next to them. "And I can assure you that George the Fifth doesn't care about our little Jewish settlements here in *Eretz Yisrael*."

"What are you talking about? The British Empire controls Jerusalem. The holiest city in the world! That is more precious than *any* jewel in his crowns, which I hear he has many," he says, turning back to Shula. "So, yes. King George cares about you."

"And so do your parents," her mother adds, dishing stew into soup bowls.

Perched on the stone counter, she watches as her father scrubs the day's dirt from his hands. The soap turning brown as he works it over his fingers. She fills the ladle with water, rinsing his hands clean.

"Abba?"

"Yes, dear?"

"Today at the well, when Eema was holding me after…" she bites her lip and looks up into the vaulted ceiling.

"Yes?"

"Mahmud's mother thanked *Allah*, Eema thanked *Eloheem* and the British soldier at the crossing called him Lord. Everyone was thanking God, right?"

"They were grateful to see you were safe."

"But I thought there was one God, not three." Yaakov chuckles and kisses her forehead.

"God is the same for everyone, Shulinka. It's what we call him that's different."

At the table, Yaakov pulls two jagged stones from his pocket.

"Here's a bit of a giant rock we broke up today." He hands one to each of the children. "Soon we'll have a proper road from Jerusalem to Tel Aviv and you will have a piece of it."

"Pieces of history!" Avraham says. Shula turns the stone in her hand then holds it up to her nose. She smells the scent of earth that covers her father each day. She decides to keep it with her for good luck.

"It can't happen soon enough for me," Rachel says. "Nazareth is nice, but I miss Tel Aviv."

"Ah, yes. The Garden City,"

"The *Jewish* city."

"My brother tells me our Jerusalem family wants us back."

"Yes, well, Jerusalem had me for a while, but my place is in Tel Aviv with my sisters. Among the Jews."

The following afternoon, Avraham bursts through the door waving an envelope.

"A telegram!"

"What do you mean, a telegram?" Rachel plucks it from his hand. Sliding her finger along the inside flap, she rips it open, pulling out a thin sheet of paper.

"What is it?" asks Shula. She isn't sure why her brother is so excited. She remembers a few months ago an envelope just like this one arrived. After reading it her mother burst into tears. She never knew why.

"It's a telegram! It's always important news when you see a telegram. So, *nu*? What does it say?" Avraham asks. Her mother smiles.

"Doda Leah and Doda Rivka are coming for *Shabbat*!" She beams at her children. "A proper Friday night Sabbath dinner with family. Now this makes me happy!" Sitting at the table, she begins to make a list.

"I need to air out the blankets and we'll need to buy some orange juice, you know how Leah loves her *Mitz Paz*! Oh, and I must remember to tell Bruria to bake an extra loaf of *challah* because with Rivka in the house one *challah* won't do. Oy vey! Friday is only two days away!"

Walking through the market the next day, Shula breathes in the spicy smell of *za'atar*; the pungent odor of cumin; the woody scent of nutmeg; the perfume of aniseed. Rachel points to the pyramids of brightly colored seeds and powders to make her choices. The man in the white turban nods, adding small brass weights to one side of his scale. After wrapping the items into paper bindles, he pats Shula's head.

"I heard what happened to you. Thank God you are well," he says and hands her a hard candy. She pops the bright red ball into her mouth, her thank you muffled by the treat. As they walk further into the market, the sound of an *oud*[1] coming from a small café draws her in. She stops in the doorway, mesmerized by the melody and the movement of the musician's fingers on the strings. As he cradles the body of the instrument on his lap, his singing follows the minor notes he plays. She watches until an exasperated Avraham pulls her away.

"We lost you to the music again!"

They pass a church, and a tall man wearing a large silver crucifix and long black tunic approaches them.

"*Gegrüßet seist du Maria, voll der Gnade,*" he says. Holding three fingers together, he moves his hand across his body right to left.

"What did the Monsignor say?" asks Shula as they walk away.

"He said, 'Hail Mary, full of grace.'"

"Who is Mary?"

"Mary? She was Jesus' mother."

"Who's Jesus?"

"Jesus?" her mother stops and rests her hand on Shula's shoulder. "Jesus is the cause of all of our problems."

"I thought that the Prophet Muhammad was the cause of all our problems," says Avraham. Shula looks from her brother to her mother. Rachel sighs.

"In Poland it was Jesus, but here in the Yishuv, it's Muhammad," she says. "But, Jesus or Muhammad, it doesn't really matter. The Jews always have problems."

Back home, Avraham lifts the violin to his chin and nods. Shula takes a breath and blows out the first few

---

1

8

measures of the song "Havah Nagila" on her recorder[2].

"There!" Rachel stops them. "You hear that, Shula? You were late coming in on the second measure — " She is interrupted by three raps on the door and a woman's voice from outside.

"Hello? Is anyone home?"

"But the telegram said they were coming tomorrow..." Rachel murmurs. Crossing the room, she adjusts her hair, then opens the door. "My Lord! What are you doing here?"

"Surprise! We decided to come up early!" her sister Leah replies, pushing her bag on ahead of her and sweeping past Rachel into the room. She wears her thick dark hair under a stylish straw hat. The pale peach ribbon trim on the brim matches the color of her long-sleeved, chiffon dress. Shula can't wait to touch the fabric, knowing that it will be smooth and silky. She rushes over to hug her aunt, smelling the Shalimar as she gets closer. But Leah stops her approach with one arm. Bending over, she kisses Shula on the cheek.

"No hugs today, *motek*. My arm has a bit of a booboo on it," she says wiping the bright red lipstick stain off Shula's cheek with her thumb. Shula smiles at her aunt, then breathes in the bergamot scent of her perfume and watches as the soft fabric of Leah's dress swirls around her legs as she twirls to face Rachel. Shula marvels at the hem and reaches down to touch the fabric with the tips of her fingers. It feels light and smooth, like whipped cream.

"Aren't you glad to see us?" Leah says, turning back to Rachel.

_____

2

"Of course, I'm glad to see you! Don't be silly, but your telegram said you would be arriving tomorrow!" she says ushering her youngest sister, Rivka, into the room.

"It was a last-minute decision, right Rivka?" says Leah revealing perfect finger waves under her hat. Shula runs over to her Aunt Rivka's open arms. Rivka wears a simple floral-patterned, dark green housedress and smells like the olive oil soap her own family uses. She notices that Rivka looks much more like her own mother then the glamorous Leah.

"Will you tell us a story tonight?" Shula asks.

"Oy vey! You little ones! Let me into the house first," Rivka says smiling widely. Avraham picks up their leather suitcases and carries them into the children's small bedroom with Shula on his heels. She picks up a small tin from her dresser, and races to join the sisters at the table, the contents rattling against the metal container as she runs. Settling onto her Aunt Rivka's lap, she listens to her brother answer questions about his newest obsession, flying airplanes. Handmade models and rudimentary sketches of his favorite planes have overtaken his side of their room. Losing patience, she flips open the top of the box and swirls her fingers around the buttons inside. There are small silver ones, large gold ones, glass buttons in red, blue, green and yellow, and iridescent mother-of-pearl buttons, some with two holes, some with four holes. Each one holds a story of her grandfather's adventures to exotic places around the world. She picks out a bright red Bakelite button and remembers his story of a snowy day in London with his friend, Mr. Williams. Of all the things she misses about Jerusalem, she misses her grandfather's presence the most.

"And what do we have here?" Rivka says into her ear.

"Sabbah Dubno gave them to me," she says holding up her treasure.

"Ah, Sabbah Dubno! How is your father-in-law these days?" Leah asks Rachel.

"We should all be as healthy at his age. The man never stops," she answers.

"And where has the button business taken him lately?"

"Let's see, the last trip was to London, Paris and Rome."

"And Venice!" Shula adds, holding up a bright green glass one.

"Yes, and Venice," Rachel says.

"Maybe he'll take me on his next trip? I could use a getaway," Leah says picking up a mother-of-pearl button, the silvery surface catching the light. Rachel brings five delicate glass cups filled with light brown liquid to the table, along with a plate of sliced lemons, sweet-meal biscuits and a silver bowl filled with sugar cubes. Avraham grabs one and sticks it in his mouth.

"Oh, Avraham, really!" Leah says. "I have much better sweets for you to eat." Reaching into her handbag, she pulls out two chocolate bars. Shula's eyes light up when she sees the thin rectangular shapes, then darken when she doesn't see the purple Cadbury wrappers. "These are some of the first chocolate bars from a new factory in Tel Aviv," Leah says, tearing the paper off a bar. "It's called *Shamnunit*, and it is delicious!" She hands everyone a small square. The morsel dissolves on Shula's tongue, the sweet creaminess overtaking her senses. "And for my poor darling sister, stuck in this backwater place, I brought — " she rummages some more, "a tin of Shemen olive oil and bar of soap." She places the items on the table.

"Thank you, *motek*," Rachel says. "But we can get Shemen products here in Nazareth. You don't happen to have a symphony orchestra in your bag, now, do you?" Rachel kisses the top of Leah's head and hugs her shoulders.

"Ay! Rachel! That hurts!" Leah snaps and moves from her grasp. Shula looks at her aunt in shock. Leah never raises her voice like that.

"What happened? What's going on?" Rachel says. Leah looks down, wrapping her arms around herself. Rivka looks away from her older sister's gaze.

"Tell her Leah," Rivka says.

"Tell me what?" Rachel asks then pulls the sleeve off Leah's shoulder. Shula gasps when she sees her aunt's bruised body.

"Are you okay, Doda Leah?" she asks and reaches out to touch the large blue and purple marks that cover her pale chest. Rachel pulls her away, sticks her hand in her apron pocket and hands Avraham a 5-mil coin. Shula sees his palm through the hole in the center of the small metal disc.

"Here's some money. Get five potatoes from the *shuk*," she says. Only Avraham is allowed to go to the market alone. Shula's shoulders slump. Then, Rachel grabs a net shopping bag and holds it out to her. She's never been to the market before with only her brother. She stands there, waiting for her mother to change her mind.

"*Nu*? Get going before the best ones are gone!" Rachel says. Shula smiles, grabs Avraham's hand and runs towards the door.

Once outside in the narrow alley, Avraham stops and peeks back in through the arched window.

"What's wrong with Doda Leah? Is she hurt? Why are they all so upset?" she asks, and feels both the need to pull him away and to look in herself.

"Don't worry, Shula," he says and starts up the hill. "Eema will take care of it."

Shula holds tight to Avraham's hand as they negotiate the labyrinth of streets in the market area. Scared of losing him, she doesn't let herself get distracted from the music coming from the cafés, and avoids Mahmud and his goat when she sees them heading toward the well. They stop in front of a Bedouin woman sitting on a multi-colored rag rug covered with produce. Her eyes are rimmed in thick black kohl and a beard of blue tattoos decorates her chin. Her indigo dress is embellished with intricate embroidery and a black *usaba* covers her head. Avraham asks her the price and begins to bargain. Standing off to the side, she's amazed at her brother's confidence.

"Pick out five," he tells her after his back and forth with the vendor. Squatting by the mound of potatoes, she turns each one, inspecting for wormholes like her mother taught her. Between each turn of the vegetable she glances at the woman's dress, finding small birds, flowers and harps woven throughout the maze of cross-stitched colors that make up the elaborate design.

"*Yallah*," the woman says, hurrying her along. Shula puts a sixth potato in the sack and stands up.

"*La! Hamseh!*" the woman shouts holding up five fingers. Avraham grabs the sack, handing one back to her.

"Say thank you," he whispers.

"*Shukran*," she mumbles. The woman nods her head, laughs and waves them away. Avraham grabs Shula's hand and, instead of turning towards home, pulls her deeper into the alleys of the market.

"Come on, I have a surprise for you!" He leads her down one passage and up another, until she is lost.

They come to a stop at a small, dimly lit, stonewalled café. Inside, under an ancient stone arch, four older men play *sheshbesh* around a low table, clacking the round playing pieces across the triangles on the board. Next to them, a man with a light grey turban sits and sucks on a long tube connected to an ornate brass and glass *hookah*. Thick, blue smoke streams from his nostrils, filling the room with its sweet smell. Avraham sits on a three-legged stool at a low table and pats the seat beside him. She sits. This place is like nothing she had ever seen before and yet her brother is so comfortable here. A young boy appears by their table.

"*Teneh sahlab!*" Avraham says holding up two fingers. The boy nods and returns a few minutes later with two bowls filled with a white cereal. She breathes in the steam rising from the bowl and catches the scents of rose and vanilla and something else she can't quite place.

"Your eyes are about to fall out of your head!" Avraham laughs.

"What is it?"

"Taste it! You'll like it," he answers as he brings the bowl to his mouth and takes a sip. "Aaaah!" he says licking his lips. Breathing in the perfumed steam, the tip of her tongue touches the white cereal. It tastes like flowers and cream. A tall man walks over and tousles her hair.

"So, what does Shirley Temple think? *Tayeem*?" he asks. Shula grins and nods. *Tayeem*. Delicious.

At dinner that evening, Leah is back to her vivacious self and regales the family with gossip from the front lines of the Tel Aviv cafés.

"And you know that fellow, oh, what's his name, the one that looks like a bulldog — "

"You mean Boaz Frankle?" says Rachel.

"Yes, yes! Boaz Frankle! A face only a mother could love! I hear he's going to move to that kibbutz, Ein Harod."

"Isn't that where they're sending all the *Yekkim*?" asks Yaakov.

"Yes! And speaking of those Germans! Oy! They are everywhere now! All you hear around town is German these days," Leah pauses to sip her juice. "They get all dressed up in their fancy clothes to sit in the cafés, just like they were back in Berlin, except it's Tel Aviv! So, it's hot and they sweat!"

"They say there are going to be more of them, what with that Hitler in power now," Rivka says.

"We thought we had it bad in Poland. Can you imagine living in Germany these days?" Rachel says. The room falls into silence.

"But are we safe here?" Rivka asks.

"What are you talking about?" Yaakov says. "We live in a peaceful place. You live in a peaceful place. No one is taking anything away from you because you are Jewish."

"No one's taking anything away from us yet," Rivka says. "Yaakov, the papers say that Arab, Musa Kazim, and his followers hate us. They want the Zionists out of the Yishuv."

"Yes, yes. They want the British out too. I'm not so worried about Kazim and his bunch. Let me tell you, I work with Arabs every day. They are my crew and my friends. I have broken bread with them in their homes. I know they want what you and I want — to work and live in peace."

"Let's hope so," Leah says. "Because I could never live in Poland again. Not after experiencing Tel Aviv."

Shula looks over at Leah and takes a sip of her drink, mimicking the way her aunt holds her pinkie out when she lifts her cup. Tel Aviv sounds so exciting. She imagines herself sitting at a beachfront café, sipping her juice and eating one of those giant layered cream-filled desserts she loves. She closes her eyes and feels the warm sun on her face, tastes the sweet acid of her drink and can even see the pastry's powdered sugar float down onto her lap.

After dinner, she climbs into her Aunt Rivka's arms.

"Doda Rivka! Tell us a story please!" she says.

"Not tonight, *motek*. I'm much too tired."

"But you always tell us a story!" she says, pulling Rivka's hand. Avraham pushes a chair over to the couch.

Placing her hand on her thighs, Rivka lifts herself up with a sigh.

"All right, *kinder*, you win," she says heaving herself into the chair. Avraham and Shula scramble onto the couch, heads at opposite ends, feet touching feet. Shula pulls the afghan up to her neck and leans back. Rivka moves her chair closer and looks over at her sisters talking at the table. Giving the children a conspiratorial look, she holds her finger to her lips.

"Shhh! I'm telling the children a story," she says. Leah and Rachel laugh but lower their voices nonetheless.

"Settle down now," Rivka says, grabbing their toes through the blanket and giving them a squeeze. "Do you know why you are so lucky?"

"Because Mahmud's mother pulled me out of the well!"

"Yes, my dear, that was lucky," said Rivka smiling. She leans in, her lips now a tight straight line. "Because, let me tell you, in Poland, they may have just let you drown. And all because you are a Jew!"

Shula stares at her aunt and pulls the covers up to her chin. Rivka's face has transformed. Her eyes shine and her cheeks flush with color.

"Once upon a time, very far away," she begins in a deep, strong voice.

"In Poland, right?" asks Avraham.

"Yes, *motek*, in the town of Rypin, where the freezing wind blows in winter chilling you to the bone!" She holds her arms around herself and shakes. "Long ago the town was inhabited by a hardy stock of peasants, and a small number of Jews. Life was fine in the town, the Jews and Christians, living together in harmony at times, and at other times, not so much." Shula knows the story well, anticipating the broken heart of the rabbi's son's jilted lover and her promise to poison the Jews of Shula's mother's hometown. But she still shivers when the girl is lured into the witch's hut deep in the woods, and she can't relax until the Jews are safe from the evil Witch of Rypin.

"But you don't have to worry about things like this anymore," Rivka says when she finishes the story. She grasps the children's toes wiggling their feet back forth. "You live in *Eretz Yisrael*. The Land of Israel. A home for Jews." She kisses them each on the head. "Now, only good dreams tonight."

"*Layla Tov*," Shula says.

"Good night," Avraham answers. Shula turns to face the couch back and snuggles into the cushions. She thinks of the strange place her parents came from, where it snows in winter and the houses are made of red bricks, not white stones, and you live in fear of your neighbors. She drifts off to the whispering of the women at the table, their teaspoons clinking against thin glass cups.

When Shula awakens the next morning, her mother and aunts are at the table, like they had been sitting there all night. Leah peers into a small silver mirror, painting her lips a deep burgundy. Her forest green dress makes her hazel eyes sparkle. A thin black leather belt surrounds her waist, and the colorful silk scarf around her neck hides any marks from view.

"*Boker Tov*," Shula says, then stretches and yawns.

"And a good morning to you too!" Leah says. "Hurry and get your clothing on. We're going shopping." Shula jumps off the couch. She loves shopping with Aunt Leah, who knows so much about style, fabrics and colors. "My little Shulinka needs a new dress, right girls?" She turns her head and looks at her sisters.

"Something 'feminine,' she said," Rivka says, looking at Rachel.

"Maybe one of those beautiful Russian dresses," Leah pauses for a moment. "Well, in any event, she needs something that will make her look like a girl since you

17

insist on keeping her hair so short." Leah throws Rachel a look.

"When you have children, my dear, you can keep their hair as long as you like," she answers.

Passing the vegetable stalls, Shula instinctively pinches her nose shut and breaths through her mouth to block out the smell of rotting food. Not until they arrive in the textile area does she breathe freely again. Their pace slows as Leah peruses the clothing hanging from the corrugated metal roofs of the shops that line the street.

"Hallo! Sheerlie Tempell!" Mahmud says. Shula spots her friend and two other children from the well. She notices that one girl has on a white cotton dress with colorful embroidery. She looks down at her simple khaki shirt. There's no pink, blue or red threads embellishing her outfit. She feels so plain.

"Over here! Let's look at these!" Leah says as she leads them over to a small storefront. She lifts her hand and flicks through the dresses hanging from above. "No, no, no. Oy, I don't think he has what I'm looking ..." She trails off as her eyes lock on the street. A stout man, his face bright red, marches ahead pulling a woman roughly by her arm. The woman looks embarrassed and frightened, the man angry and uncaring.

"Let's see what he has inside," Rachel says, pushing Leah into the shop.

Looking through the front door, Shula watches Rachel stroke Leah's back and whisper in her ear. She raises her eyes to the colorful canopy of dresses hanging over her head; still, nothing catches her fancy. Turning to the tables piled high with textiles, she is drawn to a stack of embroidered white dresses like the one the girl wears. She runs her fingers over the threads – pink, blue, orange, purple, yellow and green. Flowers and birds intertwine the vines that adorn the front and circle the neck. The stitching is smooth and shiny in some places, bumpy in others.

"It has all the colors of the rainbow!" she says. Aunt Rivka lifts the small white dress, turns it inside out and examines it.

"It's beautiful work. Very fine stitching," she says. Shaking it out, she holds it against Shula. "Looks like a perfect fit." Shula hugs the dress and dances around.

"I love this dress!" Shula runs to the shop. "This one, Doda Leah! I want this one!" Leah throws her a disapproving look.

"But, you'll look like a little Arab girl," she says. "Don't you like this one?" She holds up a pale pink chiffon dress.

"I am a little Arab girl, right Eema? I was born here, like them!" She points to Mahmud and his friends outside. Leah looks at Rachel and stifles a laugh.

"You are a *Sabra*. A new Jew born in *Eretz Yisrael*," Rachel tells her daughter, then faces Leah. "And if my daughter says she wants that dress, then that's the dress she gets. Bring it here," she motions for Shula to hand it to her.

"Thank you, Doda Leah."

"You're welcome my little *Sabra*," she says as she tousles Shula's curls. "At least it's a dress. We can get you something more stylish when you get to Tel Aviv."

"Oh, Doda Leah. I don't think I could find anything more stylish than this," she says over the sisters' giggles.

As night falls that Friday evening, Shula, her mother and aunts gather around the two silver candlesticks framed in the front window. Each one is over a foot high and covered with twisted vines laden with grapes. The heirlooms are among the few pieces her mother was able to bring with her when she left Poland, and she makes sure that they are clean and polished every week. Once, Shula asked her mother if they were a wedding gift, but her mother just laughed.

"A wedding gift?" Rachel said. "We got married on the beach in Tel Aviv. We all got the same gift. Sand in our shoes."

Hand in hand, Shula and her mother light the wicks. Then the women hold their hands toward the flames and draw them inward three times. They cover their eyes and recite the prayer:

"Blessed are You, Lord our God, King of the universe, who has sanctified us with His commandments, and commanded us to kindle the light of the Holy Sabbath."

The family take their seats at the table and her father says the blessings over the wine and the loaf of *challah*, signaling the start of the meal. Shula dunks her bread into the hot chicken broth and bites into the savory morsel. Following the soup, there is squab and potatoes and for dessert the chocolate *babka* cake that Rivka baked that afternoon. After dinner, Shula and Avraham fall asleep to the sounds of adults talking, and the last image Shula sees as her lids fall is Leah crying into a white napkin.

In the morning, her aunts pack for their return to Tel Aviv. After only three days, the scent of Shalimar now dominates the room. Leah tosses her lingerie into her suitcase, the silky garments spilling over themselves as they land. The short sleeves of her navy-blue dress leave her bruised arms on display.

"How'd you get that, Doda?" Shula asks, tamping down the desire to touch the sickly yellow marks.

"That? Oh, it's just something my husband gave me to remember him by," Leah answers, shrugging a light jacket over her arm while shoving the last few bits of clothing into her bag. Rachel walks in and shoos Shula out. Once in the hall, she flattens herself against the wall staying close enough to hear.

"You need to leave him, Leah, you have no other choice," her mother says. Leah answers her with a sigh.

"I've tried, *motek*, I've tried. But that man hunts me down and finds me every time. Ask Rivka. It's true, right?"

"He won't leave her alone, Rachel. We need you in Tel Aviv. We need your help," she says. Shula can hear her mother strip the sheets off the beds with quick sharp movements.

"With God's help, we will be there soon. This part of the road should be finished in a few months and we'll be able to move," Rachel replies. Shula hardly remembers Tel Aviv, but knows it is a place with white, boxy buildings and a beautiful beach on a deep blue sea. And, she will sit in cafés with her Aunt Leah and drink *Mitz Paz* to her heart's content. Smiling at this thought, she climbs up to the cupboard to get one more piece of chocolate.

Chapter 2

Nazareth, British Mandate Palestine

February 1934

This is a real privilege, Shula," Rachel says on a rare evening out. "The Monsignor only had a few extra tickets and your father was lucky to get two. One for me and one for you!" She pokes her daughter gently on the nose. Shula grabs her mother's hand, entwining their fingers as they walk down the darkening roads towards Nazareth's Annunciation Church.

Entering through the main doors, she slows to a stop. Tall columns line either side of the hall, dwarfing her. Six gold chandeliers hang from the vaulted ceiling, infusing the interior with a soft glow. She feels the tug of her mother's arm.

"Come on," Rachel says. "It's only a room."

Holding hands, they walk up the aisle toward a prominent dais dominated by a large cross and gold sunburst. At its center, a piano. Sliding into a polished wood pew, she smooths the fabric of her dress before sitting, and smiles when her patent leather shoes catch the light. Her mother hands her a piece of paper with a black and white image of a young man in a gray suit sitting at a piano. Rachel takes the paper back, folds it and puts it in her purse.

"For your scrapbook," she says and snaps the clasp shut.

The room quiets and the man from the paper takes the stage. His suit is mossy green, not grey like the photo. He bows to the audience and sits at the piano, lifts his hands and rests them on his lap. His eyes are closed. Shula looks across the aisle at a group of well-dressed women, light white kerchiefs covering their heads. Behind them, a row of British soldiers settle into a pew. The room is silent. The man takes a deep breath and lowers his hands to the keyboard.

The sound comes sharp and fast as his fingers jump from key to key, note to note. Up and down his hands flow, notes following hands, at times too fast to see. At points, he switches from attacking the keys like a hammer to moving his hands with such grace it's as if they are floating. The frantic melody covers the entire keyboard, causing him to cross his left hand over his right to reach the highest notes. She feels her own fingers twitch and it's like the music is controlling her, lifting her out of her seat. When he bangs out the last chord, Shula bursts into applause with the rest of the crowd. She never knew that music could make her feel this way.

"'Flight of the Bumblebee' by Rimsky-Korsakov. Piano arrangement by Rachmaninoff,"[3] Rachel says.

"That was about a bumblebee! I knew it! It sounded just like one! Eema! I want to play the piano!"

On the walk home, she pounds out music on an imaginary floating keyboard, and bows to some future audience. Standing on a low stone wall near their house, she practices an elaborate curtsy. Her mother claps.

"Brava!" she says. Shula bows then jumps down.

"Could I really play like that?" she asks. Rachel bends over, looking her in the eyes.

"With hard work, *motek*, you can do anything."

3

That night she dreams of pianos. In one dream, she is onstage before a large crowd. Her fingers fly across the keys just like the man in the church. When she finishes, the crowd roars their approval. She is elated. She wakes with a smile on her face.

Five days later, Shula sits on the stoop of their house. Her piano arrives today. She has no idea what it will look like, if it will be big or small, grand or upright. She fingers her imaginary keyboard, then stands when she notices a movement at the end of the street. Her heart flutters when she sees a piano, *her* piano, moving closer, bobbing up and down as if climbing the hill on its own volition. As it gets closer, she sees that under the heavy weight of the instrument is an older man, the piano tied to him with a series of ropes. He leans forward and methodically walks up the hill, beads of sweat running down his face from the *keffiyeh* that covers his head. Shula dances around the front door.

"It's here! It's here! Eema! Avraham! Come see!" she shouts. Rachel and Avraham rush outside and watch as the man and the piano draw closer.

"I better make sure the space is clean," Rachel says, stepping back into the house. Shula greets the man at the door, but he does not glance in her direction. She scoots past him and points to the empty spot by the wall.

"Here! Here! It's going here!" Step by slow step, the man makes his way to the wall, turns and bends his knees. As he straightens his back he lowers the piano to the ground. Once the piano touches the floor, the man unties the ropes that bind him, disrobing the piano. As he stretches his arms behind him, she hears the pop and crack of his shoulders and back. He wipes his face with a handkerchief and accepts a glass of water from her brother. Draining it, he wipes his lips and looks at Rachel. She reaches into her pocket and hands him the money.

24

"*Shukran,*" she says. He nods at her then leaves, without uttering a word.

"Lessons start tomorrow," Rachel says.

The next afternoon, Shula opens the door for a tall, somber-looking gentleman.

"I am here for the piano lesson," he says and reaches out to her. She hesitates for a moment, then takes his outstretched hand and gives it one good shake.

"I'm Shula," she says.

"Oh, Mr. Manevich, please come in," Rachel says from behind her and ushers him into the room. "I see you've met Shula," Mr. Manevich nods and motions towards the piano. Shula leads the way across the room, then sits on the hard, wooden bench. Her teacher slides down beside her. "Tea?" her mother asks.

"Yes, please. Two bags if you don't mind. One sugar and lemon." He places a book on the piano ledge and opens it to the first page. Inside the cover, she sees a photo of a well-dressed man, his hair slicked back just like her teacher.

"Who is that?"

Mr. Manevich pulls a red silk handkerchief from his front suit pocket and polishes his round gold spectacles.

"That, my dear, is Sergei Rachmaninoff. The greatest living pianist, conductor and composer of our day."

"Rachmaninoff! He arranged 'Flight of the Bumblebee' for piano. Teach me that one, please?"

"All in good time, my dear." He smiles and replaces the cloth with a flick of his wrist. "I'll tell you a story. It was November 11, 1928 and by some stroke of luck I was in Berlin the night he was to perform. A generous patron of mine gave me a ticket, although, believe you me, it was *I* who was grateful for this chance. Sitting in a box stage left, I had a wonderful view of his hands. You know about his hands, yes?" he says. Shula shakes her head. The picture gives no clues.

"Does he have an extra finger?"

"Ha! He might as well have! No, Sergei Rachmaninoff possesses the largest hands I have ever seen. And not only that, he can stretch his fingers from here," he says as he places his left pinkie on C and grunts as he tries to get his thumb to stretch to the higher G.

"Impossible for a normal man! And with my hands these days," he rubs his knuckles and she notices his gnarled fingers. "Ach, never mind me. And with his right hand he can stretch even further, a whole octave with the thumb under!" She tries to accomplish this feat and puts her second finger on D while attempting to reach her thumb under her hand to the next highest D eight keys away. The furthest she can reach is just two notes away. She frowns at her inability to master the stretch.

Her teacher's hands tremble as he sips from his glass of tea. It is a warm day, and she can't understand why he wears a suit and tie and drinks a steaming beverage, when she is melting into the wooden bench.

"Aren't you hot in that suit?" she asks before she can stop herself. Mr. Manevich whips out his red handkerchief and blots his upper lip.

"To dress one's best is of the utmost importance," he says. "You must always look your best, even if you don't feel your best. The feeling will come with the look." When he finishes, she nods like she understands what he is saying, even though, when she feels hot and tired she is pretty sure that she looks hot and tired too.

Mr. Manevich clears his throat.

"'Rhapsody on a Theme of Paganini op. 43.'[4] I have been studying Rachmaninoff's latest work."

"Do you still study? Even though you're a teacher?"

"I never stop, my dear." He interlaces his fingers, turns his palms out and cracks his knuckles. He hovers his fingertips just above the keys for a moment before he begins to play. Shula is amazed as she watches his fingers bounce up and down on the keys. Then all of a sudden, his hands are a blur, moving across the keys at lightning speed and hitting every note with precision and intent.

"Will I be as good as you one day?" she asks. Mr. Manevich looks down at his hands, and nods his head.

"With practice my dear, you can be greater."

Later, sitting on her father's lap, she examines his fingers. Palm to palm, she measures her hand to his.

"Piano playing fingers," he says. "My mother always wanted me to play but I never did." He holds her hand in his. "You have them too. Long and lean." She spreads out her fingers and looks at them.

"Come, Avraham. Your father and I have some news," Rachel says joining them at the table. Avraham sits. Her parents eye each other. They are about to tell them some important news. Butterflies rise up in her stomach.

"Children," her father says. "We have good news." Shula lets out a breath and smiles at her brother. "It looks like the work on this part of the road is ahead of schedule and the company wants us to move to Tel Aviv sooner than we thought-"

"When?" Avraham says knocking his chair over as he jumps up. Her parents laugh. A lump forms in her throat.

4

"Your mother and I thought we could go to Tel Aviv next week to look at apartments and celebrate Purim with our family. What do you think, Shulinka?" Her eyes fill with tears.

"We'll leave Nazareth?"

"Yes!" shouts Avraham. "We'll be in Tel Aviv!" She looks around at her family. They look so happy, but she doesn't know how to say what she needs to say without crying.

"But, my piano, and, and… what about Mr. Manevich? I don't want to stop playing the piano." She can feel the tears roll down her face and can do nothing to stop them.

"Oh *motek*," Yaakov says as he holds her closer. "Your piano will come with us."

"And Mr. Manevich?"

"We'll find a new Mr. Manevich in Tel Aviv. I promise," he kisses her on the head. Hopping from foot to foot, Avraham dances around the table.

"Purim in Tel Aviv! We'll get to see the Adloyada parade!"

"Wha…What's the Adloyada parade?" she asks through sniffles.

"Only the biggest Purim festival in the world! Thousands of people come into Tel Aviv to watch the parade. It's huge! I want to dress as Haman," he says referencing the villain from the Book of Esther celebrated on this holiday.

"I want to be Queen Esther!" Shula adds flushing with excitement, the tears gone. She loves dressing as the beautiful Jewish queen who saved the Jews of Persia from certain death. It is the one time of year her mother allows her to wear lipstick.

"Yes, yes. You can be the evil Haman and you can be Queen Esther. Lucky for us, your Doda Leah lives right on the parade route, so we'll have a great view," says

28

Yaakov. Shula watches her mother's bright face go dark, and hears her mutter.

"Unluckily, she lives with that good-for-nothing Meir." Just the mention of that ugly man causes Shula to shrink back into her father's embrace.

On Purim day, Shula looks through the wrought iron bars of her Aunt Leah's apartment terrace at the activity below. For the past few days, she watched in awe as the Adloyada parade workers built bleachers, hung banners and erected elaborate *Shushan* arches across the neighborhood streets. Last night, they strung lights in the trees along Allenby Street and when they tested them, she gasped as night turned to day.

"Shulinka! It's your turn," she hears Leah call from inside. Running into the apartment, she takes a seat at the small Formica table. Her ten-year-old cousin Miriam holds an ornate silver-handled mirror in her hand, admiring her peach-colored lips and rouged cheeks.

"Just like Carole Lombard," she says, air-kissing the mirror. "She's Vashti, remember. Make her look evil," she says, pointing to Shula.

"I don't want to look evil! I want to be Esther!" Disappointment wells up inside her at the thought of the wicked Queen from the Esther story.

"Your cousin Miriam is the oldest, so she gets to choose first, and she chose Esther," Leah says. "Besides, if there's no Vashti, there's no story. Don't worry *motek,* I'm going to give you a Mae West look," she flips through a magazine. "Here!" she says pointing to a picture of the platinum blonde actress. Holding Shula's chin, she moves her head to the right, then to the left. "No, you won't look evil. You will look beautiful *and* powerful."

Looking in the mirror after her makeover, Shula bats her lashes and smiles. She does look beautiful. Her eyes are dramatic, rimmed with dark kohl. Her teeth look extra white against the deep red of her lips. She grabs her aunt around the neck.

"Thank you," she says breathing in her Shalimar, this time smelling vanilla. Leah hugs her back.

"You're welcome. Now let's clean up before Meir gets here. You know he hates coming home to a messy house," she says, a slight trill in her voice. Shula helps return the cosmetics to a leather pouch, then runs into the small galley kitchen off the living room. She finds her mother and Aunt Sarah preparing food for the party. Sarah, two years younger than her older sister, wears a faded housedress and is makeup free.

"Eema, look at me!" she says.

"Oh! You look beautiful, my dear," her mother says, and Aunt Sarah smiles.

"You and Miriam are lucky to have your fashionable Doda Leah here to make you look like a movie star. Do you remember Rachel? In Rypin? The Rebbetzin?" Sarah begins to giggle. Rachel puts down her paring knife and turns to her sister.

"Do you remember the year she covered my face with some kind of white paint that cracked when it dried? Every time I smiled or raised my eyebrows, I could feel it crinkle and flake off." With the back of her hand, she wipes a lock of hair from her forehead. "And then it rained on the way home and the paint dripped down my chin onto my beautiful red dress. Oy! Mama was so mad." Sarah chuckles.

"I think we looked more like clowns than princesses," she adds, and the two burst into laughter.

"Shula!" Leah calls from the next room. "Time to put on your costume!"

After being cinched into an old dress of Leah's and fitted with a crown of flowers, Shula is ready to show off her Vashti outfit. She twirls across the living room, her feet gliding on the smooth tile floor. Miriam joins in, their

30

skirts flowing around them. Loud applause from the crowds outside draws Shula to the edge of the balcony. In every window and rooftop people are laughing and singing. In the street below men and woman link arms and dance the *horah*, their bodies creating whirlpools in the sea of humanity. A constant roar rises from the thousands of voices packing the streets. She can't imagine anything, let alone a giant float, getting through this mass of humans.

"When is it starting?" she asks. Avraham, dressed as Haman in a black three-pointed hat and sinister greasepaint mustache, folds his arms across his chest.

"Soon," he says. "I'm not moving and losing my spot, and you should do the same." Shading her eyes from the hot sun, Shula decides to arm herself with a cold drink.

Entering the apartment, she shivers despite the heat. The front door slams and the bark of a deep male voice hits her ears. As her eyes adjust to the shaded room, she sees her mother and aunts exchange worried glances. Her father and uncle stand up from their place on the couch, raising their eyebrows at each other.

"*Ahlan Wa Sahlan!*" Meir yells as he slams the door shut with a kick of his boot, his arms hugging a huge raffia covered wine jug that looks to be almost as tall as Shula. She wants to touch it but he makes her uneasy. She runs to her mother.

"*Ahlan beek!*" her parents reply.

"Ah! See? I told you Leah," he says as he pulls Leah towards him, his arm low on her back and kisses her on the lips. "Your sister and brother-in-law have learned something living with the Arabs. How to respond properly to a welcome in the local tongue." She watches as Leah throws her head back and laughs at her husband's comment. Too loudly, compared to her parents' subdued looks. Meir drops the large jug onto the table, then reaches into his pocket. He pulls out a small satin bag and slips a delicate silver necklace from inside. He holds it out to Leah. A filigree Star of David dangles from the chain. Leah gasps.

"Oh, Meir. It's beautiful," she says and holds it up. Meir takes it from her hand, undoes the clasp and fastens it around her neck. "Isn't it lovely, Rachel?" Leah says, moving towards her sister to show off her gift.

"Beautiful," Rachel agrees, and Shula sees the pride on Meir's face. Leah rushes back over to her husband and kisses him.

"*Chag Sameach*, my love. Happy holiday," she says. Meir and Leah kiss one, two, three times. Shula turns her head away. Since they arrived in Tel Aviv, her dislike for the short, stout man has grown. She can't stand the smell of the oil he uses to slick back his hair, and she hates it when he pulls her toward him and insists that she kiss his stubble-covered (and usually sweaty) cheek.

He shakes her father's and uncle's hands then turns to her. She pushes back into her mother's leg.

"*Chag Sameach*, little Shula," he says and suddenly she is whisked up into the air. He places her in the crook of his arm. She feels the sweat through his white button-down shirt. His sweet heavy cologne does little to mask his overpowering body odor and the stench of stale smoke. He kisses her and his rough stubble scratches her face. Worrying that he will mess up her makeup and hair, she pushes away. She tries to wriggle free of his thick arms but Meir holds her tight.

"Being native born, like me, makes you strong. Believe me. We are strong!" He says raising his fist in the air, and pumping up his bicep. "This is the real *Muscle Judean!*" Meir holds onto to her for another moment, his grip tight and firm. Her heart speeds up and then he kisses her again, laughs a sharp laugh and lets her go. She runs to her father. Wrapping her arm around his waist, she wipes the remains of his kiss off her cheek with her free hand. Leah puts her arm around her husband.

"It looks to me like someone started indulging in their Purim commandment a little early this year," she says as she eyes Meir. He shrugs off his jacket and holds it out to her.

"I couldn't bring a bottle of wine home without tasting it first! What would my guests think if I brought home what turns out to be vinegar? Then they couldn't get drunk like we are commanded. Tonight, it is our God given right! Correct?" Marching over to the small wood and glass cabinet, he pulls out six short thick glasses. He fills each glass with wine, right to the brim, then lifts his glass. "*Nu*? *Ad lo yadah* — tonight we drink until we no longer know!" The other adults each pick a glass off the table. "*L'Chaim!*" he says, his voice booming. He takes a long drink from his cup. The rest of the grownups hardly touch their wine. Meir puts his glass down with a bang. "Ah!" he says a satisfactory look on his face. "Now if you'll excuse me, I will get myself cleaned up from a day rubbing elbows with half of the Yishuv out there. Have you seen it? Every year you think it can't get bigger, but it does! They say we could have 50,000 people this year."

"It's starting! I can see Mayor Dizengoff on his horse!" Avraham yells. Shula runs to the sound of her brother's voice and the light streaming into the apartment. Squeezing in front of him, she pushes her face against the railing. A dozen Tel Aviv policemen on motorcycles slowly make their way down Allenby Street, followed by a British military marching band, their music drowned out by the gunning of the engines. As they get closer, she can see the band's uniforms are adorned with leopard skins.

"Look!" Avraham points down at the distinguished older gentleman on horseback wearing a wide-brimmed hat. "That's Dizengoff and Maheera!" The city's beloved mayor and his regal horse trot by. Shula waves at the famous man. Hearing a scuffle behind her, she looks up to see Meir push his way onto the balcony, his glass now filled with a milky white liquid. Leaning over her, he pats the top of her head. She smells the sharp scent of anise on his breath.

"Hey! Mayor Dizengoff! Up here!" he shouts, raising his glass in a salute to the mayor. Shula watches as the mayor looks up in their direction and gives a short wave. Meir sticks his fingers in his mouth and blasts out a high-pitched whistle, causing her to cover her ears. Then he bangs on the railing.

"DI-ZEN-GOFF! DI-ZEN-GOFF!" he shouts, waving his arm for others to take part in his cheer. Shula looks over at Avraham and, seeing him chant, feels safe to join in. Meir drains his glass, turns to leave, then stops, his grin now a grimace. She follows his gaze. A laughing Leah stands with her father. In two strides, Meir is by their side.

"What's going on, Meir? You don't look happy," Yaakov says, pulling back.

"What are you doing with my wife?"

"Doing? *Meir*! He's just telling me about Maheera," Leah says. Taking his arm, she guides him towards the door with one swift movement. "Did you know some say that Dizengoff loves that horse more than he loved his wife?"

"Yes? Is that what *he* told you?" he looks pointedly at Yaakov.

"No, *motek*, that's what the man at the stables told me!" she says and giggles. Meir softens and smiles. "Let's get you something else to drink, all right?" Taking his empty glass, Leah leads him inside. Rachel pats Shula on her back.

"What's wrong with Meir and Abba?" Shula asks.

"Nothing. Everything's fine," her mother says.

"Are we sure about that?" Yaakov asks. Rachel looks at her husband.

"As sure as we can be."

Turning back to the railing, Shula hears shouts for Queen Esther. She spies the young Yemenite girl, winner of the contest to be this year's Jewish Queen of Persia. She is beautiful, with smooth olive skin offset by burgundy lips, dark brown eyes outlined in black kohl, thicker and bolder than the lines encircling her own eyes. Framing the girl's face is an elaborate headdress of pearls, rhinestones and white feathers. Her neck and chest are covered with a multitude of silver chains onto which tiny bells are fastened. Her long-sleeved gold and white brocade tunic shimmers in the sunlight. Both wrists are encased in five thick silver filigreed bracelets. She waves and Shula spins the wooden noisemaker in her hand. The sound from her *gragger* adds to the deafening *tak-tak-tak* of hundreds of noisemakers clacking around her.

The parade stretches down Allenby Street as far as she can see. When the theme floats go by, she yells the names of the Twelve Tribes of Israel with the crowd: Reuben! Simeon! Judah! Issachar! Zebulun! Benjamin! Dan! Naphtali! Gad! Asher! Ephraim! Manasseh! Then comes the line of commercial floats: A Model T Ford piled high with cartons labeled Fresh Eggs, a bottle of orange juice the size of a man emblazoned with the Asis juice logo, a giant cow proclaiming *From the Land of Milk and Honey*, a chocolate brown Elite candy train, and a trio of large figures caught mid-stride wearing their A.G.B. suits. Each float is alive with people, music and decorations.

"Ah! Now we see the great Zionist economic dream! Fresh eggs and Agfa film! Is this what we're celebrating? I thought it was Purim!" Meir is back on the balcony, a full glass in his hand.

"Lord! Would you look at that!" Avraham says as he points to the street. Shula follows her brother's finger and sees a massive three-headed dragon protruding from the throng. The green monster is at least two stories high, and as it inches its way up the street the mammoth heads bob up and down as a man pulls the long ropes tied to its necks. The noise of the crowd grows louder as the creature moves towards them. The monster's bulging eyes and wide-open mouths scare her. "It's the Nazi Monster!" says Avraham and only then does she see the swastikas that cover the monster's back and adorn the uniform of the rider.

"What, no Hitler this year?" Meir says.

"Last year the Mandate's German ambassador complained that the Nazi float was insulting to Herr Chancellor," Yaakov says. Meir wobbles as he holds out a glass of clear liquid to Leah. She pours water from a small pitcher and the fluid turns white. Shula has never seen water turn to milk before. She will have to ask Avraham about it later.

"Insulting? That bastard?" Meir says and takes a long sip of his drink. He wipes his lips and some drops spill from his glass. The anise scent again. "That son of a bitch is not only making it hard for Jews in Germany, but now he makes it hard for us here! The Germans are flooding in and making it impossible for us to find work or homes — "

"But Meir, that's why we're here. So, the Jews will have a place to go when things get bad where they — " Yaakov starts.

"What? Where they live? But what about people like me? And my family? We've been here for generations! We never left. And now my sister can't afford to live in the neighborhood where we grew up. The rents are sky high and they say that things will only get more expensive." Meir drains his glass and looks into the bottom of his empty cup.

SPLAT! SPLAT! Raw eggs hit the giant. The driver pulls back on one long neck and then another. Egg yolk drips down the side of the beast and the roar of the crowd

36

grows louder. A darkness clouds her uncle's face. He palms the thick glass in his hand.

"That evil bastard," Meir says as he pulls his arm back to throw the glass. Leah reaches over, grabbing his arm.

"No Meir! Not glass! You can't throw glass —- " but Meir pushes her away. Losing her footing, she hits the wrought iron balcony. Her dress catches, ripping as she falls to the floor. Rachel and Yaakov rush to her side as Meir stalks back into the apartment, empty glass in hand.

Leah moves away from her sister when she tries to comfort her.

"I'm fine, Rachel. Really." Shula's parents exchange a look and it's clear that her father has had enough. Although there is no need, he tucks his shirt into his pants. Sticking his hand in his pocket, he extracts his handkerchief and hands it to Leah.

"Are you sure?" he asks. "Because we are leaving now." Leah dabs the cloth over her upper lip and hands it back to Yaakov. She is drawn, pale. Yaakov takes her hand. "You are welcome to come with us." He looks into her eyes, but she can't hold his gaze. Shrugging her shoulders, she looks out over the crowd. The monster has moved down the street, through the arch and towards the center of the festivities. She fingers the rip in her dress and sighs.

"I sh̶o̶u̶l̶d̶ ̶g̶o̶ change. I hope you stay," she says, entering t̶h̶e̶ flat.

"Avraham! Shula! Come! We are leaving," Yaakov says, sticking the handkerchief back in his pocket.

"But Abba! The parade isn't over yet — " Avraham stops when he sees his father's face. He stands up and straightens the three-pointed hat on his head. "Come on Shula. We'll get to see a lot of stuff outside too." She takes her brother's hand and joins her parents. Leah and Meir are nowhere in sight. Rachel hesitates at the door.

"I should say goodbye," she starts towards the bedroom, then stops. Yaakov puts his arm around her.

"Not now. Let's go."

Shula takes her father's hand and the four of them leave the apartment. They head down the smooth stone steps that lead to the packed street. When they get to the sidewalk, Yaakov picks her up and puts her on his shoulders. The view is spectacular. All around her celebrants cheer and dance. Moving through the thickest part of the crowd, the family finds a vendor selling *hamantashen* from a cart. Rachel hands Shula a three-pointed cookie and she breathes in the sweetness. Yaakov pats her leg.

"No crumbs on your father, all right?" Shula laughs and bites into her treat, letting the prune filling ooze into her mouth. The tension she felt in her aunt's house disappears. She lifts her arm and triumphantly swings her *gragger. Tak-tak-tak.*

Chapter 3

Tel Aviv, British Mandate Palestine

April 1936

Shula stands at the water's edge and watches as the sand flows out from between her toes with the gentle motion of the sea. To her right, Avraham builds a castle by dripping watery sand from his fingertips. Since moving from Nazareth to Tel Aviv two years ago, when she was six and her brother eight, spending Saturdays at the beach is her family's Sabbath ritual. She wiggles her toes in the warm water, burying them deeper in the soft sand. Her aunt Leah laughs and she turns to see her mother, father, aunts and uncles all sitting in a row, canvas beach chairs draped with striped or polka dot towels. There was hardly anyone here when they arrived this morning, but by mid-day the beach is crowded with bodies lined three or four rows deep.

She remembers when they first got to Tel Aviv, her family held hands and ran down to the shore, not even bothering to unpack. After a day spent riding in a hot truck sandwiched between her brother and a large wooden crate, she relished the cool water. She and Avraham jumped into incoming waves over and over, not caring that they were fully clothed. And by the time they walked back to their new apartment at 45 Melchett Street, they were dry.

Meir leans over and kisses his wife before relaxing back into his seat. It makes Shula uncomfortable that he chooses to wear the more daring swimming trunks, rather than the one-piece suits favored by her father and uncles. He is rude and crude and makes her aunt cry. For this she can never forgive him.

He lights a cigarette then holds the match out, shielding it from the slight breeze in the cup of his hand, leaning into Leah's waiting one. Sinking back into her beach chair, she breathes in the smoke then lets it out through her nostrils. She is beautiful in her stylish white bathing suit, an elegant parasol perched on her shoulder, and with her short wavy hair — she could be in a movie with Errol Flynn.

Shula's stomach rumbles and she trudges up the beach to her parents and the waiting food. Squeezing into the chair with her mother, she is careful not to bump Meir seated beside her. She feels Rachel's warm skin touch her own and points to the bag of oranges by the chair. Her mother puts an arm around her and hands her the fruit. As she digs her fingers into the hard peel, a fine mist squirts out from under her nails, landing on Meir's bronze stomach. Snapping his eyes open, he sits up, brushing the drops off of him.

"Look what you did, you stupid girl!" he yells. "Now I've got this sticky juice on me!" He grabs the orange from her and drops it onto the sand. Wiping his stomach with a towel, he pushes the orange deeper into the ground with his foot. Rachel is up in a flash.

"How dare you talk to my daughter that way!" she hisses at him. "It was an accident!"

"Well, she should be more careful! She's lucky this time I just threw the orange," he says, grabbing his towel. Rachel turns to Yaakov sitting in the next chair.

"How can you lie there when he treats your daughter like that?" she says. Yaakov glances towards Meir as he heads off toward the outdoor showers by the concrete walkway.

"It's over, Rachel. It's best not to make someone like that angrier than he already is." He leans back in his chair.

"I don't understand how you put up with that man," she says to Leah. Her sister looks out toward the Mediterranean, drags on her cigarette, then blows the smoke up into her parasol, a tiny wisp escaping from the top. Rachel settles back into her seat and pulls Shula close, reaching into the bag for another piece of fruit.

"We all can't be as perfect as you, my dear sister," Leah says. "We do the best we can, right, Shulinka?" Not knowing if she should answer or not, she bites into the sweet juicy orange instead.

The next morning, Shula sits at the piano working on Bach's Minuet in G^5. At her last lesson, her teacher, Mr. Brandt, taught her the ornamentations, and since then she has been going over them again and again. She loves the color they add to a phrase, but mastering the new fingering while keeping the tempo is a challenge. After sixty minutes of work, the C-B-C and B-C-B transitions smooth. Her mother shrugs on her sweater, the signal for Shula to place the sheet music inside her leather satchel.

"*Nu?* Avraham! Take it with you," Rachel says. He jumps up, pad and pencil in hand. Since falling in love with architecture this year, Avraham constantly sketches Tel Aviv's modern Bauhaus apartment buildings with their rounded balconies and box-like façades.

"You should walk down Rothschild today. You don't want to run into the funeral procession," Yaakov says, handing his wife her purse.

"Oy vey. That poor man," she answers clicking it shut.

"Whose funeral?" Shula asks. "Is it Dizengoff? Doda Rivka says he's in the hospital."

"Tfoo! Tfoo! God forbid! That's all we need. Mayor Dizengoff dying as the whole country goes mad!"

5

41

"It's the farmer's funeral. Israel Khazan," Avraham answers pushing out the door before her.

"Be careful," his father whispers to Rachel, kissing her cheek. Despite her parents' whisperings, Shula knows about the rash of killings and retribution murders that have taken place this month between Arabs and Jews. How could she miss the headlines screaming out from every corner newsstand: *Anger Over Death of Two Jewish Farmers! Arabs Attacked by Jews Near Petach Tikva!* She takes her mother's hand as they head south on Melchett, then east onto Rothschild Boulevard. Walking down the center of the expansive street, Shula reads the event posters plastered on the kiosks they pass, imagining her name, *Shulamit Dubno in Concert*, in large bold letters on one someday. At 84 Rothschild Avraham stops. They look up at the white four-story building with its sharp angles, rounded corners and protruding rectangular balconies.

"Jacob Rechter designed this building after returning from his studies in Paris in 1933," he says. "Do you know why it's revolutionary?"

"Why is that, *motek*?" Rachel asks beaming at her son.

"The columns, see?" He points to the thin concrete pillars that make the structure look like it is on stilts. "They create shade on the ground floor, plus they let the breeze blow around the building. He was the first architect to do this. Amazing, right?" Shula looks up at the massive building. She likes the clean look of the straight lines, the impossible concrete curves and the building's crisp white color against the deep blue sky.

They reach the old Neve Tzedek neighborhood where the narrow streets are lined with low-rise buildings. The usually busy market is quiet. Shop windows are boarded up and padlocks hang from locked gates. Missing too are the horse-drawn carriages, laden with everything from food to fabric to furnaces, that trundle by.

"Why is it so quiet?" she asks.

"They're on strike." Avraham answers.

"What's a strike?"

"A strike is when people refuse to work to protest something," Rachel answers.

"What are they protesting?"

"They want the British to do more to protect us from the Arabs."

"Why are the Arabs mad at us? It wasn't like that in Nazareth."

Glancing at her watch, Rachel stops and sighs.

"It was a different time. The *Yishuv Ha'Ivri* was small and Europe was not as dangerous for Jews. Do you know, when your father and I arrived in 1922 there were less than 100,000 of us here? Now, we are over half a million. And why? Because of Hitler! The Jews are leaving Germany in droves and coming here, to *Eretz Yisrael*. This makes the Arabs angry because they are afraid of losing their power. They complain, but the British won't stop the Jews from coming. So, now the Arabs are trying to scare us away." Taking Shula's hand, she heads down an alley, then stops short. A group of men run toward them.

"Revenge Against the Killers! Avenge the Death of the Jewish Farmers!" they yell. First one, then another push past her. Shula trips and falls.

"Eema!" she cries, her heart pounding. Her mother's grips her hand, pulling her out of the stream of furious humans. She sinks to her knees.

"Are you hurt?" Shula shakes her head. Rachel hugs her children. "Good. We're all safe. Let's go."

They reach her teacher's rooming house and step over the thin grey cat lying on the stoop. Climbing the dark stairway up to the second floor, she smells the lentils simmering on the small hotplate Isaak Brandt keeps in his room. Mr. Brandt is a true *yekke*, wearing wool and leather even on the hottest days, like so many of the German immigrants do. They reach the landing just as he opens the door, his white dress shirt open at the top and his ever-present brown tweed vest buttoned up. The blond boy with the round glasses and violin case is leaving as usual.

"Master Mosberg," Mr. Brandt calls after him. "Remember what I told you about the second section. Practice *Da Da da da* not *Da da Da da*!" The boy nods and smiles at Shula before slipping out the door.

"Come! Come! Look at this!" Mr. Brandt says gesturing for them to follow him to a small wooden table. He picks up his glasses and perches the delicate gold frames on his nose. He points to what looks like sheet music filled with an impossible amount of lines.

"What is it?" she asks.

"What is it? It's the score for the debut concert of the Palestine Symphony Orchestra," he replies as he points at a line. Rachel gasps.

"A Midsummer Night's Dream[6]!" she says.

"Yes! Yes! You see, this is what Maestro Toscanini will look at while we play. It shows all the instruments at the same time, here," he says as he draws his finger down the large paper. "This is what I will be playing. See? It says 'violin.'" As he talks, the jumble of notes and staffs begins to make sense. Each line is assigned to a different instrument. "You know, Toscanini and Huberman chose this piece by Mendelssohn because he was a Jew and that crazy Hitler has banned Jewish composers from German concert halls." He pauses and runs his hand through his thin brown hair. "Like a long-dead Jew could hurt the great German people. Ach," he removes his glasses and rubs his eyes. "That stupid Hitler! He doesn't understand he is erasing all the best talent in Germany because of his

---

6

44

hateful laws. What difference does it make if a Jew or a gentile is first violin? How well can you play? *That* should be the only question asked. Mark my words, when Hitler is finished, there won't be a Jew left working in Germany."

"They say things will be better for the Jews, now that the Olympics are shining a spotlight on the 'Fatherland,'" says Rachel.

"Yah, yah. What they don't say is how deep the hatred for the Jews is in Germany. This is not a new phenomenon. Once the pageantry is over things will get worse." He turns the pages of the score and sighs. "Soon the world will see that a world-class symphony can bloom in the desert!" He points to the small bed in the corner. "Avraham, make yourself comfortable. Mrs. Dubno? Please, have a seat," Avraham climbs onto the bed, spreading his sketchbook over his legs and pulls a pencil from behind his ear. Rachel takes a seat by his side. Shula sets up her sheet music and waits for her teacher. "Ready?" he says. Shula nods. "Good. Let's begin."

An hour later, after drilling the lower and upper mordents and the *apporratura* in the piece until smooth, Mr. Brandt is satisfied with her performance. He stretches his arms out and wiggles his fingers. Shula mimics his movements.

"Did you know," he says. "This piece is from the *Notebook for Anna Magdalena Bach*, which was a collection of music that Bach made for his wife. This particular piece was in fact not written by the great man, but by the lesser known Christian Petzold."

"Really?" Rachel says. "I always thought that Bach composed that piece."

"Yes, most people do," he says placing his hand on Shula's shoulder. "My dear, I believe you are ready for a recital, what do you think?" He turns to Avraham. "Do you think your sister is ready to perform in public next month?" Avraham looks up from his pad.

"One hundred percent," he says. Breaking into a huge smile Shula runs over to her mother.

"*Mazal Tov, motek*," she says kissing her daughter's forehead. "Let's go home and tell Abba."

Back on Melchett Street, Shula takes the stairs two at a time and bursts into the apartment.

"Abba! Abba! Guess what?" Her father, Leah and Aunt Rivka sit on the couch. Dropping her bag, she stands in front of them waiting for a response. Only then does she notice that Leah's eyes are puffy and red, her hands held tightly in Rivka's grasp. Uncertain how to proceed, she shifts from foot to foot.

"Yes, *motek*, what do you have to tell us? We could use some good news," Leah says taking her hand. Her neck is covered with bruises. Shula gasps, takes a step back, and bumps into Avraham. Hand on her shoulder, he pulls her away. She shrugs out from under him and stands her ground.

"Mr. Brandt wants me to perform at his next recital," she says, her excitement lost in the awkwardness of the situation. "That's all," she adds. Her father holds out his arms then squeezes her tight.

"That is wonderful news. I am so proud of you," he says kissing his daughter's forehead. Rachel taps him on the shoulder and he follows her to the kitchen. Leah pats her on the back.

"You will be fantastic, I just know it," she says. "And I'll be in the front row yelling 'brava' at the top of my lungs," she adds as she lifts a handkerchief to her eyes and begins to cry. Rivka puts an arm around her sister. Purple finger marks encircle her aunt's neck. Her parents whisper by the kitchen. Avraham rests his hand on her shoulder, and this time she lets herself be led to her room.

"Do you want to play some cards?" Avraham suggests. A suitcase lies on her bed.

"Whose valise is that?" she asks loud enough for her mother to hear.

"Your Doda Leah is staying over," she calls from the living room. "You'll sleep on the couch with your brother." Shula and Avraham look at each other.

"Is she all right?" she whispers.

"I don't know," he replies. "But I don't think so."

That evening, the low coffee table is covered with small plates of roasted sunflower seeds, olives, soft white cheese, hard crusted bread, jam, eggplant salad, diced tomatoes and cucumber salad and delicious but greasy *gribenes*. Aunt Sarah arrived with her raisin-stuffed *rugaleh* and Aunt Rivka slices up the apple strudel she brought. The sisters drink tea and snack. Sarah grabs a handful of sunflower seeds and begins to snap them open with her teeth one by one.

"We have a cousin up north near Rosh Pina who has a vineyard. You could move up there if you wanted to," she says.

"What am I going to do up there, in the middle of nowhere? I'm no grape picker, Sarahleh," Leah replies. The sisters catch each other's glance and look down at the table. "No, I think I should go back to Rypin and take care of Papa."

"But it's not safe in Poland, that's why we left. Look what's happening in Germany! Jews can only be safe here," Rachel says.

"Oh Rachel, I'm not worried about the Jew-haters there *or* the Jew-haters *here* for that matter. Have you not been following the murders in the papers?" says Leah.

"Yes, of course, but — "

"But nothing. Things are good in Rypin right now and Papa is alone and needs my help. Anyway, staying here is

47

not looking like an option for me," Leah adds as she rubs the marks on her neck. "In a few years, I'll come back. I promise. But right now, Meir swears he will kill me, and I believe him."

"You can't leave me, Leah, I need your help," Rivka whispers cradling her newborn baby girl. Leah picks up a dried date, fiddles with it, then puts it back down.

"I won't be much help to you dead," she says.

"Well, I think that this is all too soon, and you are in no shape to make these kinds of decisions," Sarah says. "After a good night's sleep, you'll see things differently. There are plenty of options for you here."

"Oh, I don't know about that," Leah replies. "I don't want to live anywhere else but Tel Aviv, and I can't stay here. I'm not the kind of person who derives any pleasure from working in the dirt and wearing khaki," she says as she smooths her dark blue cotton dress. "And where would I get my coffee? Do they even have cafés in Rosh Pina? My guess is not. Anyway, my mind is made up. Papa needs my help and I can't stay here."

"Well, at least wait until the morning before you make your final decision," says Rachel.

"Of course, my big sister, of course."

In the middle of the night, Shula wakes to a loud banging on their front door. She sits up and scoots down the couch to be near Avraham. They huddle together.

"What's going on?" she whispers.

"I don't know," he says. BANG! BANG! Her father crosses to the door. Then, Meir's voice. Loud and gruff. Frightening.

"Leah! Leah! Enough! Time to come home!" Meir bellows from the other side of the locked door. Yaakov looks over to Leah and Rachel standing by the bedroom door. He places his palm on the front door.

"Meir, it's three o'clock in the morning. Enough. You'll wake the neighborhood. We'll talk in the morning," he says. There is a moment of silence and then the banging begins again.

"Leah! I know you're in there! Come out now!" Meir says. Leah steps toward the closed door.

"No! Go away Meir. I'm not coming back!"

"How dare you! You are my wife!" BANG! BANG! Shula starts as Meir's fist hits the door again. Leah steps back.

"Take the children and lock yourselves in Shula's room," Yaakov says. Rachel motions for Shula and Avraham to come to her. She closes the door and turns the key, then stands by the door listening. Shula holds her breath and hears her father's calm voice.

"Meir, I'm going to open the door and we are going to walk downstairs and talk." The front door opens, there is a slight scuffle, then the door shuts. The faint sound of footsteps on the tile stairway are followed by the soft sound of male voices. Rachel opens the door and they run to the balcony. The two men stand in the street. Meir lights a cigarette and paces back and forth. Leaning over the balcony, Leah says:

"Go away, Meir! I'm not coming home with you!" Meir looks up and throws his cigarette to the ground. He points his finger at her.

"You're coming home! Now!" Yaakov steps towards him.

"Meir, it's the middle of the night. Let's talk about this in the morning, okay?" he says. Across the street, a window scrapes open. Mr. Schiffer sticks his bald head out.

"People! People! It's three o'clock in the morning. Some of us have to work in a few hours," he says.

"I'm sorry, Mr. Schiffer. My brother-in-law was just leaving," Yaakov replies.

"Meir! Go home! Have you no shame?" Mrs. Litvak yells from next door. The adult voices echo off the white buildings illuminated by the moonlight. A third voice joins the chorus.

"Shhhh! Quiet! Enough now!" the disembodied voice says. Yaakov looks at Meir and shrugs his shoulders.

"Meir. I'll bring Leah home tomorrow and we can all talk like human beings. Please, go home now and let the neighborhood rest," he says.

"Yes, listen to Yaakov," adds Mr. Schiffer. "Everything will look better in the light of day." Meir looks at the faces staring down at him from the open windows. His eyes fall on Leah. Shula shrinks back from the balcony's edge when she sees him look their way.

"I expect you home tomorrow by the time I get back from work. If not, I will drag you back by your hair, you hear me?" Leah looks down, at Meir then pulls herself back into the flat.

"Maybe if you weren't such a brute, your wife wouldn't run away from you," Mrs. Litvak says. Meir looks up at her.

"Maybe if you weren't so ugly, your husband wouldn't have died!" he shouts. Shula gasps as Mrs. Litvak slams her window down.

"You hear me? I can't see you but I know you can hear me! I'll expect to see you tomorrow, or I'll be back. And this time," he says pointing at Yaakov, "I won't leave without her." Shula peeks back over the balcony and watches as Meir stomps down the deserted street. Yaakov looks up at Mr. Schiffer.

"Sorry, Mr. Schiffer. You can go back to sleep now."

"Ha! At least I can try," Mr. Schiffer says as he closes the window.

Shula hears her father climb the steps and open the door of the apartment. She runs towards him and he picks her up in his arms. Yaakov rubs her back and she closes her eyes squeezing him tighter. He carries her into the bedroom where Leah and her mother sit. In her aunt's hands is a deep purple velvet bag with golden tassels. Shula wriggles out of her father's embrace and sits on her mother's lap. Yaakov leans against the doorjamb as Leah dumps the contents of the bag onto the bed. Shula gasps when she sees the riches displayed against her plain blue blanket. There are gold rings and earrings, and a pearl necklace she remembers seeing Leah wear last week. There is a small set of silver candlesticks and an intricately carved silver Kiddush cup, and the silver Star of David Meir gave her on Purim. It looks like a fortune to her. Leah picks up a ring and slips it onto her finger, then takes it off.

"Once I sell this, there will be enough here for me to book a passage all the way back to Rypin. I already looked into a ticket on a boat that leaves the day after tomorrow," she says looking down at the pile of precious metals. Rachel looks through the pieces and picks up a thick rose gold wedding band.

"This is Mama's," she says. "Are you sure you want to sell it?"

"If it will save my life, then yes. You saw him, Rachel. It's not going to get better, and if I stay anywhere in the Yishuv, he will find me and kill me. He's not sane. He's a madman. I have no choice. I have no choice," she says over and over again. Shula gets up from her mother's side and sits on Leah's lap. "Oh, my Shulinka. I will miss you so much."

"But you won't miss my recital, will you?"

"We'll see. We'll see," she says, tears falling down her cheeks.

"Come on you two, to bed!" Yaakov says motioning for them to leave the room. Back on the couch, Shula climbs under her afghan. Pushing her cold feet against

Avraham's warm legs, she falls asleep to the grownups' whispers.

The next morning, Shula wakes to Leah singing along to "Heyvenu Shalom Aleichem[7]" on the *Hebrew Hour* of the new Palestine Broadcasting Service. Jumping off the couch she dances the *horah* with her aunt until the song ends. She hopes that last night's nightmare-visit by Meir had all been just that, a bad dream. Maybe Leah decided not to leave after all. A man's voice begins to expound on the importance of the Hebrew language. Leah walks over to the radio and turns it off.

"Oy vey! It's too early to be preached at, don't you think? Okay, children, what would you like for breakfast this beautiful morning?" she says as she twirls around in her pale pink dress, the bruises around her neck hidden by a cream-colored scarf.

"Where's Eema?"

"Out running errands. My God! That woman never stops!" Leah says as she adds butter to the hot pan. "Avraham? Are you hungry?" Shula peeks out into the living room at her brother wrapped up in a sheet on the couch. "He'll get up when he smells the food. That's how boys are," Leah says, turning back to the eggs in the pan.

"So, Avraham, what are the plans for the day?" she asks as the three sit for breakfast.

"I have a Scouts meeting. We're learning how to build shelters for our overnight hike," he replies, straightening the green and white scarf around his collar. "And when you're old enough to join, you might even earn yourself

---

7

52

one of these," he leans over to Shula and holds out the pin attached to the pocket of his khaki shirt, teasing her with his smirk. Pulling away, she looks down at her eggs.

"Oh, don't look so sad, *motek*. Since Avraham is otherwise engaged, today, my dearest niece, we are going to shop for a new dress for your recital." Shula nods her head, her mouth full of eggs. "Something elegant, don't you think? I've been looking through some of the latest issues of *British Vogue* and I have some ideas, for your — "

"Doda Leah? Are you really going to go back to Poland?" Avraham blurts out. Shula stops chewing; the whole nightmarish scene with Meir floods back, making her sick to her stomach. She lowers her egg-filled fork. Leah sighs, then takes their hands in her own.

"Sometimes, my beloved children, life does not turn out the way we plan and we have to make the best decisions that we can in the moment." Trailing off, she looks out towards the balcony.

"But does that mean you are leaving us?" Shula asks, a slight panic in her voice. Leah holds out her arms and Shula climbs into her aunt's lap.

"One thing at a time, *motek*," she says as she hugs her close. "We'll see what today brings."

Walking the few blocks down Balfour, they make a right when they get to Allenby. Shula loves the tree-lined avenue with its glass-fronted boutiques, wide sidewalks, and the occasional car rumbling down its center. She feels proud to be with her beautiful aunt, the silk scarf around her neck flowing behind her, her hat cocked at just the right angle on her head. Bright red lipstick colors her lips, and her cheeks look blushed and healthy.

They stop in shop after shop, but nothing catches Leah's eye. A few times, Shula spots something she likes, but her aunt dismisses it with a curt response.

"Too blue," she says when she picks out a bright blue top or "With your hair so short, you'll look like a boy," when she picks out a sailor suit. "No, we have to find something that reflects your femininity and is stylish as well." Shula isn't sure what that means, but decides to trust her aunt. But, after walking up one side of Allenby then down the other, she begins to tire of the shopping expedition. All she wants is a cold drink, but Leah isn't satisfied with anything.

"Doda Leah, I'm hungry," she says for the tenth time.

"I know, *motek*, just one more store and then we'll get something to eat, okay? I promise. This place has the newest dresses from England and America. I'm sure we'll find something here," she says, dragging Shula into the next shop.

The clean and orderly space surprises her. It's not like the other shops with their tables piled high with fabrics and garments. This feels like a clothing sanctuary. Cardboard mannequins with painted faces line one wall, and racks of dresses hang on wooden dowels behind a long glass counter, out of reach to anyone but the proprietor. Of all the stores they have been to, this one intimidates Shula. Towards the back of the store she spots five cardboard mannequins that look like Shirley Temple. Drawn to them she touches the first dress. It is a pale green cotton and has a broad white collar and puffy short sleeves, just like one Shirley wore in last year's film *Curly Top*. Shula looks up at Leah standing beside her.

"You like it?" Leah asks.

"I love it!" Shula replies.

"Then let's get you to try it on." She turns to the storeowner. "Can we try this dress on? We are in a hurry. This little girl will die of starvation if I don't get something into her stomach soon!" The owner smiles and disappears into the back of the store. He returns with the dress in several different sizes. Leah helps her change behind a curtain. She tries on the first dress and it is a perfect fit. She twirls around the shop, looking at her reflection in the mirrors as she passes by. Then she stops. Her face falls.

"But, my shoes," she says, her eyes filling with tears. She looks down at her brown scuffed shoes and then over at the mannequins with their shiny white ones.

"Oh, sweetie, we can fix your shoes. We'll polish them up so bright that we'll have to shade our eyes when you walk into the room," Leah says.

"You can also buy the white shoes, if you want," the owner says as he brings out a pair of the exact shoes and places them on the counter.

Shula runs over to the counter and holds the shoes in her hands. She sees her reflection in the high gloss of the patent leather. She looks up at Leah.

"Please? *Doda*, please?" Leah looks into her purse and counts her money. She sighs and turns to the owner.

"Well, I was going to do this later, but I might as well do it now. Please hold the dress and shoes," she says as she hands him four coins. "We'll be back to get them soon." The shopkeeper nods and places the items behind the counter. "Come Shula, we'll get something to eat then run an errand and come back to pick up your new outfit. Thank you, sir. We will be back," Leah takes Shula's hand as they leave the shop and head south. Along the way, they stop and buy a sesame *bagele* and a *Mitz Paz*, eating as they walk.

Leah's joyful mood is now tempered. Holding her niece's hand in a slightly-too-tight grip, she pulls her along the narrow streets of Neve Tzedek. The *muezzin* sings the call to prayer from the minaret of Jaffa's mosque as they head down a small alleyway off Ahkva Street.

Stopping at a well-worn wooden door with a large bronze Star of David knocker, Leah bangs twice. A chair scrapes against a tile floor. Uneven footsteps approach, and the door swings open. An old man with wrinkled olive skin stands there, his corkscrew sidelocks hanging from under a striped turban. A thick white rope encircles the waist of the robe-like garment he wears. He motions for them to enter. A short old woman steps out of the narrow kitchen into the one-room space.

"Coffee or tea?" she asks Leah.

"Coffee, please."

"Come little one," the woman says and smiles at her, wrinkling her already wrinkled face. She hesitates, but Leah nudges her along, then takes a seat at a small table near the high rectangular windows. The surface is covered with gold and silver trinkets, candlesticks, rings, bracelets, wine goblets and menorahs.

"Let's make your mother a cup of coffee," the woman says as she steers Shula away from the living area.

"She's my aunt," Shula says. The woman's hair is covered by a blue cotton kerchief, which hangs down the back of her simple housedress.

"Oh, you have a pretty aunt, don't you?" she answers, filling a brass *feenjan* with water from a bucket. She pours a heaping teaspoon of powdery coffee and one of sugar into the wide-bottomed narrow-topped receptacle. Stirring the mixture with a silver spoon, she places the container on a small kerosene hot plate. "They say the best coffee is boiled seven times," she explains as they watch the small vessel. She puts two little porcelain cups into matching brass holders and places them on a brass tray engraved with an intricate pattern of vines and flowers. Shula looks back at her aunt, and watches as she pulls the velvet bag from her purse and pours the contents onto the table. She recognizes the gold ring that belonged to her grandmother, a silver *mezuzah*, several pairs of gold earrings, the small

56

silver candlesticks, an ornate *b'samim* box that once held fragrant cloves. The old man examines each piece with a large magnifying glass, then places it on a small scale and writes in his notebook.

"Ah! See? Now the coffee is boiling." The woman lifts the *feenjan* off the flame by its thin straight handle and lets it settle. "That was one, now we boil it again," she watches as it bubbles up again. "Come here, *motek*, count with me," she motions as she removes the coffee from the heat once more. Shula looks back at Leah and sees her dab her eyes with a handkerchief. "That's four, now you try," the woman wraps a cloth around the handle and holds Shula's hand as they count together. "Five," they say and lift the *feenjan* off the flame. "Six...and...seven! Wonderful! Now let's serve the coffee." She pours the thick brown liquid into the cups and brings the tray out into the main room.

Placing the tray on the table, she puts one cup in front of Leah and the other in front of her husband.

"When you are finished, I can read your fortune," she says pointing to the cup. Leah looks up at her and laughs a sharp laugh.

"My fortune is not very good, I'm afraid," she says, her voice low and gruff.

"Ah! You never know for sure," the woman answers and walks back toward the kitchen. Shula leans into her aunt. Leah pulls her close, lifting her onto her lap. Looking around the room she notices the small bookshelf filled with Hebrew books, the narrow bed in the corner, the few pictures on the walls, the peeling paint. The place looks old and worn, not like the Tel Aviv she is used to with its new white buildings, wide streets and parks. And this old couple with their old-fashioned clothes and withered faces match their surroundings perfectly.

The man finishes going through Leah's pieces and writes some numbers in his notebook. He circles the total and turns the book towards Leah. She looks at the figure and bites her lower lip.

"It's not enough," she says.

"It's what it's worth, madam," he answers.

Leah looked down at her hands and twists her thick gold wedding band. She pulls it off and hands it to him.

"How much for that?" she asks. The man looks at her for a moment and picks up the ring. He weighs it and makes a note in his book. He turns it towards her once again.

"Are you sure?" he asks.

"I'm sure," Leah replies. Standing, he walks to the corner of the room, unlocking a double door cabinet with a key. The old woman takes his seat.

"Let me read your cup, please," she says. Leah gives a nervous laugh and hands her the small container. The woman removes the porcelain cup from the brass holder and slams it down on the tray. They jump at the suddenness of the gesture and the sharp sound of porcelain hitting metal. She turns the cup right side up and looks inside. The grounds now cover the whole interior, creating a brown and white pattern of streaks and clumps. The old woman turns it around and around in her hand and studies it for a long time. She looks up at Leah.

"You have troubles," she says. Leah shifts in her seat.

"Yes, but who doesn't?"

"You need to get away from your troubles," the old woman says. "But getting away might not be the way to a longer *or* happier life," she adds. The woman looks at the cup again then shakes her head and sighs. The old man returns and his wife leaves the table, taking the cups and tray with her. He counts the bills out onto the table. Shula has never seen that much money before. Leah scoops up the cash and stands.

"This," she says holding up the money, "this is what will get me away from my troubles! Thank you," she turns and bows to the man. He returns the gesture and walks them to the door.

"Good luck," he says. "and, may God go with you."

After picking up her new dress and shoes, Shula follows Leah to Dizengoff Street to meet her aunts at Café Noga. They pass a multitude of cafés with rows of seats facing the parade of pedestrians who watch the watchers. Walking by one favored by German immigrants, she admires their fancy outfits as they sip their drinks over white cloth-covered tables and feast on large pieces of flakey layer cakes.

The short walk drags on as Leah stops and talks to every single person she recognizes. Dragging her feet and hanging her head, Shula scrapes the tops of her shoes on the sidewalk.

"Enough, Shula, we're almost there," Leah says patting her back. "Go ahead, I see Sarah and Rivka at a table in the third row. Have them order me a coffee like I like it and a *Mitz Paz* for you." Shula races up the street to the café. Sarah holds out her hands and gives Shula a hug and a kiss on her cheek, leaving a red lipstick print. She rubs it off with her thumb, but it is quickly replaced by a kiss from Rivka.

"What does Leah want?" Sarah asks as she raises the paper menu signaling a waiter.

"Coffee like she likes it," Shula replies.

"Yes, coffee like she likes it. Lucky for her I am the keeper of this important information." She pauses before looking up at the waiter. "And a *Mitz Paz* for you?" Shula nods and plops down on the woven chair. A waiter brings their drinks just as Leah gets there.

"A snail could go faster than you today," Sarah says.

"I had a lot of people to say hello to," she says and sips her milky coffee. "Not to mention goodbye, right?" She sighs and looks down at her purse for a moment.

"Well, I got the money." She looks up at her sisters. Sarah looks at Rivka, who bursts into tears.

"I don't want you to go ——"

"Shh!" Leah says reaching for her hand. The table falls into silence, each sister looking down at her drink. Shula fidgets, uncomfortable with the somber mood.

"I got a new dress today!" she bursts out. The three sisters look at her with surprise.

"Really?" Sarah says. Leah breaks out of her trance and smiles at Shula.

"And new shoes, right?" she says as she holds up the gleaming white shoes. The women ooh and aah and Shula feels happy for a moment before her face falls. She turns to Aunt Leah.

"Doda Leah! If you're really leaving, then who's going to yell 'brava' at my recital?" Her eyes fill with tears before she can stop herself. Leah looks at her and holds out her arms. Shula crawls onto her aunt's lap and rests her head against the silk scarf, breathing in the Shalimar that lingers there.

"Oh, *motek*, we'll be there and we'll yell 'brava' as loud as we can, isn't that right, Rivka?" Sarah says.

"Of course," Rivka adds.

"What's happening here?" Rachel says from behind her. Jumping from Leah's lap, Shula grabs her mother around the waist. Leah sniffs, dabbing her nose with a handkerchief. She pulls the velvet bag, now folded flat, from her purse.

"We're all a little upset," Rivka says as she holds her baby girl over her shoulder. Rachel gives her daughter a squeeze. She looks over at Leah.

"Did you get the money?" she asks.

"Yes, I did. And I bought Shula shoes to go with her new dress," Leah adds and holds up the shoes still in her hand. "Did you see Meir?"

"It took more than an hour, but in the end, Yaakov and I convinced him that you needed another day and then we promised we'd bring you home," Rachel replies.

"Do you think he believed you?" Leah asks.

"Yaakov had to give him some money. But to keep that man away, I would have paid double," Rachel says as she pretends to spit on the floor.

"I still don't think you should go," says Rivka. "You could go to that kibbutz up north where Avigdor lives. You'd be safe there. They would protect you."

Leah leans toward Rivka and lowers her voice.

"You didn't see him. You didn't stare into his eyes. Look at me," she pulls the scarf away from her neck, revealing the handprints still visible around her neck. "He is going to kill me."

"You don't know that," Rivka says.

"Oh, yes I do. He tried to kill me once, but I got away. I might not make it next time." Leah sips her coffee. She drops her shoulders and sighs, as if crushed by a heavy burden. "If I stay here, I will live every moment in fear for as long as he lives. At least in Poland, I will be able to enjoy my life now *and* help papa. I promise, I will be back." For a moment, no one speaks.

"We worked so hard to get here. To the 'Promised Land!'" Sarah says.

"Well, there are dreams and there is life. Right now, I have to live my life." Leah takes a deep breath and sighs. "I will miss it so," she says, raising her face to the sunlight streaming through the trees. They each take a sip of their drinks.

"You know what I miss sometimes?" Rachel said. "That old woman, Masha the Pickle Lady. Every Thursday she would be at the market square and I would make sure to get one of her pickles. I haven't found one like it since we left Rypin." She looks at Leah. "Will you eat a pickle for me?" Leah laughs despite herself.

"Never mind the pickles, what I wouldn't give to have a *babka* made by Duved the Baker!" says Sarah. "Does anyone know if Dr. Bronz is still in Rypin?"

Leah sits back in her chair.

"So, it's real. I'm going back to Rypin. I never thought I would ever see that town again," she says gazing at the street. Shula sits up from the comfort of her mother's lap and turns towards her aunt. Leah holds out her arms and Shula falls into her embrace. "I will miss you the most, Shulinka. You will write to me often, yes?" Shula nods. "Good. And you listen to your mother and father, and practice piano a lot so you can come give a concert in Poland someday soon."

"And you'll come see me play?"

"I will be in the front row yelling 'brava,' my dear," Leah says as she presses her soft lips against Shula's warm forehead.

Chapter 4

Tel Aviv, British Mandate Palestine

September 9, 1940

"No, Abba! You're wrong!" Avraham yells. Shula's eyes widen when she hears the tone of her brother's voice.

"Avraham, there is no need to shout. We are having a discussion. You and I are not at war," her father says. "Besides, the British Mandate will never allow for a Palestinian Jewish battalion here." She breathes a sigh of relief. Hopefully, her father's calming tone means this argument will not escalate. Since Avraham turned fourteen he is like a different person, and looks like one too. Large red pimples pop up on his face and his body stinks. Lately, her brother is plain icky.

"But there was one in the Great War! Why not now? We want to defeat the Nazis more than anyone!"

"I know, I know. Believe me, they tried to recruit me in '21. But that was before the riots. It's only one year since the last fighting between Arabs and Jews. The British can't afford to anger the Arabs right now, and arming the Jews will reignite the fire. It's relatively quiet here in Palestine and they need to keep it that way. Maybe when the Germans stop this Blitz they will reconsider, that is, if London hasn't burned to the ground."

"You just don't understand," Avraham said, grabbing his book bag and heading to the door.

"Where do you think you're going?" Rachel asks.

"I'm going to Danny's to study. I'll be home in a couple of hours."

"You have two hours. Dinner is at 6:30."

"Fine," he says banging the door shut.

Her parents don't mind; her mother is back to her sewing and her father turns the page of his newspaper. Shula hasn't told anyone, but seeing her brother so agitated upsets her. She goes into her room and sits at the piano. She pulls out the Hanon exercise book and opens to the first page. Setting the metronome for 80 she syncs to the tick tock of the machine. One…two…three…begin[8].

Twenty minutes later the baby's cries interrupt her, breaking her concentration.

"Yisrael's awake!" Rachel yells from the kitchen. Shula pushes herself up from the piano.

Since his birth two years ago, she's been helping with her baby brother's care. Most days she doesn't mind, but sometimes she would rather not have to interrupt her piano practice, homework or letter writing with naps, baths and feedings.

She finds him sitting up in his crib, rubbing one eye with the back of his hand. He holds out his arms to her and she picks him up. Laying his head on her shoulder, he then rubs his face back and forth against her neck. Back in the kitchen, Rachel dries her hands and takes the baby in her arms.

"Get the tub ready while I feed him, Shula. Then you can give him a bath." Shula hurries to the bathroom and, taking the zinc tub out from under the sink, places it in the bathtub. She swirls the water around with her hand to make sure the hot and cold mix. As her mother enters the

8

room, Shula holds out her arms to take Yisrael when she loses her balance as the floor falls out from under her.

"Eema!" she cries grabbing the edge of the tub. A second blast knocks her to the floor. Glass rains down on them as the window bursts inwards. An invisible hand punches her body. Yisrael screams. Blood on his face. Eema! She tries to scream but she can't unclench her teeth. A high-pitched tone rips through her head causing a stabbing pain in her ears. Rachel screams at her but Shula can't hear what she's saying. Another bomb shakes the building, bringing her to her hands and knees. A wave of bathwater splashes across the floor, soaking her as she scrambles over to her mother.

"Yaakov!" Rachel screams. Shula barely hears her. Her father rushes into the room.

"Stay down! Stay down!" he yells and covers them with his body. Only then does she realize the blasts are receding.

"*Yallah*. Everyone up. We're getting out of here!" He grabs Yisrael in one arm and pulls his wife up with the other. Rachel stops. Tears stream down her face and the baby is crying. Shula can see her mother say Avraham and her father answering but all she hears is a loud ringing. Hurrying to the front door she is shocked at the damage to their home. Glass shards cover the floor in front of each window, books, chairs and knickknacks are scattered across the floor. Looking up she sees a long crack in the ceiling from one end of the room to the other. They leave footprints in the plaster dust covering their way. Yaakov jerks open the front door and ushers them down the stairs. They run into their neighbors, Ephraim and Esterka Horowitz, on the ground floor landing.

"Thank God you're safe," Esterka says hugging Shula and kissing Yisrael on the cheek.

"Yaakov! What the hell happened here?" Ephraim yells, and Shula hears him. The ringing is subsiding. They huddle by the wall of the Horowitzes' ground floor terrace. Bewildered, dust-covered neighbors from the surrounding apartment buildings fill the street. A black column of smoke rises in the distance; the smell of burning dust fills her nostrils. The buildings on the street look fine, until she notices that all the windows are gone, blown out by the blasts.

"Where's Avraham?" Esterka asks Rachel, who looks at Yaakov and bursts into tears.

"He's fine. He's at a friend's house studying. Once we know it's safe, I'll get him," Yaakov says as he puts his arm around his wife. A distant rattling silences the street. Worry covers the adults' faces. It makes her nervous. Her throat is dry.

"Do you know what is going on? Who's even bombing us?" someone asks.

"I bet it was those damn Italians. They've been dropping bombs on the Haifa port all summer," says Ephraim.

"But why drop bombs in this neighborhood?" cries Rachel. "It's families! With children!"

"They probably meant to hit the ports in Jaffa or Tel Aviv. This was a mistake," Yaakov says.

"A mistake?" shrieks a neighbor. "Dropping bombs on innocent civilians you call a *mistake*? We don't know where our Davidele is..."

"The damn British! They've got to let us form a battalion. We need to defend ourselves!" Ephraim shouts.

"Ephraim, even if they let us carry weapons, they will never give us planes. Besides, didn't you read that there was a dogfight over the Houses of Parliament today? The Brits are distracted with their own mortality," Yaakov replies.

Looking at her father's watch Shula sees that five minutes have passed since the first bomb fell. It seems like hours. A man runs by holding a bloody rag to his face. He stops, looks their way and collapses. Rachel hands Esterka the baby and runs to his side. Ripping off her apron, she tears it into strips.

"Ephraim! Come here and help me," she says, lifting the man's head while slapping him gently on the cheek. His eyes flutter open and he tries to sit. Rachel and Ephraim prop him up by the wall. She turns to her husband.

"Go find Avraham."

"I'm coming with you," Shula says blocking her father's path.

"No. You stay here with me," says Rachel.

A sudden panic grips her, her eyes fill with tears. "I'm the only one who knows where they might be if they're not at Danny's." She holds her father's gaze, willing him to let her accompany him.

"She'll be with me," he says. Rachel looks from her husband to her daughter.

"All right, but hurry back," she says.

Shula walks quickly up the street by her father's side, gripping his hand. Mr. Abramowitz, the owner of the corner shop on their street, grabs her father's arm, his eyes bugging out.

"We don't know where Amit is! Batya is going crazy with worry," he says, looking crazy with worry himself. Yaakov puts a hand on his shoulder.

"I'm sure he's fine. We're going to look for Avraham. I'll keep an eye out for him," he says and keeps walking.

"I see him! He's coming!" Batya yells from her balcony lookout. "Benny! See! He's right there!" Running towards his son, Mr. Abramowitz grabs him in a bear hug and holds him tight. After a moment, he pushes him away and slaps him on the side of his head.

"That's for scaring us half to death!"

The building at the end of their street was hit. Part of the roof and third floor balcony are gone. Where they once were, is now a gaping hole. Shula can see into what remains of the kitchen and through to the books in the living room. She stops and stares. Her father looks towards the building, then pulls her along.

"Let's go." They continue west, and all around them are people — injured on the ground, helping the wounded, shouting orders, amidst a constant din of ambulance sirens, human moans and cries. Making a left onto King George she sees Danny's mother hanging over their balcony, turning and turning the ring on her finger. She spots Shula and her father and waves at them.

"Where are they?"

"They're not with you?" Yaakov asks.

"No! Oy vey. I thought you had news." She looks up and down the street and twists her ring. Shula pulls on her father's arm.

"I know where they are, Abba."

"Where?"

"You promise you won't get mad?"

"*Motek*, nothing could make me mad at Avraham right now."

"They might be at the Esther Cinema."

They turn down Dizengoff Street to the main square. All around the central fountain bodies are laid out and being tended to. Men, women and children. Black plumes of smoke from the fires burning in the shanty town by the square cover the sky. Her hearing returns, but now she feels that her senses are under attack. Shading her eyes, she keeps her gaze on the pavement in front of her feet. She wishes she could cover her ears as well, not to mention hold her nose. She sees a crowd milling in front of the theater, and then sees her brother.

"Avraham!" she yells, and a minute later she is burrowing her head between her father and brother.

"Thank God. Thank God you're safe," Yaakov says into his son's hair. Avraham pulls away.

68

"I'm sorry, Abba. We were about to come home. Eema must be so worried." Avraham says.

"Eema wasn't the only one who worried. Listen, I want you to walk Danny home with Shula and then head straight to our house. I'm going to stay and help out." Yaakov pulls his hat out of his back pocket and rolls up the sleeves of his work shirt. "Do you understand?" He looks Avraham in the eye. They are almost the same height.

"I understand," her brother answers. "Come on, Danny. Let's go."

That night Shula comforts herself by sleeping on the couch with Avraham, toe-to-toe like when they were little. But sleep evades her. How can it be so quiet now when earlier it felt like the world was breaking apart?

"Avraham," she whispers after tossing and turning for hours.

"Hmmm…"

"Avraham, wake up. I can't sleep." Feet touching feet. She wiggles her toes against his foot and he answers her back with a touch of his own.

"I keep thinking about all those hurt people on the ground. Do you think they're all right?"

"I don't know. Some of them are probably fine, others aren't." Avraham shifts over, pulls the blanket up. She tries to sleep, but images of the injured people on the street keep her awake for hours.

At midnight, she falls asleep, only to wake two hours later not from nightmare but from severe stomach pains. She pulls her knees up to her chest, but it doesn't help. Feeling something in her underwear she slips her hand down and feels a wetness. Turning on the light she looks at her hand. Blood covers her fingers. She's been injured. Jumping off the couch she tiptoes to her parents' room.

"Eema," she whispers while shaking her mother's shoulder. Rachel sits up.

"What? What's happened?" she asks blinking away the sleep from her eyes.

"I've been injured."

"What? Where?" Rachel is fully awake now. Heat rises, flushing her face. She wants to tell her mother. She doesn't want her father or brother to wake.

"Come. I'll show you," she whispers leading her mother towards the bathroom. Once inside she pulls down her underwear.

"See, blood. My stomach is hurting. I must've got hit by some glass," she says pulling up her nightgown examining her stomach for puncture wounds. She looks up when she hears Rachel laugh. "Why are you laughing?" she says as her mother envelops her in a hug, kissing her head.

"Oh, *motek*, I'm sorry. I don't mean to laugh. It's just that with all this craziness, life goes on." She holds her daughter's face in her hands. "You are far from injured. You have started to menstruate, that's all. In fact, you are now a woman." She helps Shula off with her soiled underpants, washes her off with the handheld shower, and folds the cloth that she puts inside the menstrual pad harness Shula now has to wear. Rachel fills a hot water bottle and shows her daughter how to hold it over her belly to keep the pain at bay. When she is clean and dry, her mother gives her a long hug. Pulling back, she looks Shula in the eyes.

"I'm sorry I didn't prepare you better. I didn't start bleeding until I was fourteen. I thought I had another two years." She kisses her daughter on the forehead. "And do you know what my mother did when I started to bleed?" Shula shakes her head. "She slapped me! Hard! Across my cheek. Right here," She points to her face and rubs her cheek.

"Why did she do that?"

"Why? That's what I asked her. Why did you hit me, mama? And she said, because that's what my mother did. So, you know what I decided, right then and there?" She leans over and kisses Shula gently on each cheek. "I decided that I would never do that to my daughter, no matter what. We have enough *tsoris* in the world without adding unnecessarily to the bad times." Shula hugs her mother tight, then yawns. "Let's get you to bed, my big girl."

Exiting the bathroom, Shula starts towards the couch and her brother's warm feet, then stops and heads to her own room. *The world is changing, and so am I.*

The next morning, she wakes to the sound of the radio blasting through the apartment.

"Italian aircraft raided Tel Aviv and the adjoining area yesterday afternoon and dropped bombs indiscriminately far from any possible military objectives."

"For God's sake! For no reason, they dropped their bombs, as if there's ever a good reason," her mother says. Her parents must have been cleaning for the past few hours. The floor is free from plaster and glass, the books and knickknacks are back in their places. The only glaring difference is the lack of glass in the windows. "Ah, Shula. Good morning. How are you — "

"Quiet, Rachel. I want to hear," says Yaakov. He is carefully gluing pieces of a broken vase. He nods at Shula and puts a finger to his lips.

"Full details of the casualties are not yet available. But it is known that over fifty persons were killed, of which twenty-three were children. The majority of the victims were Jews. The Arab casualties in the village of Sumail included five children."

"Did you hear? Children!" Rachel says as Avraham walks out of the bathroom.

"Now do you believe that we should have a Jewish Brigade, Abba? The British did nothing to protect us."

"And what would you have done with your brigade to protect us from an air attack like that?"

"Maybe we couldn't prevent it, but we would have warned people. They weren't even looking — "

"You don't know that — "

"Shh..." says Rachel. "They are making an announcement about the funerals."

"At eleven o'clock this morning a caravan of trucks will leave the Balfour Municipal School and head to the Nahalat Yitzhak Cemetery where workers have been busy digging all night to prepare the grave sites. A ceremony will be held at the cemetery at noon today."

"That's it. Let's finish up and walk over to the school. Shula, come. I'll help you with your room."

As her mother sweeps up the bits of glass that were missed last evening, Shula arranges the photos and knickknacks that were knocked off her dresser. There is the photo of her grandfather in front of his house on Mekor Chaim street in Jerusalem. His frozen smile warming her heart. Picking up another frame, she sees the glass covering her favorite photo of her Aunt Leah is gone. Brushing the dust from the picture, she gives the photo a kiss. Since Hitler invaded Poland a year ago, they have had no communication from her aunt in Rypin. Rachel puts an arm around her and replaces Leah's picture onto the dresser.

"Oy, my baby sister. Who knows where it's safe in this world these days?"

"Does this mean the war is coming here too? I thought the war was in Europe."

"I don't know, *motek*. Let's hope they keep the fighting on their continent."

"Eema, do you think we'll hear from her soon?" Rachel picks up the photo of her sister.

"Once this terrible war is over. I'm sure we will. And before you know it she'll be leaving the scent of her Shalimar wherever she goes."

As they make the short walk to the school on Shprintsak Street, the streets fill with people, all heading in the same direction, like a parade. But unlike parades in the past, this crowd is somber and silent. On the way, she sees stores are open, the owners still putting items back in place on the shelves. They walk by a café where people sit amongst broken glass and rubble.

"Nothing stops some people from their coffee," her father quips, and she isn't sure if his comment is condescending or proud that these enjoyments return so fast after such devastation. Reaching the school, they find a spot by the wall that surrounds the yard. She stands on a concrete block to see over the crowd. A man's voice blasts over a loudspeaker.

"*Yitgaddal veyitqaddash shmeh rabba,*"

"*Be'alma di vra khir'uteh, veyamlikh malkhuteh,*" she mouths along with the words, hypnotized by the ancient Aramaic, the words similar to modern Hebrew yet foreign at the same time.

"*behayekhon unyomekhom, uvhaye dekhol bet Yisrael, be'agla ubisman qariv ve'imru Amen.*"

"Amen," she says along with the crowd. As Chief Rabbi Amiel continues with the *Kaddish*, the prayer for the dead, she counts nine trucks in the school yard, each one loaded with eight white shrouds. She can't believe that these are all bodies, people she may have seen on the street. Grieving families surround the trucks: mothers, fathers, sisters, brothers, in various stages of anguish. Jumping down from her ledge, she wraps her arms around her mother. She feels lucky to have her family around her, and moves her arm to embrace her father. Avraham leans into his father on the other side. She clings to her family until the final Amen is said.

The trucks start up, the sound of the diesel engines fill the courtyard and bounce off the walls of the buildings. British soldiers line the streets and hang off the vehicles, their pith-like rounded steel helmets punctuate the crowd of local residents flowing after the trucks. On the twenty-minute walk to the cemetery they are stopped over and over again by neighbors with news, mostly bad.

"Did you know Amnon Lipavsky?" asks a woman from next door.

"The one who works at the store on Sirkin and Bograshov?" her mother answers.

"Gone! Completely gone. The store, Amnon, all the people inside who were buying a loaf of bread on the way home from work. The Limeys should have warned us!"

"Is your family all right?"

"Yes, yes, thank God. And I see everyone in your house is accounted for." The woman reaches over and pinches Yisrael on the cheek.

"Avraham gave us a bit of a scare, but we found him at the Esther Cinema."

"Which is reopening already! Who could sit through a movie right now? In any event, everything should be good for you from now on."

"For you as well."

Crossing the bridge over the Ayalon river, Shula looks at the few boats out today. A man with a soft cap sits in a red wooden rowboat, the newspaper spread over his lap, a fishing rod in hand. Ripe figs peek out from between the large fig leaves on the shore. Her baby brother Yisrael is now asleep on his father's shoulder, his dark brown curls matted against his damp forehead. On the other side, they pass a man affixing a poster to a kiosk. The image contains a frightened woman holding a baby, running from a looming swastika. "Join the Army" it proclaims, in

English and Hebrew text under the British Coat of Arms. She shivers, as he paints the glue over the paper.

"Abba, look!" says Avraham pulling his father towards the sign. "The Brits are doing it! They are starting a Jewish Brigade!" Avraham throws his hand out and points to the crowds of people lining the streets. "Now, do you agree with me? Now you think there should be a Jewish Brigade?" Yaakov rubs his chin, then shifts the baby in his arms.

"The boy is right," the man says while gluing the poster to the post. "The Axis Powers must be defeated. You know, now they say that over 100 people were killed here. Fifty of them children!"

"They should all go to hell for killing children," Rachel says.

"Maybe when your son is old enough, he will join the fight, eh?" The man winks at Avraham.

"You bet. I'll be flying for the first Jewish Air Force!" Avraham grabs an imaginary gunner and rat-tat-tats at the sky.

As they get closer to the cemetery Shula grows nervous. The crowds are thick and she tries to keep her panic at bay. They walk by a truck as it idles in line to enter the cemetery. Up close she can see the shrouded shapes are human beings, and not only that, some by their size, she recognizes, are children. A lump grows in her throat and she pulls close to her mother and closes her eyes, blindly letting her guide her through the crowds. She opens her eyes when they near the cemetery entrance, the crowds so thick she can barely see the trucks as they pass through the gates. She sees her piano teacher, Mr. Brandt, blotting his eyes with a handkerchief. She pulls on her mother's arm and points in his direction.

"Mr. Brandt," Rachel says. He turns to them, his eyes bloodshot. Grabbing her hand, he kisses it, then breaks into tears.

"Did you lose someone?"

Mr. Brandt's lip trembles. "I lost a dear friend from Berlin and a dear, dear student." He turns to Shula and his eyes widen. "You know him! He's the boy that comes before you on Thursdays. Remember? He carries a violin. A blond with glasses?" Shula shrinks back into her mother again. She doesn't know anyone who has died, she can't know. But then she remembers walking past him on the stairs to Mr. Brandt's room.

"He lived near me?" she asks.

"He did. He did. I never thought to mention it, I don't know why. He was so gifted, such a special boy. Maestro Huberman himself asked me to teach him. It was such an honor and now..." He wipes his eyes. "If you'll excuse me, I must go and find my friend's wife," he says disappearing into the crowd. Shula feels sick to her stomach and a sharp cramp in her lower abdomen. She can't stay here. Yisrael cries and reaches for his mother.

"He's hungry. I'll take him home. You stay here with Avraham and Shula." Rachel says to Yaakov.

"No, Eema. I want to come with you," Shula interjects. Rachel looks at her and puts her hand on her forehead.

"You're clammy. Are you sick?"

"My stomach," she says and reaches down to her belly. She doesn't know why, but she feels that she is going to cry from pain, or fear or sadness. *Maybe all three?*

"Come on," her mother says. Shula can't get away fast enough and the farther away from the crowds and noise the better she feels.

That night she dreams of the boy. She is standing in the wings of a stage in an auditorium. She looks out into the crowd but can't tell where she is. It looks like her school but feels like the Habima theater. It's an important concert, that much she knows. The boy stands nearby. He is slightly taller than her and his blond hair shines in the light, like she remembers it did when he walked down the stairs from Mr. Brandt's apartment. He smiles at her and pushes up his glasses. Good luck, she whispers and he walks out onto the stage. The floor starts to shake and she falls to her knees. The boy loses his footing and falls as an explosion rips through the ceiling. She feels the shock, the heat, the bang. When she looks up, it's all gone — the stage, the seats, the audience, and the boy. She wakes with tears in her eyes.

Two weeks later, Shula is on bus heading up north for an overnight Scout trip to a new kibbutz. First the trip was called off, then it was back on, back and forth it went for two weeks. Finally, they got the word that the trip would continue as planned. Shula couldn't wait. Since the bombing, her mother wanted her to stick close to home even though the rest of the city had moved on.

During the three-hour ride, her friend, Lilach, falls asleep on her shoulder, her red hair plastered against her freckled face. The three-bus convoy pulls up to the high wooden gates of a walled settlement. Shula shrugs her shoulder to wake her friend. They peer out the window as two armed men, each wearing khaki shorts and shirts, rifles slung over their shoulders, push the doors open. The vehicles roll into the compound, the gates close behind them. Looming over the center of the enclosure is a lookout tower. Three guards pace around the small platform up top. Toward the far end of the settlement two dozen tents are set up in rows. Three prefabricated buildings sit along a far wall. On one hangs a hand-painted sign that reads "Dining Hall."

"Fall into formation!" Moshe shouts, and the troop arranges itself into straight lines. When they settle into place, he barks commands:

"*Hakshev*! Attention!" Every child stands ramrod straight, hands down at their sides, eyes front and center.

"*Amidah Hofsheet*. At ease." In unison, the children move their left legs out to the side and clasp their hands behind their backs. Shula relaxes her shoulders.

"*Hakshev!*" Moshe shouts again. All eyes are focused on him.

"*Amidah Hofsheet.*"

"*Hakshev!*"

"*Amidah Hofsheet.*"

"At ease, my friends," he says. He turns to a tall, muscular man beside him. Shula recognizes him as one of the men from the gate. "I'd like to introduce you to Ze'ev Livney. He is a founding member of this kibbutz and he'll be our guide while we are here."

Ze'ev smiles at Moshe, removes the soft cotton *Kovah Tembel* hat he wears, and scratches his head. He turns and faces the group.

"*Bruchim habayim*, and welcome to Kibbutz Hanita. How many of you have been to a kibbutz before?" Shula raises her hand and looks around. About half the group has their hands up. "Can anyone tell me what a kibbutz is?" Shula keeps her hand raised. "You, the boy with the blond hair. What is a kibbutz?"

"A kibbutz is a communal settlement."

"Good, but what does that mean? Do we all sleep in one big bed?" Shula's hand shoots up again.

"You with the curly hair," says Ze'ev looking at her.

"From each according to his ability, to each according to his need," Shula says. Ze'ev smiles at her.

"Very good, and do you know who said this?"

"Karl Marx," she answers.

"Correct! My friends, a kibbutz is a communal settlement where each member works according to his ability and takes according to his need. We work together, we eat together, and we even do our laundry together. We believe that tending the land of our forefathers is the way to honor our homeland. We are also creating a viable socialist model for the future, not just here in the Yishuv but for the entire world. We don't just talk, we do. Understand?" Shula is pretty sure she understands what Ze'ev is saying but isn't clear on what a "viable socialist model" is exactly.

"This kibbutz is only six months old, and we are standing in what is called a Wall & Tower Structure. In order for us to secure an area, the British say we have to have a legitimate structure with four walls. So, six months ago, the Jewish National Fund purchased this land from the owner in Turkey, and a group of us drove here with six trucks loaded with prefabricated walls and in one afternoon we had a legal structure. We even put up a small dining hall and hung a sign on it, which is right over there," he says pointing to the crooked sign she noticed earlier. "So, today, after you set up your tents, we invite you for dinner. Then tomorrow you will help us clear a field where, soon, oranges will grow."

As they walk back to the buses to gather their packs and tents, Lilach leans over and whispers.

"This place scares me, you know? Do you think we're safe?" she asks. Shula looks around and sees her brother unloading packages from the bus, the men in the tower with their weapons, and the other kibbutz members with guns on their hips or rifles slung over their shoulders. She shakes off the shiver that runs up her back.

"Yes, Lilach. I believe that we are."

Before sunrise the next morning, she joins her groggy group as they gather around Ze'ev. Avraham greets her with a warm bread roll and a cup of sweet dark coffee. Ze'ev clears his throat.

"Listen up, children! We are surrounded by acres of land that have been fallow for years and years — generations, even! But we know that with some hard work we can make the land fertile and the desert will bloom, am I right?" He looks around as the group voices its agreement, then claps his hands for silence. "Today we are going to clear a nearby field by pulling the rocks from the ground one by one. When the field is cleared and the soil tilled, then will we be able to plant our oranges. Grab something to eat and drink, make sure you have your hat and canteen, and we'll meet at the entrance gate in fifteen minutes!" Shula watches as Ze'ev and a second man mount two brown horses. The second man is muscular like Ze'ev, and has a thick black bushy moustache. He wears a wide-brimmed Australian army hat and has a rifle slung over his shoulder. He takes a long drag off his cigarette and throws the butt onto the ground.

The gates open and Shula and her group follow the men on horseback, staying far enough away to avoid the dust the horses kick up. They turn toward an abandoned stone house. The roof is missing, the walls are crumbling in places, and the whole structure is infiltrated with weeds. Right by the building a large area is marked off with wooden stakes and string. A barbed wire fence surrounds that.

"Friends, here we have marked off the plot that needs to be cleared. Ephraim and I," he points to the man with the moustache, "will patrol the area, while our newest member, Ariel, will collect the rocks you dig out." He points to a pale, skinny boy of about fifteen with a donkey and cart. Ariel lifts a too-large cap off his head and scratches his straight black hair. He waves to the group and puts his hand in his pocket, a gesture that almost pulls his pants down. Lilach elbows Shula in the side and rolls her eyes. Shula puts her finger up to her lips shushing her.

After an hour of digging up rocks, Shula stops. The work is slow and her nails are packed with dirt. She stands and takes a sip of water. She offers the canteen to Ariel who heaves stones into the wagon. He nods.

"Thank you. I forgot mine," he says.

"You have to drink water here!" Lilach says. "It's very important."

"I know, but I'm not used to this weather, I've only been here three weeks," he answers.

"Where are you from?" asks Shula.

"Berlin." Shula and Lilach look at each other. The recent news from this German city has been plastered on front pages across the country.

"Were you there on *Kristallnacht?*" Lilach asks eyes wide.

"Yes, I was." The girls gasp.

"Were you scared?" Lilach pushes.

"Terrified."

"What was it like?" The boy shifts his feet and pulls at his pants. His voice is soft when he speaks.

"The noise was so loud. Hordes of people were yelling 'Death to the Jews!' and smashing windows. It went on all night long. My father's shop was destroyed. They broke the windows before setting the place on fire. Luckily, my family and I were able to hide. The next day though, my parents arranged for me to come here." There is no emotion in his voice.

"Did you come alone?" she asks.

"Yes, I did." He says looking around the barren fields. "I did not expect this."

Shula is about to speak when she hears the sound of a goat's bell. She turns to see three men wearing *keffiyehs* walking toward the group with a herd of about thirty goats. Ze'ev and Ephraim trot over on their horses. The riders tower over the men. Ephraim turns his horse this way and that, causing the tallest man to flinch. He steps back only to be confronted by the flank of Ze'ev's muscular horse, which forces him to reverse direction. He smiles at the mounted men and greets them.

"Assalaam Alaikum."

Shula starts to pick up stones again, while listening to the men talk. Ze'ev asks the men what they want. The men gesture to their herd then to the area where her group is working. Lilach leans over to Ariel.

"Shula lived in Nazareth so she speaks Arabic. *Nu?* What are they saying?" she asks.

"They say that this is where their herd grazes. They have been using this land for years," Shula says.

"Well, not anymore!" says Lilach. "This belongs to the kibbutz, right?" Shula looks over to the men and watches as Ze'ev pulls an official-looking document from his shirt pocket.

"We bought the land from the owner six months ago," he says. "This is ours now. See, here is the deed," he holds up the paper so the men can see. The men study the paper.

"But, sir, the man who owns this land lives in Turkey, not here," says the tall one. "We live here," he says pointing at the ground. "This is where our goats graze." Shula is aware of how polite the goat herders are being. The way they keep their voices low and start each sentence with a formal salutation. The youngest goat herder looks toward Shula. She looks down at the ground.

"With all due respect, sir, where will we go now? Our goats need to eat," the tall one asks. Ze'ev shrugs his shoulders.

"There's plenty of land down the road," he says. The youngest herder circles the animals, using his long stick to keep the goats from wandering into their usual grazing land. The two older Arab men lean their heads together. Ephraim rides up to Ze'ev then throws his head back and laughs a loud deep laugh. He swings his horse around and the men step back. She wonders if they are scared.

"Sir, we will have to go speak to the authorities about this," the tall man says. "We have been here for generations."

"Go ahead, talk to the authorities!" Ze'ev says. "We have this on our side," he adds as he waves the deed at them. The older one looks at the other two and motions for them to head back down the path. Lilach puts her hand on Shula's shoulder.

"What happened? Where are they going?" she asks.

"They said they are going to talk to the authorities, to tell them that they have been here for generations," Shula stops when she sees Ariel's face. He looks agitated, his face blotched with red. In quick succession, Shula sees first anger, then fear, then hatred in his eyes. He balls his hands into fists held rigidly by his sides.

"We own this land now!" he says. "We are safe here. No one can make us feel fear ever again." He looks at them with an intensity that startles Shula then jabs his thumb to his chest.

"*Am Yisrael Chai*! The nation of Israel lives!"

Chapter 5

Tel Aviv, British Mandate Palestine

May 1941

Shula looks up from the piano and sees that it is almost four o'clock. The shops on Allenby will be open again, and she is on the hunt for a new dress for her upcoming recital. She brushes her hair and looks at herself in the mirror. Pulling her thin cotton dress tight across her chest, she checks on her growing breasts. At thirteen she still doesn't see much change, at least compared to Lilach. Her friend's breasts have grown so large her shirts are on the verge of popping open. She moans about how uncomfortable they are but Shula suspects that she is secretly proud at how developed she is compared to her friends. She pushes her own chest out to no avail.

"I'm going to meet Lilach to look for a dress?" she says to her mother as she heads for the door. Rachel hands her two coins.

"Here, take this," she says. "It's enough for a deposit if you find something you like. If not we'll go out later this week," Shula kisses her mother on the cheek and places the coins in her small brown purse.

She finds Lilach at the corner of Allenby and Ahad Ha'am streets standing in front of a wall of posters. There are advertisements for concerts, announcements of local deaths, and poster after poster urging support of the defensive brigades. She scans the event posters first to see if any new concerts have been announced. She notices a sign for the newly formed *Palmach*, the Jewish fighting unit. The soldier pictured wears a rounded helmet and blows a whistle. "Prepare!" it urges. Lilach stares at a poster featuring a soldier, his forehead covered by a curly forelock, his khaki shirt open exposing his chest.

"Oh, he is handsome, don't you think?"

"Hmm," Shula agrees. "Good-looking for a cartoon and much better looking than this one," she points to a Gan Rina Cinema poster for Charlie Chaplin's *The Great Dictator*.

"I have no desire to see a movie about Hitler, even if it makes fun of him," states Lilach.

"Agreed," says Shula. "What about *Kathleen*?" she points to the new film starring her childhood idol, Shirley Temple.

"I heard that Curly Top is not so fun to watch now that she's a teenager, but her dress is nice," Lilach runs her finger along the picture of the actress in a light blue dress trimmed with a white Peter Pan collar.

"Do you think we can find something that nice?" asks Shula.

"Of course," says Lilach. "We'll find something even better. Come on. Let's go to Esther's," she takes Shula's hand and pulls her down the street.

The girls walk down Allenby arm in arm, passing a bookstore, a camera store, and a store that sells silver and gold Judaica items — from wine goblets, to candlestick holders, to the thin rectangular *mezzuzot* that hang on the right-hand doorjambs of Jewish homes. Welcoming the coolness as they enter Esther's shop, she sorts through the counters covered with mounds of clothing. She picks up a thin cotton dress. Scanning the garment for pulled threads and holes, she looks up when she hears footsteps coming from a back room.

In clomps Esther, an obese woman with thick glasses, wobbly arms and a swollen left leg.

"Welcome, girls. What can I help you with?" she asks.

"My friend needs a dress for her recital next week. It's the end of the year concert at Herzliya Academy. She's been invited to perform even though it's her brother who goes there. It's very prestigious," Lilach says before Shula can open her mouth.

Esther's eyes widen and she looks impressed. "But of course," she says with a smile and turns to Shula. "What are you doing? Singing? Dancing?"

"I'll be playing two pieces on the piano."

"Very good. And, what will you be playing?"

"'Shir Haemek' and 'Hatikva.'"

"'The Valley' describes the beauty of our land and 'The Hope' our desire to be here! A real Zionist recital," Esther says. She claps her hands together. "How old are you? Twelve? Thirteen?"

"Thirteen," Shula replies. Esther examines her as if she is a specimen under a magnifying glass.

"What do you like to wear when you perform? What's your style?"

"Umm…" she stalls, flashing through her favorite pieces. She's never thought about her outfits as a reflection of a personal taste.

"She likes the dress that Shirley Temple is wearing in the poster for *Kathleen*," Lilach says. Shula nods in agreement.

"Ah! I just got something in that I think would be perfect for your concert. Wait here, I'll be right back," she says as she waddles her way to the back of the store. The screen door squeals open, then bangs shut.

"Yankle! Where is he? *Yankle*?" she yells.

"What?" answers a man's voice from far off.

"Bring me the bag that Boaz brought by yesterday," she commands. The girls hear a grunt and then silence. They giggle, but stop when the back door opens. Esther returns with a basket in hand and places it on the counter.

"Come," she says motioning for the girls to join her. She unfolds a pale-yellow dress with exquisite Yemenite embroidery.

"Oh!" says Lilach. Shula gasps then reaches to touch the fabric. The Peter Pan collar and sleeves are adorned with a simple red zigzag pattern, and across the chest are three large sunbursts made from circles of thick gold thread surrounded by alternating rims of green and red. Red and green petals burst from the outer circles. The skirt's gentle pleats hang from red zigzag stitching that wraps around the waist. Shula touches the soft cotton and runs her fingers over the raised threads. She has never seen this kind of embroidery on a dress Shirley Temple might wear.

"You like it?" Esther asks.

"Yes, very much so," she replies.

"I think it's the perfect dress for a *Sabra* like you."

"What's going on? You scared me!" Shula says when Avraham races up to her on the way home from school the next day.

"I thought Miss Shula wasn't afraid of anything," her brother teases. She smirks and continues to walk, her brother at her side.

"Guess what?" he asks. The excitement emanating from him causes a buzz in the air.

"*Nu?*"

"We have a ride out to the airfield tomorrow and there's enough room for you to come along!" Shula's heart flutters. She rarely gets to the airfield to watch her brother's glider club. She breaks out into a huge smile squeezing her books tight against her chest.

"*Yallah!*" she says as she starts to run. "Let's get home and tell Eema!"

Avraham opens the front door and stops, blocking Shula's view. Squeezing around him, she sees her mother and father on the sofa, a rail thin girl between them.

"Ah ha! Here they are," Yaakov says as Shula and Avraham shuffle over. "Children, please meet our guest, Naomi."

"Hello," says Shula.

"Welcome," says Avraham. The girl smiles and pushes her straight brown bobbed hair behind her ear. Shula notices how narrow her forearms are and how pale her skin looks. *Like tissue paper.* Purplish circles surround her brown eyes.

"Naomi is staying with us for the night. Tomorrow, Dr. Levy will pick her up and take her to her new home. We want to make her as comfortable as possible as she has come a long way." Avraham and Shula nod in agreement. "Now, you must be tired. Shula, show Naomi to your room and help her get settled." Shula smiles at Naomi and motions for her to follow.

"When did you get here?" she asks as Naomi places her worn canvas bag next to the narrow cot against the wall.

"A week ago. I was living in a tent in the middle of nowhere until last night. It's how I imagine the surface of the moon must look." She looks around the room, stopping at the light bulb hanging down by a long black cord. "In my house in Munich, we had beautiful chandeliers," she says, the familiar pain of loss in her voice. "I'm tired. Would you mind if I slept?"

She moves to help Naomi with her jacket, but the girl flinches, and looks down at the floor. *I was just trying to help her*, she thinks.

"I'll close the shades," Shula says, shutting out the bright afternoon sun. "I'll wake you up for dinner," she adds, and turns to see the girl already asleep, still wearing her threadbare jacket, arms wrapped around her waist.

Yaakov and Yisrael roll a wooden ball back and forth between them. It is so rare for her father to be home at this time of the day, and she can tell that Yisrael is giddy with excitement. Smiling at her little brother, she joins her mother in the kitchen. Rachel hands her a knife and an onion and she begins to chop.

"The poor child," Rachel says. "She's been traveling by foot, train and boat for weeks." Shula tries to imagine being on a crowded and dirty boat for weeks on end, and shudders. She wipes her onion tears and sniffs. "Poor, poor dear," her mother says shaking her head. "They are *children* for God's sake!" she says, scrubbing deep red beets in the sink.

"Where are her parents?" Shula asks.

"We don't know. They were separated at a train station in Constantinople." Shula sniffs again, this time not sure if the tears are her own or the onion's. She feels sad for this girl. She has never seen anyone look so wounded.

"Where will Dr. Levy be taking her?"

"She has relatives in Holon. He's taking her there tomorrow. He had some kind of emergency today and needed to make sure she was safe for tonight."

"So, he brought her here," she smiles at her mother. Her mother blows her a kiss and washes the magenta juice from her hands.

"After dinner, I want you to see if you have any clothing that might fit her. She's small for sixteen," she says. Shula can't believe that Naomi is sixteen. She doesn't look any older than herself.

"Well, maybe she could stay with us for longer than one night," she says. Rachel puts her hand on Shula's shoulder.

"Shula, I am so glad to hear that you want to help Naomi, but we can't do more for her than we are already doing. Dr. Levy is working with a group that has a plan and they know what's best." She takes the cutting board away from Shula and adds the chopped onions to the hot skillet. They sizzle and pop as they hit the oil, then turn translucent, their scent filling the air.

After a meal of cabbage and beet stew, Naomi's cheeks have blushed pink, like one of those hand-tinted photographs. Sitting at the coffee table, they sip hot tea and eat cookies from a German bakery on Ben Yehudah Street.

"These are delicious," Naomi says as Shula watches her stuff a fourth cookie into her mouth. A few minutes later, the girl can't keep her eyes open and goes to bed. Climbing into her own bed later, Shula watches Naomi breathe in and out, her body so slight she can hardly see her shape under the covers. She lies back and looks up at the ceiling. The moonlight streams in through the window, creating silvery lines through the slatted shades. Does the moon look the same in New York? Munich? Paris? Is it as bright as it is in Tel Aviv? While she sleeps, she dreams of the moon's reflection shimmering over the Mediterranean Sea.

"*Nein! Nein!*"

Shula sits bolt upright as the shouts rip her from sleep.

"Are you all right?" Rachel says rushing into the room. She sits on the edge of Naomi's cot. The girl is like a divining rod. Stiff and shaking. "Bad dream?" Naomi nods. "Do you want to tell me?" She shakes her head. Rachel pats her on the leg and makes shushing sounds. The girl begins to relax. "Can you sleep now?" Naomi nods and slips down under the covers, pulling the blanket up to her chin.

"Yes, I think so. Good night," she whispers.

"Good night," Rachel says. She kisses Shula on the forehead. "*Layla Tov.*"

Lying there, Shula stares up as headlights dance across the dark ceiling. After five minutes of complete silence, she hears a sigh.

"I'm sorry I woke you," Naomi says.

"No problem."

"Well, I'm sorry if I scared you."

"No problem." *Should I ask her a question? Leave her alone?* She clears her throat. The girl sighs again.

"My father owned a bookstore in Munich, not a Jewish bookstore, just a bookstore that sold all kinds of books, but in the Jewish section of town. One day the brown shirts came and destroyed everything. For hours, we hid in a crawl space under the floorboards, their boots stomping around just above our heads."

"Were you scared?"

"My heart was beating so loud, I was sure they would find us."

"I'm so sorry."

"Don't be. We were lucky. We were able to escape." Silence fills the room.

"Where did you go?" Shula asks, hoping the girl is still awake.

"We moved to the French countryside. My father, mother, my three younger brothers and I all lived in small loft of a barn with just a blanket hiding us from view. For a whole year, I wasn't allowed outside during the day."

"Why did you leave?"

"The farmer's wife began to get nervous. A local man was arrested after the police found a family hiding in his shed. The farmer felt bad, but told us we had to go. My father paid a truck driver to take us to Constantinople. In the middle of the night, we climbed into burlap sacks and buried ourselves in a mountain of potatoes."

"Potatoes?"

"I've learned it could have been worse. I met a girl on the boat over here who hid in a truck surrounded by

91

chickens. She had to hold her nose for days." Shula shivered. If she ever had to hide in a truck, she hoped it would be filled with oranges.

"How did you get separated from your family?"

"At the train station, my mother sent me to look for my father at the ticket counter. I couldn't find him, and then I couldn't find my mother. The station was so crowded and noisy. No one would speak to me," she cries softly. After a minute her breathing calms. "I wandered the station for hours. I had no money, no food, nothing. Then a man approached me and in Yiddish asked me if I was lost. I burst into tears when I heard his words. He was from the Jewish Agency and promised me that I would find my family in *Eretz Yisrael*."

"Are you happy to be here?" A long silence, then a deep sigh.

"I'm sure I will be someday," she answers, detachment in her voice. "But right now, I'm not sure what that means. Right now, I feel nothing."

The next morning, Shula wakes to the sound of Avraham's banging.

"Eema! Where's my bag? The one with my helmet and goggles? I put it in the closet, I'm sure!" Shula yawns and stretches. Naomi's eyes pop open. She sits up straight. Blinking, she looks around the room, recognition dawning on her face.

"Good morning," she says.

"Good morning!" Shula replies, throwing her blanket off and jumping out of bed. Pulling the shades up, the bright sunlight streams into the room. Naomi shields her eyes.

"Come! Get ready! We get to watch Avraham fly today!" she says pulling on a pair of khaki shorts.

"But he's just a boy," the girl says.

"Avraham is a member of the Herzliya Gymnasium Flight Club! Come on, you'll see."

Ten minutes later they are down on the street. Naomi's borrowed hat slides down over her eyes. Shula folds the brim up over her forehead.

"There," she says. "Now you can see." Naomi smiles and for the first time, there is a lightness to her face.

A British Army staff car rolls up. Avraham's friend Danny pops his head out of the passenger seat and waves. Danny's father, Reuven, salutes the group from the driver's seat. Yaakov whistles in appreciation.

"What a beauty!" he says running his hand over the car's top. "So, there are some perks to working for the British."

"Isn't she though? Brand new 1941 Austin with enough room for at least ten kids," says Reuven.

"Well, we have three kids for you here," he says. "This is Naomi. She just arrived in the Yishuv this week and we thought this would be a nice treat for her."

"Nice to meet you, and welcome," Reuven says, reaching back to open the passenger door from inside. Avraham pushes past the girls, jumping into the seat next to the boys. Climbing in after him, Shula smiles at Danny, hoping to catch his eye. She slides into the last row of seats pulling Naomi with her.

"Come, sit with me. I'll keep you safe," she says as the boys begin talking at each other. Naomi leans into the window as far she can.

"Attention!" Reuven's voice booms out from the front seat. The boys all quiet down. "Everyone, this is Naomi, please introduce yourselves." Turning toward the girls, Danny smiles. Shula's heart melts.

"I'm Danny," he says. "Welcome to the Yishuv. This is Benny, Doron, and Amichai — "

"And *we* are the future pilots of the *first* Jewish Air Force!" Avraham says, and the boys erupt in cheers of *El Al*, the slogan of their flight club.

During the hour-long drive to the airfield, Naomi leans her forehead on the window and stares out at the houses that dot the farmland along the way. For most of the ride the girls are silent, while the boys shout their flight plans to each other. One of them breaks into the chorus of "*Shoshana*" and Shula joins in the singing of her favorite new song.

Shoshana, Shoshana, Shoshana
The moon has risen high into a cloud,
And like the rising moon, Shoshana
The captain will sail out of the sea to you.
The sea was stormy and the mast broke.
The prow of the ship was almost smashed,
But Yoske took control of everything and sang such a happy song.
Oh! Shoshana...
What a sorry figure shorty Shmulik cut when he was brought to Cyprus.
But he sat behind the fence and sang this happy song.
Oh! Shoshana...
The journey over the seas came to an end.
The ships and their crews reached the shore.
And then all the men streamed towards Shoshana,
Singing this happy song[9].

"Listen, if you think the Nazis won't be in Moscow by the end of this summer, you're crazy. Your whole plan relies on the fact that the Soviet Union won't fall to

---

9

Hitler," Avraham says when the singing ends. Shula feels Naomi tighten up.

"Well, we can revise our plan if that does happen. Anyway, the way this war is going, we'll have to be revising our plan daily!" Danny replies.

"I can't wait to fly with the RAF and bomb the hell out of the Reichstag!" Doron says, pulling his helmet over his red hair. He lifts an imaginary machine gun. "Rat-tat-tat-tat-tat!!" he says, aiming at the olive trees whipping by them. Naomi flinches.

"Enough, you guys! Not everyone wants to play war games," she says, taking the girl's hand. A dead silence fills the car as the boys look down at their feet or out the window.

"She's right. Enough of that for now. How about some music?" Reuven says, breaking the quiet. He reaches over and tunes the dial. Bob Eberly's deep voice fills the vehicle. Shula feels Naomi relax.

When they get to the airfield, the boys pile out of the car. Shula sees the glider tethered to the prop plane, and pulls Naomi to it. They run their hands over the machines, look into the cockpit, and try to move the propeller. When the boys begin their safety checks, Shula and Naomi sit on dry scrub at the edge of the runway.

"Have you ever been this close to a plane before?" she asks Naomi.

"No, never," Naomi replies.

"Well, it's loud, but exciting. You'll see."

Up first, Avraham pulls on his leather helmet, adjusts his goggles and secures his safety straps. A wave of excitement courses through Shula as the prop plane starts up. She grasps Naomi's hand, still cold despite the heat. The girls release their hands to cover their ears as the plane taxis down the runway, waving to Avraham when he gives them the thumbs up. The aircraft soars into the clear blue sky, her brother trailing behind in his wooden glider. The plane makes a wide arc and flies right over the girls, the vibration of the engines thrilling them. Soon, Avraham will release the towrope and glide back down to earth. She is so proud and jealous of her brother at the same time. Maybe, she too can fly high above the world one day.

When they return home that afternoon Dr. Levy is there. Shula begs her mother to let Naomi stay one more night, but the adults say no.

"The quicker she settles down, the better," Dr. Levy explains. Shula gives Naomi a hug and hands her a bag with her old clothing, and memory book.

"See? You already have your first inscription," she says showing her the page. Under a delicately drawn rose it says: *To Naomi, on her first days in Eretz Yisrael. Remember me forever. Love, Shula.*

Later, Shula sits down at the piano to practice for her recital. She relaxes into her warm-up exercises, letting the repetition of the notes lull her into a meditative state. Her short time with Naomi raised so many questions. What is it like to lose your family, your friends, everything you know? How can she not feel frightened after living so long in fear? Would Shula ever see her again? She hopes so, making a promise to keep in touch with her new friend.

The next day is Sunday, a school day, and Shula races home after dismissal. A wrapped package sits on her bed. She tears the brown paper open to see her dress. Changing into it she twirls out into the living room.

"Eema! Come see my dress!"

"Coming!" Rachel says as she leaves the kitchen carrying Yisrael on her hip. Her little brother squirms out of his mother's arms and runs to Shula, hugging her around her legs.

"Careful! Yisrael! It's my new dress!" she says as she pulls his arms off her legs.

"Oh! It looks beautiful, but I think I need to bring up the hem, no?" Rachel picks up the edge of the dress and looks at the hem.

"No! Not now! I want to wear it! To show Lilach!"

"What? You want to wear it out today?" Rachel says as she grabs a pincushion from the table. "If I know you, you'll sit on that dirty wall by the beach and come home with a big black stain on your *tuchus*. No, my dear," she says as she helps Shula stand on a chair. "This dress is for tomorrow's concert. Period. We don't have the money to waste on expensive *schmates*."

When Shula gets to Avraham's school the next day, the butterflies in her stomach flutter around making her feel sick, then elated, sometimes at the same time. Walking over to the auditorium, she stands in the empty hall, acclimating herself to the cool, dark interior. Her shoes echo as she walks onto the stage. Ten steps to the piano. She should be outside right now, watching her brother stand with the rest of his class in the closing ceremony, but these few moments alone will calm her once she performs. She sits at the piano and lifts the fallboard. Running her fingers above the keys, she practices the fingering for the first piece without making a sound. She closes the cover when she sees her teacher, Mr. Brandt.

"I see you are preparing like I taught you," he says. Shula laces her fingers together and pushes out her arms into a forearm stretch. "Are you ready?" he asks.

"Yes, I think so."

"You will be wonderful, I'm sure," he smiles. "Now, go find your family and I'll see you shortly."

A short while later she stands in the wings of the stage, watching a group of children perform an upbeat *debka* dance in five short lines. She finds herself jumping along to the music played by a small ensemble and tries to remember the steps. *There is always a new folk dance to learn*, she thinks, trying to follow their feet.

After the group clears the stage, Shula walks towards the piano. She counts the steps in her head, one…two…all the way to ten. She stands next to the instrument, one hand resting on the edge and curtsies to the audience. Sitting with his friends, her brother leads a round of applause. Her parents sit a few rows behind them and she gives them a small wave. Taking her seat at the piano she rests her hands on the keys for a few moments before she begins.

She starts with "Shir Haemek, The Song of the Valley." As she plays, she sings the lyrics along in her head, remembering a trip through the Galilee with her Scout troop.

Rest has come to the weary and calm to the toiler.
A pale night unfolds over the fields of the Jezreel Valley.
A cry rises high, from the fields of the Jezreel Valley.
Who fired and who fell between Beit Alfa and Nahalal?
Oh, what a night of nights
Silence over Jezreel
Sleep dear Valley, land of glorious beauty
We will guard you.[10]

The applause upon her completion warms her, and she stands and bows. The next piece is "Hatikva," the Hope. She remembers Mr. Brandt bursting into tears when she first played it.

"Do you understand what this song means?" he asked her, eyes brimming. Shula had been too taken aback

---

10

by this display of emotion to respond. Of course, she knew what the song meant; it was in Hebrew after all. But she knows that Mr. Brandt is talking about something else, not just the literal translation of the words, but what it symbolizes for him and so many others. After the formal musical introduction, she recites the words with the melody:

As long as the Jewish spirit within the heart yearns,
With eyes turned East, toward Zion,
Then our hope will not be lost
The 2,000-year-old hope
To be a free nation in our land,
The land of Zion and Jerusalem[11].

She thinks of Naomi and the look of fear on her face as she sat on the cot, knees pulled up to her chest, arms gripping her legs. By the time she reaches the end of the piece, she is pounding the piano keys. Looking out into the audience to catch a glimpse of her brother, only then does she see the entire crowd up on its feet singing along with her. Her heart swells, and at that moment she feels at one with herself, at one with her country, and at peace in the world.

Towards the end of the week, Shula sits on the couch and reads through Avraham's memory book. Her father brought the book home from work on the new Tel Aviv canal last week. It is small, with a blue and gold bumpy cover, and features an etching of the canal and the word *Remembrances* embossed in gold. Running her fingertips over the raised cover she flips through the

---

11

pages, stopping at a new entry by his friend Amos Kenan. Underneath a poem is an elaborate drawing with cacti, birds, grape vines, and a *hanukkiah*. Over the image, he wrote their names — Amos and Avraham. She flips through some more and smiles when she sees her little brother's drawing of an orange flower in a brown pot.

Then she turns to Danny's entry. There is a cartoon drawing depicting Avraham as a pilot wearing a too-puffy flight suit, medals hanging from his chest. He leans out of the cockpit, ready to drop a bomb by hand. Below him, planes soar above a battlefield, dropping bombs onto tanks marked with Nazi swastikas. *The Battle of Berlin with Danny and Avraham* is written below. Shula shudders to think of Avraham going to war, and it saddens her when he and his friends talk about joining the forces fighting the Nazis. She doesn't want Avraham to leave her.

She turns to a blank page and smooths it with her hand. Friends and teachers have written such beautiful inscriptions she feels that she can't match up. Pen in hand, she hovers over the page and then, in the neatest handwriting she can manage, she writes:

Avraham!
A memento forever
From your sister
Shulamit Dubno

She draws a single rose rising up from the ground, delicate petals decorating its stem. In one corner, she puts the Hebrew date (*Monday, 4ᵗʰ of Tamuz, Tasha*) and in the other the English date (*29.6.41*). She draws three lines across the bottom to mark the end. Blowing on the sheet to dry the ink she holds out the book and examines her work. It is neat and simple, but something is missing. Another picture? A joke? She flips through the pages and stops on Danny's piece. Turning back to her entry, she draws a little triangle in the top left-hand corner. Writing in the smallest of letters she adds: *My wish is to see you bomb*

Berlin. As much as she dreads the thought of her brother going to war, this is what he wants most in his life. She blows on the page once again and closes the book.

Chapter 6

Tel Aviv, British Mandate Palestine

December 1944

S hula looks through her closet and wonders what she should wear to tonight's holiday *simcha*. Since the British instated a curfew due to a rash of violence by guerilla Jewish groups, they aren't leaving the house after dark. Her mother, though, insisted on having at least one Hanukkah party on the sixth night of the eight-day celebration.

"I will not let those Irgun hooligans ruin the holiday. We'll eat at four o'clock, light the candles, and everyone will be home before the curfew begins," she argued. "I don't think God will mind if we start a bit early, considering."

"If God minded, he wouldn't have made gangs like Lehi, Stern and Menachim Begin's Irgun. How dare they assassinate Lord Moyne, the highest-ranking British official in the Mandate, in Cairo! On Egyptian soil! It's Jews like that that give the rest of us a bad name," Yaakov replied.

The Zionist paramilitary arms of the Jewish resistance had stepped up their attacks on the British in recent months with a series of bombings of government buildings and murders in Jerusalem, Haifa and Tel Aviv. Since the killing of the British minister of state in Egypt on November 6, just one month earlier, security intensified. Checkpoints were erected all over Tel Aviv, blocking streets with hoops of barbed wire and making it impossible to get around the city. Shula agrees with her mother. It will be nice to celebrate, even for a few hours.

Digging further back, she finds clothes she hasn't worn for years. She comes across the pale-yellow dress she wore three years earlier for the recital at Avraham's school. She holds it up and marvels at how short it is on her sixteen-year-old frame. Maybe she can try and wear it as a tunic over a pair of red or green pants, like a Yemenite woman. She smooths down the soft cotton fabric and returns it to her closet. She now owns several performance dresses, one of the few indulgences her mother insists on. Flicking through the dresses in her closet is like looking through a photo album. Each one elicits the memory of a performance and is linked to a specific piece of music. The yellow was Mozart; the green chiffon was Rachmaninoff, and the black with the silver trim, Beethoven. Just seeing the collar of a particular outfit can put her back on stage, as she remembers how each fabric felt against her skin, or tickled the back of her neck.

For the party, Shula decides on the light blue dress she bought last week. Lilach told her about a store on Shenkin that held a few of the coveted well-made and stylish British Utility brand pieces in back, but you had to know to ask for them. She slips on the rayon garment and admires the way the black trim around the neck, sleeves and sides outlines her figure. Curling her hair under like Lauren Bacall in *To Have and Have Not*, she looks in the mirror and ties the thin black belt around her waist. It makes her look sophisticated, glamorous and smart.

First to arrive is Aunt Sarah carrying a bowl filled with hardboiled eggs.

"Well, at least we'll have enough eggs!" Her husband Yosef jokes as she places the bowl on the table.

"You think that my wife would allow anyone to go hungry?" Yaakov says, shaking Yosef's hand. "With Rachel, there are always contingency plans."

By four o'clock the apartment is filled with people, most of whom Shula knows, but a few that she doesn't recognize. It is common these days for people to house refugees from Europe for a day or two, sometimes even weeks. Guests bring a dish to add to the feast, even though it is clear by some of the paltry portions that this is no easy feat. She greets her cousin Miriam, her aunt Rivka and family. She sees the couple from across the hall and pats their daughter on the head. Then she sees Danny's parents, Mr. and Mrs. Goldberg. Ever since Danny chose to join up with the Irgun he stopped coming around, and the girlhood crush she had on him is long gone.

Her mother carries over a fresh batch of *latkes*, and the savory smell of the potato pancakes makes her mouth water. Reaching for the basket piled high with dried dates, she bites into one right then. The soft, rich, sweet meat of the fruit always reminds her of Nazareth. Sarah replaces the empty bowl of peeled eggs with a fresh batch, sprinkles them with salt, then throws a pinch over her shoulder.

Reaching for the bowl, Shula touches someone's hand. She turns to apologize and sees a young man she doesn't know.

"I'm so sorry, please go ahead," she says. She notices his deep brown eyes and thick black eyebrows over long lashes. His face is narrow and his cheekbones high. His black hair is slicked back and comes to a point on his forehead. He is attractive in that Humphrey Bogart way. Ugly-Beautiful.

"No, no. I insist. Ladies first," he says.

"Please," she says, pulling her hand back. They lock eyes and she feels the blush rise in her cheeks. She smiles and averts her eyes. They both hesitate, then she reaches out once more only to knock hands with him again.

"I'm so sorry," he laughs, "You first." Shula places an egg on her plate. The man does the same, then balancing his plate on one hand, he put his right hand out to shake.

"Solomon Shapiro, at your service," he says.

"Shulamit Dubno, but you may call me Shula," she answers. His egg starts to roll and he rights his plate. Shula laughs. Solomon draws back, raising his hand as if to shield his eyes from a bright light.

"My God, but your smile almost blinded me!" he says, and she bursts out laughing. Her cheeks turn bright pink. Eyeing a plate piled high with slices of noodle *kugel*, she takes a corner piece with the crispiest noodles, then offers the serving fork to Solomon.

"Shulamit. That's a musical name," he says. Shula feels her cheeks heat up again.

"Thank you…um…Are you visiting the Yishuv or do you live here?" she asks.

"Working, I'm afraid, but temporarily. I just started at the British Mandate headquarters. Mr. and Mrs. Goldberg were kind enough to invite me tonight, as I haven't been able to light candles this week. There are no other Jews in my unit. Do you know if this is dairy or meat?" he asks.

"Dairy," she says. "It has cheese in it. Do you keep kosher?"

"Yes, yes, I do. You don't?"

"No, no, I don't."

"Well, that *kugel* looks delicious, so I'll stick to the dairy tonight."

"Are you sure? My mother's beet and beef stew is delicious." Solomon laughs.

"I'm sure it is. The smell is heavenly. But I am a sucker for a crispy noodle, as I can see you are too," he says, pointing to her *kugel*. He bites into a large piece and chews, rolling his eyes back. "Wow! That was the most delicious thing I have eaten in weeks. I must thank the hostess for inviting me." He looks around the room. "Do you know Rachel, the woman who lives here?"

"Yes, as a matter of fact, I do. She's my mother."

"Ah! You must be the pianist. I hear you are quite gifted." Out of the corner of her eye she sees Lilach standing behind Solomon giving her the thumbs up. She ignores her friend and looks towards the balcony.

"It's getting a bit crowded in here. Would you like to stand on the terrace?" she asks. Moving outside, they eat in silence for a few moments and look out over the quiet street. She wracks her brain for something to say.

"How has your stay been so far?"

"Wonderful. Inspiring. Enlightening. The biggest surprise being the people. You Yeshuvniks are a funny lot."

"Funny? How?"

"Well, for a number of reasons. Let's take keeping kosher. Here, you know what the laws of *kashrut* are, meaning you know *how* to keep kosher — "

"Of course, I do. I learned it at school a hundred times," she replies.

"But you don't follow the laws in everyday life. And if you don't keep the laws of the Bible, what makes you a Jew?" Shula feels like rolling her eyes. She has had this conversation before with other foreign Jews who come to visit the Yishuv for the first time. How can you be Jewish, they ask, if you don't *act* like a Jew?

"I speak Hebrew, I follow the Jewish holidays, I was born in the land of my ancestors, and I don't have to live in fear of living life as a Jew."

"You don't?" he asks. A shiver runs up her back. She looks down at her plate and tries to spear a chunk of tomato onto her fork.

"I'm so sorry. How rude of me," Solomon says. "Only days in the country and I've already insulted a lovely lady." Shula smiles and looks up from her plate. "Let me make it up to you. Can you meet for coffee, say tomorrow?" She nods.

"Great. Tell me when and where," he says.

"How about Café Tamar on Shenkin. At 2 p.m.?"

"It's a date then," he replies. She holds his gaze and smiles. Opening his mouth to speak, he is interrupted when Rachel bustles out to the balcony.

"People are getting nervous and want to leave soon," she says.

"Eema, this is Solomon."

"Pleased to meet you, Mrs. Dubno, and thank you for your hospitality. You are a wonderful cook and you have a charming daughter," he says, shaking her hand.

"Ah! You are the young man who came with the Goldbergs. Welcome to our home, and please join us for the candle lighting."

"That's why I'm here, although I need to get back to the barracks myself."

"Yes, everyone is worried about the curfew. Come, let's light the candles." Rachel takes Shula's hand and leads her to the living area. She, her mother and father stand behind her younger brother as he says the blessing.

"Blessed are You, Lord our God, King of the universe, who has sanctified us with His commandments, and commanded us to kindle the Hanukkah light," he says touching the six candles in the *hanukkiah* with the flame of the helper candle, the *shamash*. He replaces the seventh candle back in the central holder.

"Amen," Shula says with the rest of the guests. She steps back to see Solomon, when her aunt Sarah says:

"Shulinka! Play your piano for us. We need to hear some music to lift our spirits."

"Please do, Shula," Yisrael says pulling on her sleeve. She looks around the room again. No Solomon. She lets herself be led to her room by her little brother and sits at the piano.

"*Maoz Tzur!*" someone yells. She places her fingers on the keys and pounds out the stirring melody to the holiday tune she has played so many times before.

My refuge, my rock of salvation! It is pleasant to praise you.

Repair our house of worship, and there we will offer You our thanks.

When You have slaughtered the barking foe.

Then we will celebrate with song and psalm the dedication of the altar[12].

She finishes the piece with a flourish and starts to get up, but Yisrael is by her side before she can move.

"*S'vivon Sov Sov Sov*[13], Shula! Play the one about the dreidel," he says.

By the end of the fourth song requested, the guests begin to leave. Shula jumps up to see if she can catch Solomon. She scans the room, but he is gone.

Standing on the balcony later that night, Shula looks out over Melchett Street. Shining in window after window is a candelabra with seven candles. Looking higher she sees on roof after rooftop electric *hannukiot* glowing in the night sky. She feels her father's hand on her shoulder and leans back into him.

"You know," Yaakov says. "In Poland, sometimes we could put the candles in the window, and other times we had to hide them in the back of the house. The locals knew we were Jewish, but somehow there were times when we knew not to show it off, you understand?" Shula nods. "But here? In *Eretz Yisrael?* In Tel Aviv, the first Jewish city in 2000 years?" He sweeps his arm out pointing to all

---

12

13

the sparkling lights within view "Here we are like the mighty Maccabees. We are proud we are Jewish. We don't have to hide anymore. And we will do everything within our power to feel secure here. Where we belong."

Heading toward Café Tamar the next day, Shula turns left onto Shenkin from Allenby and runs into a long line of people. She groans when she sees coils of barbed wire blocking the street. Half a dozen British soldiers man the checkpoint. She glances at her wristwatch and sighs. A woman in front of her turns and smirks.

"Be patient my dear. This may take a while."
She pulls a postcard from her purse, a picture of the Tower and Stockade settlement where Avraham is stationed with the Palmach. She rereads the postscript: *I'll see you at Sachne soon!* She hasn't seen him for weeks and can't wait for her trip to the hot springs, and her chance to get out of the city.

The wait is so long she manages to play *Rhapsody in Blue* twice in her head before making it to the front. Avoiding the soldier's eyes, she hands over her identification card. He checks her face against the picture stapled inside. They lock eyes for a moment and she looks down, knowing that any sign of impatience will make the soldier move even slower. An older man pushes up to the front, jostling her into the barbed wire to her left. The soldiers grab him and pull him aside, but he forces himself forward again.

"I have to get home. My wife is sick! She is sick!" he says over and over again in Hebrew. One of the soldiers grabs his arm.

"English, please. *Ahn-gleet*! I don't speak Hebrew," he says. The old man looks panicked and Shula wants to help, but a second soldier pulls at her, moving her past the bottleneck. Feeling a tug on her dress from below, she sees her hem is caught on the barbed wire. Bending down, she tries to unhook it when the soldier pulls her arm again. The fabric tenses, then releases as it rips, and she gasps at the torn material. A wave of anger engulfs her.

"Now look what you did!" she says. The soldier shows no emotion on his face.

"Move along, miss. Move along," He waves her through and turns back to the next person in line. She hates these checkpoints, she hates these British soldiers, she hates the old man who pushed her into the hated barbed wire. Standing there, she takes a deep breath, looks at the ripped hem, then turns so they won't see her tears of rage.

When she makes it to Café Tamar she is taken aback when she spots Solomon wearing the familiar British uniform. Looking down at her dress, she decides not to tell him about the soldiers. He lifts his eyes from his paper when she approaches and jumps up, spilling his coffee.

"Oy vey! How clumsy of me," he says. Shula can't help but laugh. She feels like she can finally relax after the stress of the walk over. She sits down and looks at her hem once again.

"Is everything all right?" he asks.

"It is now that I made it here. But look what happened at the last checkpoint up the street. It wasn't this hard getting around Tel Aviv a few months ago," she says.

"I'm so sorry about that," he answers looking at the torn fabric. "You will be able to get that fixed, won't you?"

"Yes, at least I hope so. But enough about my poor dress, tell me how you are," Shula says, deciding then and there to enjoy herself despite what happened. She is curious about this man and wants to get to know him. She looks around the café, waving at Mr. Sternberg, the owner, to order her drink. Mr. Sternberg, a gruff Polish Jew with a potbelly and thick eyebrows, walks over.

"Yes, what can I get you?" he asks as he surveys his café kingdom.

"Coffee, white, please," she says. Mr. Sternberg nods and makes a note on his pad with the stub of a pencil. He looks over at Solomon.

"More coffee?" he asks.

"Actually, no. Do you have tea?"

"With lemon?"

"Milk, please," Solomon replies. Mr. Sternberg nods and turns away.

"You may want to stick with coffee. Mr. Sternberg serves Wissotzky Tea and most of the British complain that it's too weak and often tastes quite stale. A group of them once begged Mr. Sternberg to carry some strong British tea, they were even willing to get him some from the British Commissary, but Mr. Sternberg will only sell products made in *Eretz Yisrael*."

"Hmmm, weak and stale…kind of like this coffee," he replies.

"One doesn't come to Café Tamar for the beverages, Solomon," she says. "We come for the artistic and intellectual atmosphere."

"But don't artists and intellectuals like good drinks?" Solomon asks. Shula laughs.

"Ah! But Mr. Sternberg says it is good, and it's his place, so we agree. Anyway, like I said, you don't come to Café Tamar for the coffee." Solomon smiles at her, cradling his chin in the palm of his hand.

"Well, I certainly didn't come for the drinks. I'm so glad you made it," he says. She feels herself blush again. She has never been around someone who made her feel this way, uncomfortable and excited.

Just then Mr. Sternberg returns with their steaming beverages, places them on the table, and stalks away. Solomon lifts the tea bag in and out of the cup a few times and watches the water turn a light brown.

"It does get darker than this, right?"

She smiles and shakes her head. She can't think of a thing to say. The best she can come up with is something about the weather. *Oy,* she thinks, *how boring.*

"Have you been enjoying the weather?" she says.

"Yes, indeed. Definitely not like the cold winters of England."

"How long will you be staying?" she asks, dreading the answer.

"Not long, I'm afraid. I'm conducting a training, so I'll be here for six to eight weeks." Shula doesn't press him for more information. She is used to soldiers not divulging much.

"So," he says. "What do you do when you are not playing the piano?"

"I'm attending secretarial school right now," she replies as they lapse into silence and watch the people walk down the street in front of them.

"You know, it's funny, in England you would never sit at a café and face the street, just to watch the people walk by. It would be considered rude, whereas here, it's normal." Solomon looks at Shula. "So many things here are the same yet so different. Like you. You look European, but then again, you're not."

"I'm a *Yishuvnik.*"

"I know! It's wonderful! It's unbelievable! Jewish people from all over the world living, working, building, and studying in the land of our ancestors? It's just so new! I guess that's what I'm trying to say. There's no word for it yet," he says.

"But there is," she answers. "*Sabra.* The fruit of the cactus."

"Ah, yes. Prickly on the outside and sweet on the inside, isn't that what they say?" He leans back and looks at her. "May I make a suggestion?" he says.

"And that is?"

"You might consider playing the Royal Albert Hall one day." She widens her eyes at the mention of the famed London concert hall.

"Oh, I would love to! Have you been there? Is it as beautiful as the pictures? I suppose every concert must sound wonderful in a place like that," she says. He laughs at her effusive response.

"Well, yes, I have been there. My mother teaches music at a Jewish school in Bromley and we go there as often as we can. Have been since I was little. Sometimes we stand in the back when we can't afford actual seats. I love it now, but when I was a little boy, I must be honest, it was hard to stand through certain arias, if you know what I mean," he says laughing. She is thrilled to hear this. Few of her friends show an interest in classical music, frustrating her at times. She likes to have company at a concert.

"I saw that Hanna Rovina may star in *The Dybbuk* at Habima Theater soon," he says. Shula lights up at the name of her favorite actress.

"I saw her once at an outdoor theater, but when the wind shifted, we couldn't hear her. I would love to see her there," she says.

"Well, if it happens, let's go together," he says, glancing at her, then looking back down at the table. Shula is about to answer when she hears a man yelling from behind. Mr. Sternberg is arguing with a middle-aged gentleman in a dingy white suit.

"What is that all about?" Solomon asks as he turns to look.

"That man, Nachum, owes money on two separate tabs and Mr. Sternberg just figured it out. Nachum says he can't pay either of them. Poor man. He left Poland with just the clothes on his back. Now Mr. Sternberg is sending him to Siberia," she says.

"Siberia?" he laughs. "Is that what you call it? That's funny. Haven't heard that one before." She looks at Nachum hovering by the tables at the outer edge of the café.

"He won't let him sit. He has to finish his coffee standing. Nachum practically lives here. He doesn't have anything else in the world but this café."

"How much is the fellow in to Mr. Sternberg for?"

"About 100 *grush*," she says. Solomon reaches into his jacket and pulls out his wallet.

"Well, I always try and do a *mitzvah* when I see the opportunity," he says and fishes out the bills. He gets up from the table and approaches Mr. Sternberg, standing at the entrance to the café, his thick arms crossed over his chest, his dark eyes glaring at Nachum. Solomon talks to the café owner and hands him the money while pointing to Nachum. Mr. Sternberg hesitates for a moment before taking the bills and slipping them into his pants pocket. Smiling, he slaps Solomon on the back. He speaks with him for a few minutes then signals to Nachum to take his regular seat by the door.

"That was interesting," Solomon says as he sits down. "Did you know Mr. Sternberg's daughter is joining the British Army's Women's Brigade?"

"Yes, I heard. That was a very nice thing to do," she replies.

"Once he calmed down, he was downright friendly." Leaning in toward Shula, he lowers his voice. "Which was a relief, I tell you. I never know how I'll be treated these days when I'm wearing my uniform."

Then it hits her. He is wearing the same uniform as the checkpoint guards. A waiter comes by carrying a plate filled with *rugelach*.

"Compliments of Mr. Sternberg," he says. She takes one of the small cinnamon rolls stuffed with raisins and bites into the sugary treat.

"*Bon Appetit,*" says Solomon.

"*B'Tayavon* to you too," she replies.

After an hour, Shula has to start home. She tries to think of when she might be able to meet Solomon again, when she has an idea.

"Have you been to Sachne?" she asks.

"No, I haven't. In fact, I'm not quite sure what you are talking about," he says.

"It's a place just south of the Sea of Galilee with these amazing hot springs. My brother is stationed nearby, so a group of our friends are going up there this Friday to meet him. You should come. We'll be back by Sunday," she says, amazed at her bold invite.

"Why, thank you, Shula. I'd love to join you. I'm hoping to see as much of the country as I can while I'm here." They lock eyes for a moment. The blush rises in her cheeks and she looks down at her wristwatch.

"I'm sorry Solomon, I have to start home. It may take extra time to get there." She stands, and Solomon takes her hand and kisses it. The warmth of his palm and the softness of his lips surprise her.

"I must be getting back myself. It was a pleasure talking to you and I look forward to seeing you on Friday," he says as he walks away from the café. "I say," he says stopping. "How should I get there?" How stupid of her for not telling him the whole plan.

"We're meeting at noon on Friday at the Central Bus Station. Near the Haifa queue. A friend is borrowing a car for the weekend. Don't forget to bring your swimming costume!" Solomon smiles and tips his hat to her.

Standing for a moment, she calculates the shortest route home given the street closures she encountered on her way over. She clips her purse open and shut, open and shut, then decides that heading north on Shenkin is her safest bet. As she wonders if she will have time to stop at Esther's and get her hem fixed, an uncomfortable feeling comes over her. She scans the crowded cafe searching for the source, and to her surprise, sees Danny sitting at a table four rows back, slumping in his chair, arms folded across his chest. His bright blue eyes bore into her.

One year ago, he came over to their home to try and convince Avraham to enlist in the Irgun with him. The conversation devolved into a fight where friends, family, and actions were all attacked. After that, Danny slammed out of the house and disappeared from their lives for good. But seeing him now makes her think of Avraham and all the times they shared. She smiles at him and Danny curls his finger signaling her to come to him.

Making her way toward Danny's table, she notices how different he looks now that he is eighteen. Gone is the slight boy with the gangly arms and legs, so excited about flying, so excited about life. Danny looks mean — it is the only way she can describe it. His blondish hair is short but left longer in front, the curls falling down over his forehead in the fashion of the *Yishuv*. The sleeves of his white button-down shirt are rolled up to his elbows, and his khaki pants are shabby and worn. He furrows his brow and squints his eyes as he watches her move through the labyrinth of tables and chairs. Approaching him, she holds out her hand.

"Nice to see you, Danny. It's been a long time." She stands there with her hand out but instead of taking it, he motions for her to take the seat next to him.

"You want me to touch your hand right after you shook the hand of our enemy?" he says. Shula starts to sit but stands up again. Her stomach tightens up and she feels her neck get hot. *Bristling like a cat.*

"I am not here to argue with you, Danny. I came to say hello. If you want to fight, find someone else," she says adjusting her purse on her arm.

"Sit. I have something to tell you," he says, and the way he looks at her, commands her, makes her stay.

"So, talk," she says sitting back down. She looks around searching for anyone else she might know there, feeling self-conscious for sitting with Solomon. "How is your father these days?"

"Still working for the occupying forces. I don't talk to my parents," he says as he stirs his coffee. Shula watches his spoon go around and around.

"But Danny, they are your parents," she says. Does she even have anything in common with this boy any longer? She can't imagine not seeing her parents on a regular basis. "They love you so much and are proud of you." Danny laughs, but it comes out more like a bark.

"They aren't proud of me. They think I'm a terrorist," he says. Shula decides not to engage in this. She will give him five minutes for old times' sake, and then she is leaving. She checks her wristwatch. Danny looks away and lights a cigarette. He offers one to Shula. She shakes her head.

"How's Avraham?" he asks as the smoke streams from his nostrils.

"He's fine, Danny. What do you want to tell me?"

"That's good, that's good," Danny says and flicks the ashes off onto the ground. "Send him my regards, would you?" She nods and waits for him to continue. Danny leans in toward her.

"I need to warn you, Shulamit. Some of the gangs are capturing girls like you if they are found with a British soldier. They shave their heads, even tar and feather them. Did you know that? You have to be careful, and you have to choose your side. This isn't a game. We are at war!" His tone is quiet but urgent. The heat rises up in her, not out of embarrassment, but with fury.

"I don't need you threatening me, Danny."

"I'm not threatening you. I'm telling you the truth," he says. Shula feels her ears burn.

"The truth?" she says, clenching and unclenching her fist. "The truth is I can't walk down the street without going through rolls of barbed wire at every turn. I sleep with my clothing on sometimes and my shoes at the ready so I can run to shelter at any moment. The truth is we sit at home most nights and don't go out because we are too scared, not of the British and not of the Arabs, but of our own people — the Jews." She takes a deep breath and looks him in the eyes, the eyes she had dreamily stared at a few years ago. Now she only feels anger and huge disappointment. "The truth is that I don't care for you. I don't care what you or your idiotic gang says. You aren't acting like human beings!" She stands up knocking his cup off the table. She watches as it crashes to the floor, splashing a few drops onto his pants. *Good*, she thinks, *a stain to remember me by.*

Arriving home, she finds her mother, father and aunts gathered together on the sofa. Her mother sobs out loud, while Sarah and Rivka cry in silence. Yaakov sits by Rachel holding her around the shoulders. Shula drops her book bag on the floor and sinks down at her mother's feet.

"Eema, what happened?" She looks at the grave and tear-stained faces of her family. Rivka's eyes are liquefying and Sarah blows her red-tinged nose into a handkerchief. Panic rises inside her. *Avraham!* Rachel's bottom lip trembles.

"It's true. It's all true. Worse than we even knew." Her mother lifts the newspaper spread over her lap, then leans into Yaakov and begins crying again. "My poor family! My poor Leah!" Shula looks at her father for some kind of explanation. Yaakov sighs and slips the newspaper from Rachel's lap.

"The Americans released a report today," he reads aloud, smoothing the paper. "Document estimates 1,765,000 Jews gassed to death in one camp," he reads.

Shula sinks back to the floor, her arms holding her up for support. "The report gives a 'careful estimate' of the number of Jews gassed to death in Birkenau between April 1942 and April 1944: 1,765,000 total Jews, of whom 900,000 came from Poland; 300,000 from Polish camps for foreign Jews; 150,000 from France; 100,000 from Holland; 60,000 from Germany; 50,000 each from Belgium and Lithuania; 45,000 from Greece; 30,000 from Slovakia; 50,000 from Yugoslavia, Italy and Norway together; and 30,000 from Bohemia, Moravia and Austria together," he reads. Shula can barely hear him at this point. The numbers are so huge. Almost two million killed for what? For being Jews? And what about Doda Leah? It had been years since they heard from her; did this mean she was dead?

"Where we came from is gone. All gone," Sarah says as her shoulders begin to shake. She stands up. "I'll make tea," she says walking to the kitchen.

"What else does it say?" Shula asks, looking at her father while taking her mother's hand.

"The atrocities reported in detail are characterized by the report as 'so revolting and diabolical' that 'the minds of civilized people find it difficult to believe that they have taken place' — "

"Enough! I can't hear this anymore!" Rachel cries. There is so much pain in her eyes that Shula almost doesn't recognize her.

"We told her not to go back," Rivka says. "We told her she would be safe here. But now it's too late. It's too late," she says as tears roll down her cheeks.

"And what about Papa? And your cousins in Krakow?" Rachel turns to Yaakov with panic in her eyes. "And the worst part is that the British won't let the Jews into the Yishuv!" she says, then bursts out. "That stupid British Mandate White Paper with their immigration quotas. Why do they limit the number of Jews fleeing from those that want them dead? Well, here's a new White Paper!" She grabs the newspaper from Yaakov and holds it up. Shula sees the lists and lists of numbers. "Now, do you think they'll change their minds? After the facts have been revealed?"

Shula looks towards the kitchen and sees Sarah standing there, staring out the small window, the water boiling away on the stove. She picks the paper up off the floor where her mother has dropped it and spreads it out in front of her. She scans the article. She reads about medical experiments performed on inmates of the camps called Auschwitz and Birkenau, about the Jews given a sliver of soap and a washcloth and then crowded into shower rooms, only to be gassed to death in less than three minutes. And all the while, Nazi officers watched them die then counted the bodies, keeping meticulous records throughout. It is too much to take in. She tries to finish the article. There were rumors of the camps and what was going on in Europe, but it was just that, rumors, stories, jokes that the kids would tell in the playground or adults would whisper about around the dinner table. But reading this report, researched and published by the American government, she finds the horror just too much to take in. A wave of nausea overtakes her and she escapes to the balcony.

Outside, she breathes in the cool evening air and leans over the concrete wall. The street is quiet. A man with a pork pie hat walks his little black terrier down the street, the red lead connecting them. She sees the proprietor of the corner store moving the merchandise that dangles outside the front door back inside before closing. It is all so ordinary, so quiet, so peaceful. Nothing makes sense to her at all. Danger, war, and hatred are spread all over the world. Did there exist a place in the universe where one could live in peace?

As planned, a few days later Shula arrives at the Central Bus Station in Tel Aviv just as Aryeh pulls up in the British officer's station wagon. She waves to the group and clutches the straps of her backpack as she runs over to where they are loading up the car. Lilach gives her a hug, then swings her arm around Shula's shoulder, giving her a squeeze. She looks around for Solomon but doesn't see him

"Do you think he'll show up?" she asks Lilach.

"Don't worry! He'll show up," Lilach says. Shula looks around again. *Well, even if he doesn't show up, nothing could ruin this trip.* She knows the second she sees Avraham the slight irritation in her stomach will subside and she can relax her shoulders again. She looks forward to cleansing herself in the waters of the warm springs and not worrying about barbed wire, road blocks, checkpoints, random identity checks, bombings, assassinations, and the horrors of the death camps, at least for a few days. Then she sees Solomon and waves. He is wearing khakis and what looks like the light blue, button-down Utility shirt her brother has. She decides that she likes the way he looks out of uniform so much better. Solomon waves back, and Shula feels Lilach's hand on her shoulder and her warm breath by her ear.

"I told you he'd be here," she teases, then scrambles into the car just as Solomon strides up. He and Shula exchange a quick hug.

"I heard from someone at the base that this place, Sachne, has healing powers," he says as they get into the car.

"They say if you have something that you are sad or mad about, the waters will make those feelings go away," she says, settling into her seat.

"You don't seem to be a sad or mad person," he says.

"I'm not," she says. "But I do want to wash away all thoughts of war for a few hours. That would be nice."

During the bumpy, dusty five-hour ride to Kibbutz Tel Amal, the friends play "Name that Tune" by seeing who can guess the song on the radio first. Shula and Solomon win each round, discouraging the rest of the players. Pulling up to gate of the settlement she sees Avraham, rifle slung over his shoulder, walking towards them, a big smile on his face. She scrambles over Solomon, and before the car stops, she is out the door and running to her brother.

"Avraham!" She jumps into his arms and he twirls her around in a big brother hug. After weeks of uncertainty and tension, she feels safe and happy.

After settling into their tents, Shula and her friends meet up at the new dining hall. Windows line three sides of the building and steam rises from large pots in the open kitchen. Hungry *kibbutzniks* and soldiers sit side by side at long tables while others stand in lines waiting for their turn to fill their plates. The room is alive with people arguing, complaining and talking. Shula grabs Solomon's elbow and steers him to the food line. She hands him a wooden tray and they walk by station after station, collecting portions of soup, meat, and vegetables from the women and men serving them from behind the counter. She shows him where to fill a small porcelain cup with water. Avraham waves them over to his table just as she feels the first pangs of hunger.

Shula feels all eyes on them as they sit. She always gets this feeling when she visits a kibbutz. Anyone new is sure to stand out in such a tiny settlement where all members work, eat and live communally. They sit across from a young couple still wearing their work clothes. The woman wears a bandana over her hair, her black curls sticking out here and there refusing to be contained. The man is tan and wears his cap pushed back on his head, his shirt stained with dirt and sweat. He smiles at them.

"Maybe I should have dressed for dinner," he says to the woman. "I didn't know we had guests." He looks as Solomon says the blessing over his meal. "You believe in God?" he asks.

"Yes, yes. Of course, I do," he replies.

"Ach! I used to when I was young and lived in Poland. Then this happened." The man points to the deep scars on his forearm. "A group of Poles unleashed their dogs on me when I was walking home from the market one day. That's when I decided that God isn't some imaginary thing that may help me someday. That's when I decided that God is here," he picks up his cup, "and here," he picked a piece of lettuce from his plate. "God is in the things I can see and feel. You understand?" He looks at Solomon with such intensity that Shula feels the need to intervene.

"I'm Shula and this is my friend Solomon. We are visiting my brother Avraham," she says pointing to her brother.

"Oh, such a lovely fellow. So talented!" the woman says. "He helped design and paint the backdrops for our last play. It's a pleasure to have him here. We wish he would stay."

"He is gifted," answers Shula. "But I'm afraid that he has his heart set on two things; architecture and flying."

"Yes, he told us all about his studies. But, maybe he will come back afterwards and help us build this kibbutz. And where are you from?" she says looking at Solomon.

"I'm here from London. Err…England."

"Are the skies this blue in London?" the man says as he points out the window.

"Well, the skies are usually covered with clouds, although we do have some beautiful summer days," he says.

"There is no place on earth with skies like *Eretz Yisrael*," the man continues. "Are you planning on staying here? To help the Jewish people?" He looks Solomon in the eyes.

"I'm afraid not," Solomon says. "I'm signed up with the British Army for the next two years, and then there's my family's business —"

"We need young men like you here, you understand?" the man interjects. "We need to build up our own army. The British won't be able to stay here much longer. They'll be leaving soon enough. It's inevitable." His eyes bore into Solomon's.

"Well, I believe that right now, I can do more for the Jewish people in the British Army. Hitler must be stopped and the Allied Forces can do that."

"I've heard that argument from those here who choose to join the Jewish Brigade of your British Armed Forces. 'I can do more good fighting the Germans!'" he says in a sing-song voice. "As far as I'm concerned the Germans can and will go to hell. What we need to do is defend what we have now! You think that you're safe in England? That the English people won't turn on the Jews there? Ha! That's what we thought in Poland and look where that got us!" The man pushes back his chair and picks up his tray. The woman puts her hand on his arm.

"Chaim, enough. The boy is just visiting," she says.

"It may not be easy here, but it's the only home we Jews have!" he says as he stalks off towards the kitchen.

"I'm so sorry about Chaim," the woman says as she stands and lifts her tray. "Sometimes he's not very polite. Enjoy your stay." Shula looks after her until she is sure that the woman is out of earshot.

"Sorry about that. He was pretty mean," she says.

"No worries, Shula," he says. "Don't think I didn't think about this long and hard. I think every Jewish man in the world is thinking about it. But I made my decision and I believe it was the right one for me. Some of these people," he turns and looks around the room. "Some of

124

these people are hurt. They are damaged. I can't judge them after what they've been through." Solomon lifts his cup in a toast. "To Jewish people everywhere," he says, "*L'Chaim*, to life!"

The following morning, Shula wakes early and pulls on her swimsuit. She can't wait to be in the magical water where it feels warm when it's cool and cool when it is hot. And the waterfalls! She looks forward to the power of the water beating down on her shoulders.

After filling a basket with sandwiches, fruit and water from the dining hall, the group walks to the springs. When they arrive, Shula catches her breath. It is beautiful. The slow-moving river is a mix of blues from teal to sapphire, and flows through small ponds at different levels, creating constant waterfalls. The shore is sloped in some areas and in others are light brown cliffs, not too high, but high enough. She watches two young Arab boys run, then jump off the edge. They hold hands while they fly through the air then land in the water with a loud splash. The group of friends finds a small grassy spot under one of the palm trees and lays down their blankets. Then, not wanting to waste another minute, she runs to the water's edge.

Diving into the warm waters, she feels a weight lift off her chest. The waters are clear and feel cool in the hot sun. She turns back to the shore as Avraham, Aryeh and Solomon walk to the cliffs. The three young men yell like Tarzan, then jump into the water.

"Let's take a shower!" Lilach says, and they wade through the water towards the nearest waterfall. The two girls stand under the rushing stream and Shula lets the water crash down on her head. She looks through the liquid curtain and sees the boys swimming languidly in the pool. Avraham stops and waves at her to join him. The group gathers around her brother.

"Now that you have all experienced the glory of the Sachne springs, we will do our cleansing ceremony," he says.

"Do we have to say a prayer?" asks Aryeh.

"No, no prayers. This is a ritual, although," he says, turning to Solomon, "you can always say one if you want."

"I'm sure if I feel the need, I can think of an appropriate prayer to say."

"Good, good! Okay friends," Avraham says, turning back to the group. "Think of something that is making you sad, or angry, something that you just want to get out of your mind. Now hold that image, take a deep breath and dive under the water. Hold that thought and your breath for as long as you can manage and then, only then, come up for air. And you'll see that thought will not feel so bad any longer. Now close your eyes, and when I count to three, dive under the water." Eyes closed, Shula hears Avraham say, "One…Two…Three…"

She thinks about her image. She would like to erase the unrest in the Yishuv from her mind. She wants the war in Europe to end, her brother at home, and she doesn't want to worry walking through her neighborhood.

"Dive!"

She ducks down into the pool. Opening her eyes, she sees her friends, her brother, all of them, holding their breath, eyes closed, suspended in liquid. Lilach furrows her brow, then her face relaxes and she rises up for air, her red curls billowing around her like an ethereal mermaid. Aryeh bobs up next, then Solomon, and then it is just she and Avraham. He looks over at her and gives her a thumbs-up. She nods her head. He waves and lifts his head above water. Only then, when her lungs feel like they are about to burst, does she push up towards the light and breathe in the fresh air.

Chapter 7

A Trip to the Galilee

July 1947

It is mid-July and a *hamseen*, a heat wave, blankets the country. Shula's legs stick to the hot seat of the bus on her way to the Central Bus Station. It's funny how close she feels to someone she hasn't seen in two and a half years, she thinks, pulling the most recent letter from Solomon from her bag. She was sixteen when she met him, and since then, the occasional postcard they exchanged turned into weekly letters where they discovered a mutual love of Rachmaninoff and most recently, Leonard Bernstein.

"Dearest Shula, It was a great joy to receive your last letter. I laughed out loud when I read about your Leonard Bernstein experience. I had no idea you didn't know who he was. I'm glad your friends convinced you to go. I've seen him twice in London and both times he was breathtaking. I think you would agree that he is quite a talented man." She laughs when she reads that last line again. Saying Leonard Bernstein is "quite a talented man" is like calling Albert Einstein smart. She pulls out the small photo he included and flips it over. *"The Royal Albert Hall, of course! Fondly, Solomon."* She'd love to visit Solomon in London one day. *When things quiet down here. When things quiet down.*

All around the crowded bus passengers fan themselves with their morning papers. The headlines scream out: *"EXODUS 1947! BRITISH REFUSE ENTRY TO PALESTINE TO 4,554 VISALESS JEWS!"* All morning she hears talk of the refugees stranded in the Mediterranean. She looks over the shoulder of an older

127

man sitting next to her, trying to read his paper. He smiles at her at her and moves it so they can both read.

"Thank you," she says.

"We all need to be informed these days," he replies.

"The President Garfield left the port of Marseilles on Friday and was spotted by British reconnaissance planes yesterday afternoon. This blockade runner has been in contact with the Jewish Haganah forces in Palestine."

"You know, time is running out for the British here," the man says. "World opinion is shifting in our favor now. The great empire is falling!" He chuckles and turns to face her. "Did you hear that a delegation from the United Nations is here researching a partition plan for a Jewish and an Arab Palestine?" He shrugs and turns to the next page. "Who knows? It's been 2000 years since the Jews had a home. I never get my hopes up."

As they pull into the bus station, she catches sight of the giant square clock suspended from the overhang and scans the crowd for Avraham. As the bus parks in its berth she tosses her backpack over her shoulder, her canteen strapped across her chest.

"Going on a hike?" the man asks.

"Yes, my brother and I are hiking across the Galilee."

"Ah! From sea to sea?"

"Yes, from the Galilee to the Mediterranean," she replies. She feels a jostling behind her as a woman with a large package and baby in tow tries to push past her down the narrow aisle.

"*Nu*? Young lady! Are you moving or staying here? This isn't a café, you know," she says, and Shula starts down the aisle.

"Have a wonderful trip!" the man calls after her. "Enjoy every minute, because you never know what tomorrow may bring." His words make her shiver despite the heat. She doesn't want to think about the future right now, unless it has to do with the next two weeks.

Running to the Haifa queue, she pushes through the crowds milling about the metal stanchions that curve around the platform. No sign of Avraham. She wanders over to the food stalls and buys a round bread covered with sesame. She breaks off a piece and watches as the small white seeds sprinkle down to the ground. *The streets of Tel Aviv are littered with sesame and sunflower seeds.* She looks at the clock again — 7:20 and no Avraham. Typical.

At eight o'clock, she feels a pinch at her waist. She whirls around to find Avraham laughing.

"Avraham! I've been waiting for almost an hour!"

"What can I say? The King takes his time in the mornings," he replies. Shula rolls her eyes and pretends to bow to him as she reaches down to pick up her pack. She hitches it onto her back.

"It's not polite to make your subjects wait."

"I'm a King! I don't have to be polite. Come on. The bus to Sefad is over there," he says leading the way.

The crowds are thick now. People mill about eating their *bageles*, drinking hot tea or steaming coffee by the food stands, reading newspapers and talking about one topic. The *Exodus.*

"Did you see the *Exodus* when you left Haifa this morning?" she asks.

"No, it's too far out to see from the docks, but they did bring in a few people by boat and loaded them into ambulances."

"Were there a lot of sick people?"

"I couldn't tell. It's crazy though. People at the docks were yelling at the British that if they didn't let the refugees in, they would be sending them back to their deaths. Really, we have the room here! Let them come! We'll take care of our own, right?"

Spotting their bus, she hurries toward it. She can't wait to get out of this hot and crowded place. She wants to escape the bad news surrounding them. She wants to be in the country.

The bus pulls out of the station, winds through the busy Tel Aviv streets and then heads north. People with their packages get on and off every few kilometers, loading the larger items onto the top of the vehicle. At one point a man climbs onto the roof and a second man hoists a goat up to him, which he proceeds to tie onto the roof rack. Shula can hear the faint bleating of the animal for the next hour as they continue up the increasing hilly terrain. And, although she has never warmed to that particular animal, she still feels bad for the creature above her head.

They reach the mystical town of Sefad, its ancient stone buildings glowing brilliant saffron in the setting sun.

"Come on, we have to get to the top before dark," Avraham urges. "We'll be at one of the highest points in the country!"

"Yes? And then what?"

"And then? We'll dance the *horah* to celebrate." He grabs her hand and they run the rest of the way up the narrow streets.

When they reach the top of the hill they indeed dance the *horah*. Shula laughs so hard tears run down her cheeks, and she sits. Avraham dries her tears with a handkerchief and gives her arm a squeeze.

"What's bothering you, my sister?" She sighs.

"Where do I begin?"

"Tough luck that your recital was canceled," he adds.

"I don't get it, Avraham. Every time I think I am going to get a break, something happens beyond my control and once again, I put my dreams aside 'until things quiet down.' I spent weeks working on 'Notturno in G minor.' I even bought a new dress. Mr. Brandt had two men from the symphony coming to hear me. Now we'll just have to wait."

"There'll be another performance in the near future, I'm sure. Be patient."

"Patient? That's what Eema and Abba always say. I don't feel like I have much choice, but playing concertos in my bedroom is not my idea of moving forward," she says.

"That's true, but just think, if they hadn't cancelled your recital, you wouldn't have been able to take this fantastic trip with me! What could be better than that?" He bumps his shoulder to hers and they grin at each other. Closing her eyes, she lets the breeze cool her. It's quiet and peaceful. She hasn't felt this calm in months.

Sitting back to back, Avraham sketches in his notebook while Shula looks out over the white limestone buildings. She works on her recital piece, pushing the pads of her fingers into her thigh. After a few minutes, she turns to peek at his sketches, but he pulls the book away.

"Not now! When I'm finished, you can see!" he says, shielding his pad from her view.

As the sun dips behind the hills, they leave their perch and head towards the Old Town. An older Yemenite man sweeps the steps outside a large synagogue, his black and grey corkscrew side locks waving back and forth under his turban.

"*Bruchim Habaim,* welcome," he says.

"Good evening," replies Avraham.

"Where are you from?" he asks.

"Tel Aviv," Shula says.

"Ah, the Jewish City. I have never been. Concrete buildings and Hebrew in the streets, yes?"

"And the beach," adds Avraham.

"God willing, one day I will see. This is the Ari Synagogue, the sacred place of the great kabbalist Rabbi Luria, the Lion of Sefad. If you have some time, you may ask God for something. Here, inside." He motions for them to follow. Shula looks at her brother and shrugs her shoulders.

"Sure," Avraham says and starts up the steps. Following the man through a side door, he leads them to a small chamber. Along one wall is a shelf covered in thick layers of candle wax. Burning flames illuminate the room. Shadows dance around them.

"This is the room where the Holy Ari himself studied and where Elijah the Prophet visited him not once but several times." The man steps aside, letting Avraham and Shula enter while he stays just outside the doorway. He points to the long counter.

"If you light a candle in here you may ask God for something." He hands them each a candle to place on the counter. "In here, you are protected from the evil eye. Feel free to ask God for anything."

Shula closes her eyes. She doesn't believe in this nonsense, but figures she might as well ask for something. She wishes that her recital will be rescheduled, that she will be chosen to perform as a soloist with the symphony, and that she can take a trip to Italy with her brother next year. Avraham opens his eyes and turns to the man.

"You don't want to ask God for something?" he asks. The man takes a step backwards and shifts his feet.

"I don't go in that room," he replies.

"Why not?" The man looks at them and sighs.

"It used to be called the Death Room," he says. "It was said that if you walked into that room, you would die. But in 1921 Baba Sali, the holy Praying One, came here and he broke the curse, so now it's safe."

"Then why not come and ask God for something?" she asks. The man wraps his forefinger around a side lock and pulls.

"My mother was seriously ill when I was young. Late one night, my father brought me here. He wanted me to light a candle, but I was too afraid. He lit a candle, said his prayers and then we left. The next day he had to go to Tel Chai. It was 1920. He was caught in a vicious battle between the Zionist settlers and the Arabs. He was killed. Even after Baba Sali came the next year and took away the curse, I still wouldn't go into the Death Room." He pauses and looks at them.

"My family has lived here for ten generations. We never had problems with the Arabs until the Zionists came.

The following day, they decide to hitchhike north along the Sea of Galilee. Within minutes a truck stops and the driver motions for them to jump onto the mounds of oranges in the back.

"Just try not to eat too many," he says as they climb aboard. She watches Avraham as he leans his arm over the side and rests his chin on his forearm, his hair blowing in the breeze. She breathes in the sweet smell of the oranges and lets the wind wash over her face. Looking out over the sparkling blue water of the lake, she can't wait to wash the dirt and sweat off her body.

"Coming to the Sea of Galilee was a brilliant idea," she shouts over the rumble of the truck's diesel engine. Avraham laughs.

"It was my idea, right?" he shouts back. She tosses an orange in his direction. Peeling it, he hands her half. She bites into the warm citrus, relishing the sweet juice as it soothes her parched throat. After twenty minutes, Avraham bangs on the side of the truck. The driver stops and they jump off the back. Cutting through an olive grove they reach the lakeshore. Fresh water glistens in the sunlight and Shula catches her breath.

"It's lovely," she says.

"I told you," Avraham replies as he plops his pack down on a patch of grass. "This is the spot we used to come when I was stationed in Tel Amal." He takes off his shoes and socks. "The trick is," he continues, starting towards the rocky shore, "You have to run as fast as you can," and bolts for the shoreline. Shula laughs as he runs into the water yelling like Johnny Weissmuller's Tarzan.

Shula takes her time. Laying out her towel, she folds her clothes and tucks them in her pack. She ties her hair up with her kerchief. Two girls about her age sit off to the side staring at Avraham and giggling. Her brother always attracts that kind of attention, especially when he shows off. He spits out a stream of water as he floats on his back. Shula steps out onto the rocks and starts towards the shore. Rocks jut into the underside of her feet, making each step hurt.

"Avraham! The rocks are cutting me!"

"I told you. The trick is to run," he yells back.

"This is crazy! Ouch! What a stupid idea! I'd much rather deal with the crowds at the beach in Tel Aviv then walk over these godforsaken things," she complains. The girls laugh. She calculates it will take her eight strides to get into the lake. "Watch out! Here I come!" she yells leaping towards the shimmering water. She dives in headfirst, cleaning the day's grime from her skin. Flipping onto her back, she looks up at the blue sky. Fresh water feels so different from the sea water she is used to. Cleaner, clearer. No wonder Jesus washed here. She swims over to Avraham.

"I take it back. Whoever thought of this idea was a genius," she says.

"And who would that be?"

"You," she replies. He smiles, glancing over at the girls on the shore.

"I'm getting out," he says. "You coming?" She shakes her head.

"No, I'm going for a swim." On shore, her brother grabs his towel and dries off. He waves at the girls who, of course, wave back.

"Where are you from?" one of the girls asks.

"Tel Aviv," he replies.

"Oooh! A Tel Avivi," she teases. "And your girlfriend? Is she from Tel Aviv, too?"

"That's my sister, not my girlfriend," he tells them. The two girls look at each other and giggle. Shula has seen enough. She swims away as Avraham sits with the girls. She knows that one day he will get married and have children of his own. That one day she will become Doda Shula and not be his best friend. It will come and that is fine. She just hopes it doesn't come too soon.

An hour later, the wind picks up, blowing stray leaves and dust in their direction. The two girls pack up their belongings and make Avraham promise to meet them at a café later on.

"Bring your sister," one of them says and Shula smiles from her spot on the shore and waves goodbye, knowing that there is not a chance in hell she is going to spend her precious evening with those two. She grabs her bag and begins to stuff her book and towel into it when she spots a small fishing boat close to shore. It is painted white with dark blue trim around the windows of the small onboard cabin. All of a sudden, Shula feels the urge, no the need, to get on this boat.

"Hey!" she yells at the sailor. "How about a ride?" Avraham looks at her like she has lost her mind.

"Shula, what are you doing? Can't you see the waves? It's too rough out there," he advises. But she waves him off and walks towards the shoreline. She waves at the boat.

"Hey! Mister! Can we have a ride on your boat?" she yells. The sailor smiles and laughs.

"The sea is dangerous right now, *motek*!" He tips his hat in her direction. Avraham joins her at the water's edge.

"Tomorrow we'll hire a boat. Right now, let's go to that café and meet the girls," he says. Shula turns to her brother and smiles. Her face is flushed. The wind whips her wavy hair.

"You can go sit in a café with some dumb girls," she says as she kicks off her shoes and wades out to the boat, holding her pack above her head, "or you can have an adventure with me. Hey!" she yells to the sailor. "I'm not afraid of some wind! Can you take me now?" The sailor shakes his head and laughs.

"*Yallah,* come on." He leans over the side and holds out his hand for her. The boat wobbles back and forth as she climbs on board. Her brother is close behind, wading into the water with his pack held high. A strong breeze causes a wave to splash him up to his neck. Shula laughs as he climbs aboard and shakes the sailor's hand.

"Thank you, sir. My sister acts a little crazy at times," he says.

"Crazy or fearless. Sometimes they are the same thing," the man answers as he guides the boat away from the shore and towards the choppy waters of the wide lake.

The first big wave they hit knocks Shula off her feet. She lands on her behind and Avraham helps her up. Finding her balance, she shrugs off his hand. Her goal is the front of the boat. She wants to stand there, feel the wind in her hair, the wild water around her. After so long dealing with the stress of school, piano studies, and the disruption of daily life in Tel Aviv, she needs this. She feels it. She wants it. The waves jostle her as she moves up the hull. She can barely hear Avraham and the sailor talking from the stern. The bow lifts off the water and slams back down again. She loses her balance, rights herself, and hangs onto the railing, pulling herself hand over hand. A few meters never felt so far.

"Hang on!" the sailor yells. Turning to face him, she smiles. She takes the last few steps to the front of the boat. How lucky those women carved into old sailing ships were, right out front, watching the whole world from this vantage point. She feels her foot slip on the wet floor, and then Avraham is at her side, his arm around her waist, his hair blowing in the warm wind. He kneels down and holds onto the tip of the bow. Shula rests her hands on his shoulders. Together they go up and down with the waves and the wind, and she feels more alive at that moment than she ever felt before.

Thank God for the kibbutznikim, because there is no way I would be able to live out here, she thinks when they arrive at Kibbutz Dafna a few days later. The landscape is barren. Shrubs cover the rocky ground. In the distance, a dry *wadi* wends its way through the parched terrain. Avraham points towards the mountains in the east.

"That's Syria over there," he says. Then pointing north, "And Lebanon over there. You can see why this kibbutz is so significant strategically. Come on, let's go find my friend Shaul."

When they enter the settlement gate she is pleasantly surprised. There is a green lawn with picnic tables near the kitchen under shade-giving trees. A young woman pushes a cart with five little children and sings an old Polish lullaby. She turns to see Avraham talking with someone.

"And this, my good friend, is my beautiful and talented sister, Shula. Shula, this is Shaul."

"Nice to meet you," she says shaking his hand. His bright blue eyes shine against his bronze skin. His light brown hair is cut short and the tips of his curls have been bleached blonde by the sun. He smiles at her. Something about his look makes her blush. She drops his hand.

"Nice to meet you too, Shaul. Avraham told me a lot about you."

"Should I worry? We told each other a lot of things sitting in that tower for hours on end." Shaul laughs and punches Avraham on the shoulder. "Come, I'll show you where you can rest up before dinner." He winks at her. Her heart flutters. She needs to wash her face.

After a short nap, Shula wakes disoriented. Avraham sleeps, his khaki shirt pulled tight over his shoulders, which move up and down with each breath. It reminds her of when they were little and lived in Nazareth. Sometimes, if she woke up in the middle of the night, she would watch her brother breathe, his chest moving up and down, up and down, and when the world felt right again, she could fall back asleep.

As the sun sets outside their tent, children's laughter mixes with the high twitter of little swifts darting around the trees. It is dinner time.

They pile their plates high with food from the dining hall, then join a group of young people at a picnic table under a tree. The setting sun bathes the area in a golden glow. The grass looks greener, the flowers a brighter pink or a deeper yellow. Shula watches parents play with their children on the lawn. Each time Shula visits a kibbutz she has the same thought, *what if I lived here?* It feels so relaxed. How nice it is to not worry about cooking meals, doing laundry or even taking care of your children. But in reality, living on a farm in the middle of nowhere would drive her crazy. She loves the culture, energy and excitement of the city. She breathes in the scent of the stew and bites into an enormous chunk of lamb. The meat melts in her mouth.

"Hey, this is pretty good," Avraham says as he digs into his goulash. "You can tell that a place has a lot of Polish Jews by the caliber of its goulash."

Shula looks around and sees the other diners conversing with a new sense of urgency. There's a shift in the air. A young man rushes to their table.

"Friends! Have you heard? The *Exodus*! The British said they aren't going to let the people off the boat and into the Yishuv. Do you believe it? There are hundreds of sick people onboard who have just escaped hell, and those bastards!" The young man stops and sits down at the table. The mood shifts. The calm of the evening, the beauty of their surroundings, is overshadowed by this news.

"What are you talking about? What have you heard?" Shaul asks.

"They brought the *Exodus* into Haifa then loaded the people onto three different British ships. Now they're sending them back out to sea. They don't even know where they are taking them! The camps on Cyprus are filled. No other country will take them."

"So, what are they going to do with all the people?" Avraham asks.

"Who knows? They're Jews, nobody cares," the young man says.

"I was there a week ago when they brought the sick into port," says Avraham. "I told my sister, I don't understand why they won't just let them into the Yishuv."

"The goddamn 1939 White Paper, that's why. The British are bastards for succumbing to Arab pressure and agreeing to a Jewish quota. Don't they know they're going to lose this one? This land belongs to us now! We are the Israelites and we will fight to the death to keep it!" The young man pounds his fist on the table, causing Shula to flinch. She pushes her plate away. The calm of the evening, the smiles from this handsome young man, all destroyed by the news. Who is she fooling? There is no escape.

After two weeks away, they are now hours from Tel Aviv. They decide to spend their last night at the Carmel winery in Zichron Yaakov.

Arriving late in the day, they find the winery is closed, but Avraham sweet-talks the caretaker into giving them a private tour and tasting, convincing him that Shula must pick out wines for her upcoming wedding. She gets into the ruse, talking about her imaginary fiancé (Solomon) and what food they will be serving. The caretaker warms to them, agreeing to take them on an extensive tour of the historic winery. He leads them to the rows of grape vines, pulling on his long grey beard as he talks.

"Carmel was founded by Baron Edmund de Rothschild in the late 1890s when the first group of Zionist Jewish immigrants came to the Yishuv, in what we now call the first *Aliyah*. This great man, one of the richest in France and owner of the revered winemaking establishment Chateau Lafitte, took it upon himself to open the first wineries in *Eretz Yisrael*. He helped choose the best grapes to grow and funded the digging of the massive wine cellars below." Shula picks two ripe grapes and hands one to Avraham. He throws it up in the air and catches it in his mouth. She peels the skin off with her teeth, savoring the fruit as they walk to the main building.

"Now we go to the tasting room in the cellar. It's quite cool down there, and I'm sure it will be a refreshing change from this heat." He pulls a handkerchief from his pocket and wipes the top of his head, then leads them down a long staircase and into the cellar. Shula catches her breath.

"I've never seen anything like this!" she says. The enormous room is lined floor to ceiling with giant wine barrels, most as round as she is tall. She shivers as her body acclimates to the cool temperature. Breathing in the complex scents that surround her, she discerns grapes, wine, wood and smoke. She runs her hand over the smooth wooden surface of a cask.

"Each of these barrels is filled with wine," the caretaker says. "We keep it here for months, sometimes years, depending on the type of wine we are making. Our wine master trained at the Baron's wineries in France. Carmel wines are some of the best in the world!"

"Then we must taste," says Avraham. They gather at a wooden table in the center of the room. Shula picks up one of the glass bottles and examines the label. In the picture are vineyards and the building where they now stand. Two figures carry a long stick between them laden with a large bunch of grapes.

"What is Muscat?" she asks about the golden liquid inside. The caretaker walks over to the opposite side of the table and adjusts his black vest. He reaches down and pulls out several glasses, lining them up in front of them. He pulls the bottle from Shula's hand and places it back on the table.

"That is a dessert wine. For the end of the meal. We will start with a dry white which can go well with fish — even gefilte," he says with a laugh. He pours some into each glass. "Have you done a wine tasting before?" They shake their heads. "Well, first you look at the color. Hold it up to this candle." The light shines through her wine. "It should be clear. Next, swirl the wine around in the glass to release the bouquet." Moving her glass in a circle three times, she sniffs the wine like the caretaker does. "Finally, take a taste and swirl it around your tongue. Make sure you breathe through your nose to get the full scent." Shula and Avraham clink their glasses and sip. At first the sourness burns her throat, but her second sip releases a delicious fruit. She watches as Avraham knocks back his drink like her grandfather does when his friends from Poland come around. She takes a large gulp and almost chokes. Avraham laughs.

"Slow down, Shula! I don't want to have to carry you back to the room!" She feels her cheeks flush and lifts her glass to the caretaker. "What's next?"

The caretaker places two clean glasses on the table. He pours a red wine into them. She lifts her glass and smells. This one has a deep, rich scent and when it hits her tongue, her taste buds explode. It's not sweet, but not sour like the last one. She drinks some more and finds herself laughing at Avraham for no apparent reason. She can't stop smiling and there is a faint buzzing in her ears.

"Uh oh. You may have to stop pouring wine for my sister," Avraham says. "She looks like she's had enough already." She slaps Avraham on the arm.

"Nonsense. You just make me laugh," she says holding her glass out for more wine. The caretaker laughs and pours them each a glass of the Muscat.

"Now this wine is sweet. A dessert wine. Perfect with a *babka* cake or cream puffs. Plus, all our wines are kosher, so you don't have to worry about using them in the ceremony," he adds. Shula takes a sniff and sips. The honey flavor slips down her throat and burns the back of her mouth. It is delicious. After one more sip the lights in the cave sparkle.

"Now this, I like!" she says, laughing loudly. "I think I may be drunk. Shhhh," she whispers to her brother holding a finger up to her mouth.

"Don't worry," says Avraham. "It's sacred wine," he says looking at the caretaker. "God approves, right?"

The next morning, Shula leans her head against the bus window as they head back to Tel Aviv. Her temples throb and every so often she experiences a wave of nausea. She has never experienced a headache like this before.

"Remind me never to drink wine again," she says. She opens the newspaper and braces herself for more bad news. The bodies of two British soldiers were found hanging from a pair of eucalyptus trees in a grove not far from Netanya. The notes pinned to their dead bodies claimed their deaths were in retaliation for the execution of three Irgun members that same day.

"Two British spies held in underground captivity since July 12 have been tried after the completion of the investigations of their 'criminal anti-Hebrew activities' on the following charges:

1. Illegal entry into the Hebrew homeland.

2. Membership of a British criminal terrorist organization known as the Army of Occupation which was responsible for the torture, murder, deportation, and denying the Hebrew people the right to live.

3. Illegal possession of arms.

4. Anti-Jewish spying in civilian clothes.

5. Premeditated hostile designs against the underground.

Found guilty of these charges they have been sentenced to hang and their appeal for clemency dismissed. This is not a reprisal for the execution of three Jews but a 'routine judicial fact.'"

She is not shocked, nor horrified, by this news, just anxious. She hears a low whistle from Avraham.

"This isn't good. The city is going to explode tonight," he says. "We better get home before the curfew starts." Tel Aviv, which has been simmering with violent outbreaks for the past six months, will be a hotbed of riots with the news of these killings. She tries to shake off these thoughts by looking over at her brother's sketchbook.

"Are you going to let me see what you're doing in there?" She grabs for the pad, but he pulls it away.

"Not now! When we get home...maybe," he replies with a wicked grin. She punches his shoulder and looks out the window. Amongst all the bad news, her brother always makes her feel better. She folds the paper, tucking it between her seat and the wall.

Closer to the central bus station, the traffic thickens and this late in the afternoon the heat is unbearable. The sea of humanity swarms outside her window — donkeys and horses pulling carts across the streets; women pushing

143

carriages with babies, or piled high with packages; drivers of cars and trucks pounding on their horns in frustration. A horse-drawn wagon filled with cans of olive oil cuts off their bus. The driver slams on the brakes and Avraham's pencil skids across the paper.

"*Nu*? *Yallah*! Move over! Yah!" the driver yells. He bangs his hand on the steering wheel, and looks up at the roof. "This is hell! I tell you! This is hell!"

"Driver! Relax!" Avraham says. "There's a curfew. People are worried they won't be able to finish their business, that's all." A few other passengers join Avraham in his effort to calm the driver. He leans over and whispers in Shula's ear. "He must not have a mother at home cooking for him." Shula smiles and slides her arm around her brother's arm. "What do you think our mother is preparing for her oldest children's return?" he asks. Shula puts her head back and relaxes.

"Definitely, cabbage soup," she says.

"Of course, of course. And maybe some stuffed peppers?"

"If she can find the meat at the market. It might be squab."

"Or scrambled eggs. How does she make even scrambled eggs taste so good? At university the eggs have no taste. How can you ruin scrambled eggs?" Shula sighs.

"It will be nice to be home tonight. I'm glad you're here." She looks at her brother and squeezes his hand. He lifts his canteen towards her.

"Next year in Italy!" he says. Shula taps her canteen to his.

"Or the U.S.A...."

"I'll drink to that," he says.

The pace of their walk home is slowed by the vehicles and pedestrians clogging the street and the multiple British checkpoints they pass through. When they get to Melchett Street, it is getting dark. Shula looks up at the apartment's balcony and there is Yisrael looking out for them from above.

"Hey! Yisrael!" she shouts. "We're over here!" She sees her younger brother's face light up as he disappears from the balcony. In seconds, she hears his footsteps echoing off the plaster walls. Looking back up, she sees her mother, then father on the balcony. She runs to get to the stairs first.

After a dinner of cabbage soup, squab and stuffed peppers, she sits on the couch next to Avraham.

"Are you going to show me what you've been drawing?" she says.

"No. Not now, at least," He closes the pad and smiles at her.

"Stop teasing me!" Her shoulders slump forward. "I wish you didn't have to go back to Haifa."

"It's not for much longer," he replies. Tears fill her eyes. She doesn't want him to return to a life that doesn't include her. She leans over and puts her head on his shoulder. And although she is sad, she has something unique with Avraham that no one else will ever have. No one, not friend, not lover, not wife, will ever know Avraham the way she does. As his sister.

Chapter 8

Tel Aviv, British Mandate Palestine

November 1947

Shula squints as she looks out across the rows of her peers, all dressed in khaki uniforms, all standing in precise straight lines, all facing their Scout leaders. She pushes back her Australian Army slouch hat and adjusts the bandana around her collar. Across the field is a new neighborhood. The identical rows of three-story-high boxy, white Bauhaus buildings remind her of her Scout troop. Straight and tall and strong. Her troop commander shouts the orders.

"*Hakshev*! Attention!" Hundreds of feet stamp together as palms slap their thighs. The sound sends a shiver up her spine.

"At ease!" the commander yells and all at once the troop relaxes their arms and clasps them behind their backs, legs spread to shoulder width apart.

"Today is a historic day!" the commander says. "Remember this date! November 29, 1947! The day the United Nations votes on our future. On the future of our country! On the future of the Jewish people!" There is silence all around. Shula looks across the lines of people, to the lines of the buildings. Straight and tall and strong.

"Today we will find out what our future holds! We will find out if we must fight for our lives or continue to live in fear of our neighbors and occupiers. The British are through with us. They are through with the Arabs. They will leave us soon and then we will have to defend ourselves. Friends! Are you ready?" Shula can't help herself and shouts "Yes!" along with the other voices. She is ready. She has been preparing for this her entire life. For the first time in 2,000 years, the Jewish People will have a home.

"I want to tell you something," the commander continues. "I recently made the climb up to the top of Masada, where over 1,000 years ago a group of Jews defended themselves against the Romans to their unfortunate death. Like them, today we are preparing for the most important battle of our time. And we will not let the Arabs, the British, the Fascists — or any other future enemy — threaten our lives again. As long as we can protect ourselves, here in our own land, the nation of Israel will live!" He shoots his hand up in a salute. "*Am Yisrael Chai!* The Nation of Israel Lives!"

Shula's voice joins with hundreds of others as they answer: "*Am Yisrael Chai!*"

After the opening ceremony, Shula and her troop gather around a burnt-out campfire. She looks at the friends she grew up with — Uzi, Yael, Dan, Uri, Rutke, Dudu, Sarah — now young men and women of eighteen, nineteen and twenty. In the past, they spent their time learning how to tie knots and build fires they would then dance the *horah* around for hours, some nights to the point of exhaustion. But for the past few months, they have been training in earnest for the war that they all know is coming. Shula learned how to dismantle a Sten gun, clean it, and put it back together. She practiced shooting a Webley revolver. She remembers how surprised she was by the weight of the metal, how shocked she had been at the kickback when she fired at the target, missing wildly on that first try. But, by the time she finished her training session, she hit close to the mark every time.

On the bus ride home, Shula pulls out the most recent letter from Solomon. She sniffs the envelope and smells cedar and leather. A few months earlier, she described the scented letters Aunt Leah used to send. Since then, the two exchange scents with each letter, revealing the source in the postscript.

Dearest Shula, I must apologize for my late reply. Between my classes at the university and my job at the "fastest growing printer in Bromley!" (as my father says) I have scarce time for myself. During exams last week, I fell asleep at the table ON MY BOOKS for six days straight. Eventually one of my parents would wake me and drag me off to bed.

In general life is normalizing somewhat. We still have rations on certain items but you can also feel that people are starting to look up again. New buildings are being erected all over London and what was damaged is in the process of being fixed. The wounds of the city are healing.

How are things in Eretz Yisrael? I can't stand to think that you missed your last recital because of bomb threats. I worry about you constantly. I pray each day that peace will come to the Promised Land soon.

I've added to my list of places I want to take you to see when you visit England. (You'll notice I said 'when' and not 'if.') A friend of mine told me that the new Edinburgh Festival of the Arts is worth the trip up to Scotland. I think you would really enjoy it.

I must run. Thinking of you quite often. I've enclosed a recent photo of me so you will think of me too.
Fondly,
Solomon
P.S. Courtley Cologne

She pulls out the small black and white photo and runs her finger along the bumpy edge. He is handsome, like she remembers. She prays she will see him again soon.

A nervous excitement greets Shula when she opens the front door to the apartment. Aunt Rivka is busy cutting and rearranging her strudel on a plate, while her husband, Lev, fiddles with the radio, even though the

148

signal is clear. From the kitchen, her mother instructs Yaakov on what to bring to the table. Yisrael pulls on his sister to show her the poster-sized chart he made to keep tally of the U.N. vote. The new Goblin radio is positioned front and center on the credenza, the vacuum tubes glow through the fabric-covered slats at the top. All the furniture in the room has been rearranged to face the wooden box. Shula spots Avraham and her cousin Miriam out on the balcony. Miriam's auburn hair glows in the setting sun and the smoke from her cigarette curls up from her hand, belying the tension in the air.

"Shula! You're home!" she says, giving her a big hug and kissing her on the cheek. "Exciting, no? I can't stop biting my nails, even with polish!"

"Exciting? Yes," Shula replies. "So, what have you heard? Any news? When will they start?"

"They won't say," replies Yaakov, joining them from inside. He puts his arms around Yisrael and Shula and kisses them on their heads. "I used to have to bend down to do this, you know." Shula returns her father's embrace.

"This is an amazing day. It's hard to believe it's even real," he says as he looks up into the sky, the few clouds now streaked with pink and orange against a darkening sky. Up and down the street a similar scene plays out in each window. People pace, talk, or huddle around radios blasting the same news feed. All waiting for this vote to happen — waiting for the world to grant the Jews a home. She never felt this kind of anticipation before, knowing that her whole world would soon change. Yisrael runs out to the balcony and pulls on his father's shirt.

"How much longer, Abba?" Yaakov puts his hand on his nine-year-old son's shoulder.

"Do you know how long we've waited for this day, *motek*? Two thousand years. A few more hours isn't too long to wait," he says leading the boy back into the apartment.

The evening wears on, but not the excitement. They eat dinner over hours, first plates of pickled peppers and eggplant, olives, and salads — babaganous, hummus, *techina* — then baked chicken and stuffed cabbage, and still later, almond cookies, chocolate wafers and Rivka's apple strudel. It is late now, past ten o'clock, but still there is no vote. So, they talk and smoke, and drink strong coffee and weak tea.

And then the announcement comes from the United Nations meeting in Lake Superior, New York. The roll is about to be called. The voting to begin.

"The Jewish Agency has indicated that it is now ready through its authorized spokesman, a member of this delegation to... uh... make this statement, which they have been invited to make by the decision of the assembly," a man says.

"Who's talking?" asks Sarah.

A loud "shush" arises from the group and she waves her hand. "I was just asking," she says and is shushed again.

Shula looks back and sees her mother standing behind the couch alongside her two sisters with their husbands, their arms around each other's waists. She can tell her mother is nervous by the way she dabs her upper lip with the handkerchief wrapped around her finger. Yisrael stands by his chart holding his new ballpoint pen, purchased this week for the occasion. Shula squeezes Avraham's hand when she hears the deep authoritative voice of the spokesman for the Jewish Agency in Palestine, the Yishuv's de facto government.

"We are grateful for the opportunity to take counsel with you...which is to study the problem of Palestine...We trust that our participation in these deliberations will be helpful and will prove to be a contribution to a just solution to this grave international problem which this international community is now earnestly seeking. Such a successful solution will prove a blessing not only to Palestine, and all of its inhabitants, to the Jewish people, to the cause of world peace, but it will also enhance the moral authority and prestige of this great organization for world justice and peace upon which so many high hopes of mankind now rest."

"Thank God for the United Nations!" Yaakov proclaims and Shula smiles up at her father. She didn't think much about the U.N. when it was founded two years earlier, but now she understands its importance. The issue of Palestine is not just a Jewish problem, or an Arab problem. It is a world problem that the member countries of the U.N. will solve. The speaker continues in his proper British accent, r's rolling off his tongue.

"The Mandate in its preamble recognizes the historical connection of the Jewish people to Palestine and the grounds for reconstituting — I call attention to the word 'reconstituting' — a national home in that country." Shula and her family cheer at that last line, their sentiments echoing up and down the street.

"You cannot turn back the hands of the clock of history. We are an ancient people, and though we are often on the long hard road on which we travel, we have never been disheartened. We have never lost faith in the sovereignty and the ultimate triumph of great moral principles."

Yisrael sinks down to the tile floor, a look of sheer boredom on his face.

"Abba! What's happening?" he asks. "And when is the voting going to start?"

Yaakov makes a calming motion with his hands.

"Remember, 2,000 years, my son. Two more minutes, we can wait."

The first voice wafts from the radio.

"You all know how to vote. Those who are in favor say Yes and those who are against it will say No. And the abstainers, they always, they *always* know what to say." Shula and her family laugh along with the voices from the other side of the world.

"They're starting!" Yisrael is up again positioning himself next to the chart. An American man's voice comes through the speaker.

"Afghanistan."

"No."

The room stays silent. Shula grasps Avraham's hand tighter. He squeezes back.

"Argentina."

"Abstention."

She closes her eyes and takes a deep breath.

"Belgium."

"Yes."

Shouts of approval come from inside the room and up and down the down the block. Yisrael draws a giant check in the Yes column.

"That's one, one and one," he says. Shula looks over at her mother who holds a delicate paper fan. A gift from Leah from years before.

"Oy! This is too much for me. I'll put the water on for tea," Sarah says as she hurries over to the kitchen. The roll call continues.

"El Salvador."

"Abstention."

"France."

"Yes." The roll is interrupted by the sound of clapping from the crowd in New York. Shula starts when she hears a loud rap as the gavel smashes down on the hard surface one, two, three, four, five, six, seven times. Then the first man speaks again, his anger palpable through his voice on the radio.

"I call on you, the public, and hope that you will not interfere with the voting or the debate. I am talking about the way you behave while this assembly deliberates on this very serious decision. And I have decided not to allow *anyone* to interfere in our decisions." The hall quiets down, as does Shula and her family, the street, the entire city.

"Greece."

"No."

"Boo!" says Yisrael.

"Shh!" says Shula.

"What? They can't hear me in New York." He pauses and leans over. "Can they?" Shula shakes her head, running her fingers through his hair.

"Ukraine."

"Yes."

"Soviet Union."

"Yes."

"United Kingdom."

"Abstain."

"They have to, you know," Yisrael announces to the room. After several more minutes, Shula looks over at the chart. Only two more countries to go: Venezuela and Yemen, who will surely vote no with the other Arab countries.

"Venezuela."

"Yes."

"Yemen."

"No."

And then it is over, and the cheers climb through the balcony, echoing off the white concrete walls of her street.

"Shh!" yells Yaakov. "I want to hear them say it!" The room quiets down in time to hear.

"The resolution of the UNSCOP committee of Palestine was adopted by thirty-three votes, thirteen against, ten abstentions.[14]" A second wave of hoots and hollers is heard outside, rising higher and louder. Shula turns to Avraham and throws her arms around him. She can't believe it, but it is true. They are going to have their own country. She turns and sees her mother standing off to the side crying into her handkerchief. Her father wraps his arms around her, and her shoulders shake even more. She crosses over to them, and hugs them both. Avraham, Yisrael, her cousins, uncles and aunts are out on the balcony singing *"Heveynu Shalom Aleichem*! We Bring Peace unto You!" with the whole neighborhood. Then Avraham races over to them, his face radiant with joy.

"Come! We have to go down to the museum. We have to celebrate with Tel Aviv!" He grabs his wallet, shoving it into his pants pocket. He runs his fingers through his wavy hair and looks up at Shula.

"Are you coming?" Shula breaks into a huge smile and grabs her purse.

As she walks down Melchett Street, arm in arm with Avraham and Miriam, Shula feels unbelievable joy. At each intersection, they are joined by more and more people, some waving the white flag with a blue Star of David. Every man, woman and child in Tel Aviv is out on the street or celebrating from their balconies, celebrating the news. Now the uncertainty of life under occupation will end. Now Jews from all over the world will be safe. Now she will be able to pursue her dreams unobstructed by manmade constructs. Now the Jewish people can thrive again.

14

Chapter 9

Tel Aviv, British Mandate Palestine

January 1948

Returning home one afternoon in mid-January, Shula finds Dr. Levy on the couch with her father. Yaakov is drawn and thin, and in the late afternoon light, noticeably jaundiced. Dr. Levy wears a black suit, white shirt and tie, and thick round glasses worn low on his nose. He rests his hand on a pork pie hat. Her mother bursts out of the kitchen, tray in hand.

"Oh, good. You're home. Come sit. Dr. Levy wants to give us some news about your father," she says placing the tea and biscuits on the coffee table. Her hands shake as she passes the glasses around.

"So, doctor, what have you got to tell us?" Yaakov says stirring his tea. Shula watches the sugar crystals spin inside the glass until they dissolve. This could be bad news. She puts the sweet biscuit in her hand back onto the tray. Her palms sweat. Her mouth is dry. Her mother dabs her upper lip with a handkerchief.

"Yaakov, you know," Dr. Levy begins. "The Jews have many enemies, the Arabs and the Fascists today and before it was the Ottoman Empire, the Crusaders, and on and on. You know the story," he says. Her father chuckles.

"Yes, doctor. Very well. Go on."

"Well, mankind has enemies too. Diseases caused by germs, virus or parasites, and they don't care if you're Jewish or Muslim or Christian, or what have you. With our enemies, we know what to do. We fight with guns and sticks and rocks, or lawyers," he flicks his eyes up at Yaakov. "But, with germs it is not so easy. We don't have the weapons we need to battle, or the ones we do have

155

may not work, or in the case of quinine, may not be available."

"Quinine? Are you saying I have malaria?" His voice is calm. For years, malaria has been rampant in the area, especially amongst the road building crews, but her father has never shown symptoms. Maybe he expected this all along.

"But malaria can be treated!" says Rachel. "That fellow you worked with, Avi, he had malaria and he's now strong as a horse."

"Yes, sometimes malaria can be treated," Dr. Levy says. Then directing himself to Yaakov, "We will do everything we can. But your case is advanced, and as I said, quinine is not easy to come by these days, and sometimes not even effective. What you need is to get lots of rest and we will monitor you closely."

"Rest is all I can do these days, I'm afraid." Dread grips Shula's stomach and the fear of losing her father overwhelms her.

A few days later, Shula and Yisrael stand on the balcony waiting for Avraham to return home from his Palmach unit's basic training. After this weekend off, he will head up to the Galilee and join his platoon. The Yishuv is gearing up for war.

A horn blast signals the start of the weekly showdown. A *hassid* walks down the block wearing a long black coat, white shirt and tie. His black pants are tucked into a pair of black knee high stockings, a large brimmed hat sits atop his head. He pauses by every other building to blow his metal horn and announce the Sabbath. Across the street, Mr. Abramowitz halfheartedly sweeps the steps of his still-open store, eyeing the man's progress. The *hassid* gets to the shop and stops. Smoothing down his thick black beard, he pushes his glasses back into place and lifts the trumpet to his lips. Mr. Abramowitz stands in the

156

doorway leaning on his broom as the first note blasts from the horn. The two men lock eyes. The *hassid* lowers his trumpet, his corkscrew side curls bouncing.

"The Sabbath is coming! Prepare for the Sabbath!" He yells at the store. Mr. Abramowitz yawns and continues to sweep. The *hassid* waits for a moment, then issues another blast from the trumpet. Rachel steps out onto the balcony and looks over.

"What — Oh! Oy vey," she says as she sees Mr. Abramowitz smirking at the *hassid* outside his open shop door. "Not this racket again."

"Why does Mr. Abramowitz do that?" Yisrael asks.

"Do what?"

"Keep his shop open until that man blows his horn and yells," he replies. Rachel sighs.

"Mr. Abramowitz doesn't believe that anyone can tell him how to be a Jew, whereas this man," she gestures towards the *hassid* as he lifts the trumpet to his lips once more, "This man thinks that it's his job to do exactly that. And here, in *Eretz Yisrael*, they can waste their time with these silly arguments and no one will kill them for it. At least that's what we hope," she adds and goes back inside.

The *hassid* continues to blow his horn until, as usual, the neighbors yell from the balconies to let them have some peace. Then, a few minutes later, the corner store is closed and the man with the trumpet is moving toward Allenby Street, where the shops and cafes will be scrambling to close before sunset.

A Jeep roars down the street and stops short at their building. Avraham jumps out, tossing his duffle bag over his shoulder. He slaps the roof twice and the Jeep takes off, tires squealing along the asphalt. Shula and Yisrael wave down to him then race to the door. Her brother is home.

That evening at dinner, Avraham regales them with stories from his military training, the light from the two Shabbat candles flickering across his face.

"Tell us another one!" Yisrael says.

"What? Climbing Masada at sunrise with a broken boot wasn't good enough?"

"It was too good," Shula says. "We want more." Avraham smiles at his sister and holds her gaze for a moment.

"All right then. I have two more stories," he says. "But you can never tell anyone. Can I trust you, my brother?" he looks at his little brother. Yisrael nods his head.

"What are you doing that is so secret?" Rachel asks. "And who shouldn't we tell?"

"One act was against God's law and the other against British law."

"I wouldn't worry about God, but the British…What did you *do*?"

"So, my buddy Moti and I had a three-day furlough and — "

"And you didn't come *home*?" she adds.

"Rachel, please. Let the boy tell his nefarious tales. Go on," Yaakov says.

"We decide that we want to go to Petra — "

"But you aren't allowed to go to Trans-Jordan," Rachel says.

"Like I said, one is against British law — "

"*Oy vey zmir*! You could have been arrested!" Rachel cries.

"Did you make it? To Petra?" Shula takes her brother's hand. She has heard stories and seen pictures of the ancient sandstone city built into the mountain side, but would never dare to sneak over the border to get there. Avraham's eyes sparkle.

"Yes, we made it there. And back," he leans over and kisses his mother's cheek. "But first I have to tell you about breaking God's law. Moti and I went to Jerusalem to meet our ride to the border. That night, the two of us walked around the city for hours, talking. At one point, we found ourselves near the *Kotel*, the Western Wall. When Moti realizes where we are he stops in his tracks. 'Let's go to the wall.' 'Why?' I asked him. 'You have a note to God you want to stick in the cracks?' But he grabs my arm and we head down to the alley. It's late remember, no one is out, just us two. So, Moti walks over to the wall, looks around and pulls out a note."

"No! You read the notes from the wall?" Yaakov says.

"We did, but don't worry, only a few."

"I'm not worried, but it's not nice, Avraham," Rachel says.

"I thought you didn't believe in that stuff, Eema."

"I may not, but some people do."

"Sorry, Eema."

"So, after desecrating a holy place you smuggled yourselves over the border? Rachel? Where did we go wrong?" Yaakov says.

"Wrong? *Hitalfchut v'shatara*. Sneaking and stealing. I'd say he's acting like a *Sabra*," replies Rachel.

Later, after walking them through his grueling heavy-artillery work, he tells them about the fledgling Jewish Air Force.

"I won't lie to you," he says fiddling with his spoon. "It was hard to accept at first, not getting into the Air Force. I'd been training for this since I was fifteen. But have you any idea how big the Air Force is right now?" He turns to Yisrael. "Tell me, little brother. How many planes do you think we have?"

"A hundred?" he says. Avraham laughs.

"We have *two* planes right now and plenty of pilots to fly them. They've recruited Jewish fighter pilots from the U.S., England and Australia, most with years of experience."

"Have you seen the planes?" his younger brother asks.

"Not only have I seen them, I was there when they first landed and painted the Star of David on the tail." Yaakov gives a low whistle, leans back in his chair, and laughs.

"A fighter plane with the Star of David on it? *Wa'alah*! *This* I'd like to see," he says turning to Rachel. "Do you believe it? Fighter planes with Jewish stars!" he shakes his head in disbelief. "So, what was it like? When the planes landed." Shula leans forward onto her elbows. She knows how exhilarating it is to sit by a runway and feel the planes coming in for a landing.

"It was thrilling." Avraham winks at her. "We were standing in a large empty field on either side of a crude runway lined with kerosene cans. It was the middle of the night and pitch black out there. Finally, after hours and hours, we heard a crackling noise from the radio speaker, and the Commander gave us the signal to light the lamps. We crouched down beside the runway and waited. Then off in the distance," he points to the far wall, "I heard the sound of engines. I couldn't see them, but I heard them. You don't know how exciting that was for me," he says, shaking his head.

"Oh, yes we do," says Shula. He laughs.

"I guess you do."

"Did you get to meet the pilots?" Yisrael asks.

"I did. Out of the two British planes came two American fighter pilots."

"Jews?" asks Yaakov.

"Yes. There are rumors that an entire fleet of planes and pilots is on its way here, but no one knows for sure." He stops and shakes his head. "So, there you have it. My dream of a Jewish Air Force is now realized in two beat-up planes."

It is February 9, Shula's twentieth birthday, and she and Lilach decide to explore the proposed U.N. partition plan to separate Tel Aviv and Jaffa. They walk along the beach towards the ancient Arab city.

As they walk past the cafés on Hayarkon Street, she reads the headlines on the papers held aloft by the patrons in the cafés. *"Pasha Swears to Sweep the Jews Into the Sea!" "Arabs Want to Eradicate Zionism!" "Seven Arab Countries Prepare for War!"* A tingle travels down her spine and she opens a map.

"Where does the partition start?" she asks.

"Hmmm... It's supposed to start just past — " Lilach looks up. "God! That's going to be strange! It's like the Jewish State will be on this side of the street and the Arab one over there." Shula sighs as she looks out over Jaffa. Will she still be able to walk there? Sometimes she wants to bask in the spicy smells of the market and meander down the winding streets, so different from the white concrete buildings and planned avenues of Tel Aviv.

"It doesn't make any sense to me, this whole partition," Lilach continues. "They agree to two states, one Jewish, one Arab, but the way they carved out these territories... It's like the British took cookie cutters to divide the whole thing up. They probably did it around Christmas, which means they were most certainly drunk. Maybe that's what did it," she says. Shula smiles at her friend's attempt at a joke.

The sun is setting as they get closer to Jaffa, and the stones of the old city glow in the late afternoon light. Shula can see the destruction around the central square's tower from a recent bombing. Twenty-six people were killed, an Ottoman Empire building destroyed, plus dozens of houses and shops suffered severe damage. All this devastation orchestrated by the Stern Gang. *Jewish gangsters. That's all they are.* She looks north toward Tel Aviv and sees the endless lines of sandbags and barbed wire that line the streets. She feels the weight of this war, the weight of her country.

"Let's walk down to the water," she says. Slipping off her sandals, she buries her feet in the warm sand. They sit and watch as the deep orange sun melts into a silver sea. Lilach puts an arm around her and begins to sing the melancholy melody of "Halikha Le-Kesarya."

"My God, My God,
I pray that these things never end,
The sand and the sea,
The rustle of the waters,
Lightning of the Heavens,
The prayer of Man[15]."

As the melody builds to the crescendo, Shula's heart swells. Like the poet, Hannah Senesh, she prays that these things never end.

Two months later Shula announces to her mother that she is volunteering for the war effort with her Scout troop. She is to work at Kibbutz Hill, a two-year-old settlement southeast of Tel Aviv.

"Shula, please," Rachel says. "Your father is sick and I can't be alone right now."

"Eema, Avraham is training in the Galilee, and everyone I know is working in some way to prepare for when the British leave."

"But I need you here to help me. I'm sure they will understand." Shula feels her face flush with anger for a moment, but calms herself. She takes her mother's hand from across the table.

15

"I have to do this. You know I do. You have Yisrael here to help you and he is more than capable of taking care of Abba. I was changing his diapers when I was his age. It will make him feel good knowing that he's contributing, right?" Rachel looks at her daughter for a long time, and sighs. She squeezes Shula's hand.

"Go. But make sure you keep in close touch with me, okay? Your father is just — " She trails off. "And Avraham is God knows where! Will we ever have peace in *Eretz Yisrael*?"

"Eema, peace will come. But first we must fight this war."

Shula waits by the kibbutz's laundry building like she has every morning for the last two weeks. Young men and women slowly join her, all dressed for the heat in short pants and shirts. The scent of fresh baked bread wafts over from the bakery across the way. Long rows of white shirts dry on clotheslines connecting the two structures like tentacles. The supervisor approaches, his black hair short and neat. He breaks apart a fresh loaf of bread and distributes it among them.

"*Boker Tov,* good morning," he says. "Some British soldiers are here with shirts to launder. Let's walk over here until they leave." Walking toward a row of apple trees, she breathes in the crisp morning air, closes her eyes, and lets the sun shine on her face. It feels so good, so right. She wants to hold on to this feeling, the warmth of the sun on her skin, the sounds of the birds chirping in the trees, the smell of the fresh grass. She pulls a branch to her nose and sniffs the light pink blossom.

"Doesn't really smell, right?" the supervisor says.

"No, not really, but it looks nice," she answers. He plucks the flower from the tree and hands it to Shula.

"Keep it with you today and maybe things won't seem so bad."

163

A few minutes later, the British soldiers U-turn in a cloud of dust and drive off in their Jeep.

"Ah! Looks like we can go to work now," he says, and they head back to the laundry.

Inside the cement block structure, three large round washing machines churn. The sound of metal scraping metal is deafening. Steam erupts from a huge boiler. A woman at a large sink rubs a shirt back and forth against a soapy metal washboard. The foreman, a big strong man with a shock of thick white hair, nods as they file into the building. He wears a faded blue work shirt that pulls against his barrel chest. A cigarette dangles from his mouth.

"Even in the middle of the desert, the Brits walk around like they've just left a fancy nightclub," he says, throwing the white shirts into a basket. "Did you see any Giraffes out there?" Giraffes are the kibbutz members who are oblivious to the work being done under their feet. The supervisor shakes his head. "Then let's get to work."

The two men walk over to a large washing machine. With one pushing from behind, and the other pulling from the front, the huge barrel swings to one side, revealing a man-sized hole beneath it. The supervisor waves his hand and motions to them. They have three minutes to get their group down the ladder.

Her stomach tightens as she looks into the hole. Loud metallic banging overtakes the roar of the washers. Her mood darkens. She sighs and sticks the apple blossom behind her ear.

"Try to keep it alive, okay?" her supervisor says. She manages a thin smile, then hand over hand, makes her way down the ladder. When she reaches the bottom, she puts her earplugs in, looking up as the giant washer seals the hole.

The long underground room is hot and cramped, the noise earsplitting. She passes the machines that line the

164

right-hand wall, each one operated by one of the forty-five volunteers in her shift. Today she is assigned to work on the far end of the room. She walks by the machines that press, stretch, trim, shape, wash and pull the metal — each one a step in the bullet-making process. Like every day for the past year, this underground facility will produce thousands of bullets for the British-made Sten gun. Fittingly, these 9mm parabellums got their name from the Latin *if you seek peace, prepare for war*.

Two weeks ago, she was amazed by the secret munitions factory. Finally, she was supporting the war effort in a real way. For a week she was happy, singing at the top of her lungs like each worker did, following their own melodies together under the deafening noise of the machines. Then after a week, her mood shifted. This was not for her. She dreaded the metallic banging of the machines, hated the smell of chemicals and burning metal, hated the work that was ruining her fingertips. Would she still be able to play the piano? The lack of sunlight wore her down. She developed a new-found hatred for potatoes, the one thing they had to eat down in the dungeon, as she called it. The days were twelve hours of hell, with the assaultive noise of not only the machines but the constant rat-tat-tat of Sten guns firing in the underground testing range. Even though she stuffs her ears each day with a mix of wax and cotton-wool, every night she falls asleep to the same incessant ringing.

She pours gunpowder through a narrow funnel into the bullet casings, then tamps them down. She fills a box and moves it over to the next station where the tips are put into place. From there they are packed into bigger crates that line the far side of the workshop. A woman stands at a nearby table painting stencils on the tops of the large wooden boxes that read "Fragile — Handle with Care! Light Bulbs."

Sometime after a potato break (she never calls it lunch since it was always the same, no matter what) the foreman signals for her to follow him to the closet. Inside is a stool and a large light fixture. The foreman points and Shula sits. She sips from her canteen as the man pulls a string, turning on the bulb. Ultraviolet light from the sunray lamp fills the tiny space. She leans back against the wall.

"Twenty minutes," the foreman yells. "And don't fall asleep!"

Shula looks at her watch and takes another sip of water. Her first week of work here, a girl fell asleep in the Sun Room, as they call it. When they found her an hour later, only one side of her face had been exposed to the light, leaving half of her face bright red, the other half white. After that incident, the supervisor lectured them on the room's proper use.

"We are trying to blend in and look like people who have been working in the sun all day, not like clowns in the circus!" he admonished.

She leans her head back against the wall and feels her face warm. Closing her eyes, she imagines the sun on her face, the smell of the trees, the light breeze on her skin. Fingering the apple blossom behind her ear, she takes it out and smells. No, there still isn't a smell, but at least the flower is alive. She puts a drop of water from the canteen on the tip of her finger and dips the stem in, then sticks it back behind her ear. She is hot. The air is stifling. The noise is deafening. And if she never sees another potato in her life, that would be a blessing.

Chapter 10

Tel Aviv, British Mandate Palestine

April 1948

After Shula's been a few weeks at the bullet factory, Yaakov's health deteriorates and Rachel is desperate for her help. By early April, Shula is home.

The situation in Tel Aviv is more dangerous than ever, but she isn't frightened any longer. She does not flinch at the sound of gunfire. When out on the street, she keeps tabs on the nearest garden wall or doorway where she can hide.

On April 9, the newspapers are filled with stories of the Arabs massacred at the hands of the Jewish Irgun and Lehi gangs in village of Deir Yassin. An agitated Yaakov can't stop talking about it.

"We didn't come all this way, give up so much and work so hard..." he pauses for a moment and shivers. "How dare they kill women and children in the name of the Jews? The Arabs are our neighbors. How are we supposed to live next door to these people when we are treating them no better than animals? It's a *shandah*! They should be ashamed," he says. Rachel wipes his face with a cool cloth and rubs his back.

"My teacher said that we all have to be united behind David Ben Gurion and the Jewish Agency now," Yisrael says.

"And he is right, my son. He is right. As the head of our de facto government, Ben Gurion is the only sane voice in this insanity. The world wants to see a united front amongst the Jews and we will not survive a war with the Arabs if we are fighting each other as well."

A week later, the news is worse. Arabs are blockading the road between Tel Aviv and Jerusalem, and her

167

grandfather's neighborhood is under siege. A convoy of five hundred trucks carrying food and water makes its way towards Jerusalem, but the fighting is fierce and the news not good. Her father insists on reading the papers despite the upset it causes him. And then on April 20, some good news.

"They made it! You see!" Yaakov lifts the paper up for Shula and Yisrael. She smiles at her father, glad to hear him sound strong, at least for the moment. "Sabbah Dubno, Uncle Yehoshua, cousin Ruthie, oh, everyone! Finally, they'll get food. Ah! But the road we worked so hard to build! It is probably destroyed in so many places. *Ach.* War is a terrible thing, my children." Yaakov sinks back into the couch.

A few minutes later, there is a banging on the front door. Yisrael gets there first and flings it open. There stands her eleven-year-old cousin, Ilan, tears streaming down his face.

"What happened? What's wrong?" Shula says. The boy tries to catch his breath.

"Abba! Was shot!" is all he gets out before hyperventilating. Shula lead him to the couch. *Uncle Yosef shot? Is he dead? In the hospital?* She gets down on her knees and faces the boy.

"Ilan, take a deep breath and tell us what happened," she says, belying her panic. The boy breathes, trying to calm himself.

"He was in the Carmel market," he gasps for air every few words. "...and was shot! Eema sent me here to get Doda Rachel!" Yaakov moans and leans back on the couch.

"Oh God, no," he says. As if for the first-time she sees her father's face — yellow eyes, jaundiced skin, gaunt cheeks — and realizes that he is going to die.

"I'm getting my coat," Rachel says, rushing toward the door.

"How can they do that? Turn the one place where Arab and Jews conduct civilized commerce into a war zone? A place of human necessity should never become a line in the sand."

"Where's my purse?" Rachel says as she pulls on her coat.

"Gadi's father was shot in the leg last week," says Yisrael. "And he's home now, so don't worry." Ilan looks at Yisrael, tears spilling from his eyes. Rachel grasps his hand pulling him to his feet.

"We're going to the hospital," she says.

Five days later, an urgent shaking wakes Shula in the middle of the night. Rachel's darkened face leans over her, backlit by the harsh bulb hanging outside the doorway.

"Shulinka, wake up." She pushes herself onto her elbow, not comprehending what her mother is saying.

"What? What's wrong?" She tries to get her mother's face and voice into focus.

"Move to the cot by Abba. He has a high fever and needs to drink every two hours. I'm going to Doda Sarah. Yosef died."

"Eema! You can't!" she says, a shot of adrenaline waking her. She grabs her mother's arm. "The curfew!"

"There's a Haganah Jeep waiting downstairs. I am going to my sister. You stay here and watch Abba and Yisrael." She puts her arm around her daughter and kisses her head.

"I'm counting on you," she whispers into her hair.

"I know."

Sitting by her father, Shula places a cool, wet towel on his forehead.

"Abba, are you okay?" She doesn't expect him to answer her. She wipes the sweat from his face. At times, the high fevers cause delirium and his speech becomes incomprehensible, but that is the nature of this disease. He gets better for forty-eight hours only to fall ill again. Each time the better period is a little less better, and the worse times, much worse. She breathes a sigh of relief when she sees him pull the sheet up to his chin and smile at her.

"Ah, my Shulinka," he whispers. "What time is it?"

"Four o'clock in the morning. Time for a drink."

"Really? That's a bit early for you, isn't it?"

"Eema had to go to Doda Sarah. Yosef died." Shula looks at her father and bursts into tears. Her breath leaves her body as the reality of her father's imminent death overwhelms her. She loves her Uncle Yosef and cares for her cousins, but Yosef's death won't impact her like her father's death will. And she can see, anyone can see, that Yaakov is not getting better.

"Oh, no. No. No." Yaakov says and shakes his head. She helps him sit and gathers the pillows behind him. He sinks back and his face and body relax. As he reaches his arms out toward her, she leans into his chest. He pats her on the back, using the gentle strokes he used when she was little. Her eyes fill and she closes her lids, letting the tears flow onto her cheeks on their way to her father's pajamas. He tilts her chin up.

"You loved your Uncle Yosef." Shula looks up and nods. She doesn't want to talk about his death. Let him think she is crying for her uncle and not for him.

On May 14, Shula pushes her way through the crowds filling the streets. There is an electricity in the air as the country waits to celebrate the official declaration of the State of Israel. There will be music and people dancing the *horah*, but for her family it will be a quiet night with muted celebration. They are still in mourning for her uncle Yosef, and her father is weaker every day.

Pushing her way up to a kiosk, she hands a bill to the proprietor standing behind the rows of gum and candy.

She peruses the books, newspapers and magazines hanging from the awning of the small shack while waiting for her change.

"What's *Yom Hamidinah*?" she asks knowing that her father would appreciate the picture of the Zionist Theodore Herzl emblazoned on the front page.

"It's a special paper from *Ha'aretz* and *Yidiot*. It takes 2,000 years and the declaration of a Jewish state to get these two to work together, eh?" the man answers. Shula grabs a yellow packet of spearmint "Girl" gum and hands him another coin.

"Are you heading down to the Tel Aviv Museum for the ceremony?" he asks. Shula clicks her tongue no.

"My family is in mourning. We'll listen on the radio," she answers and picks up three more papers.

"Ah, my condolences," he says. "So many people are in mourning already. I'm worried that come this declaration, so many more will join them." The man looks straight into her eyes. "The Jewish people always pay an exorbitant price for their freedom," he adds. As she tucks the papers under her arm, a shiver runs down her spine as she walks away.

Back in the apartment, Shula distributes the papers to her family. Yisrael sits on his father's lap, her mother, on the couch. Tinny voices chatter from the radio in the corner.

"How do you feel?" she asks her father, resting her hand on his forehead.

"Tired, but happy. Did you hear the news? We are going to have a country," he takes her hand in his. "Believe me when I say this is incredible. Yisrael, read me the headlines." Closing his eyes, he leans his head back.

"*At Four in the Afternoon the State of Israel will be Established,*" Yisrael reads aloud.

"*Jewish Forces Have Entered Jaffa,*" Rachel reads from her paper.

"It says here '*Haganah on Alert for the Danger of Invasion,*'" Shula says shaking her head.

"*Seven Surrounding Arab Countries Poised to Declare War on Israel come May 15,*" Yisrael reads. The room falls silent. Yaakov opens his eyes.

"Listen! Ben-Gurion is talking!"

The voice of David Ben-Gurion, the nation's acting leader, comes from the radio. Lowering their papers, the family focuses on the glowing machine.

"I will read before you the Founding Charter of the State of Israel, which has been approved in its first reading by the People's Council," Ben-Gurion says.

"Did you hear that? He said, the State of Israel!" Rachel gasps.

"In the Land of Israel arose the Jewish people," Ben-Gurion continues, "where a spiritual, religious and national image was formed, where an official sovereign life was created, where its people created national and universal cultural treasures, and bequeathed to the entire world the eternal Book of Books."

Shula listens with rapt attention as Ben-Gurion lays out the steps that led to this momentous declaration. How the Jewish people throughout history always return to this land; how this last generation began to return in droves; how in 1897 Theodore Herzl declared the right of the Jewish people to its land; how the 1917 Balfour Declaration recognized the historical connection between the Jewish people and the Land of Israel; how the Holocaust led to the slaughter of millions of Jews in Europe and proved anew the necessity of a Jewish State; how in 1947 the United Nations recognized the right of the Jewish people to establish their own homeland; how the Jewish people have the right to a sovereign state.

"Therefore we have convened," Ben-Gurion continues, "we members of the People's Council, representatives of the Hebrew community and the Zionist movement, on the day of the termination of the British Mandate over *Eretz Israel*, and from the power of our natural and historical right and on the basis of the resolution of the Assembly of the United Nations we hereby declare the establishment of the Jewish State in the Land of Israel, to be called the State of Israel."[16] An extended applause coming through the radio is drowned out by the voices outside their apartment. Up and down the street people shout "*Am Yisrael Chai* — The Nation of Israel Lives" amongst the occasional gun shots into the sky. Rachel sits on the arm of Yaakov's chair, resting her cheek on his head. Yisrael perches on his lap. Shula wraps her arm around her mother's shoulder.

"We are so lucky to see this day," her father says.

The sound of the Palestine Symphony Orchestra fills the room. Leonard Bernstein conducts the first playing of the country's national anthem, "Hatikva," the Hope. Shula and her family stand at attention and sing along to the radio. Her eyes fill with tears, not from sadness but joy. *We made it. We are here.*

The next morning Shula dreams that she is sitting at a café with Solomon. He stirs his coffee and she watches as the silver spoon goes round and round in the white porcelain cup. He looks up at her and smiles and a delicious warmth spread through her body. He reaches for her hand and holds it, and it is like he is right there with her and not thousands of miles away. She smiles at him, and as he leans in to kiss her, bombs explode around them. Shula screams and dives under the small café table, knowing that it is no protection. As she tries in vain to find

---

16

a spot that isn't covered with shards of glass, she uncovers Solomon's severed hand, the blood-spattered silver spoon still tight in its grip. She rears back in horror and wakes with a startling realization that the explosions are real. Her heart pounding, she jumps out of bed, her nightgown soaked in sweat. She runs into Rachel in the doorway, startled by the panic on her mother's face.

"Yisrael went out. The Arabs! They're bombing Tel Aviv. There wasn't an air raid signal! We have to find him!" she says. She grabs Shula's arm as sirens go off. "Help me get Abba downstairs, then go look for him," Rachel yells above the sirens. Pulling on her pants and coat as she crosses the living room, she puts her father's arm around her shoulders. They make their way down the steps, first one floor, then the next, then into the Horowitzes' first floor apartment. The living room shutters are sealed shut, blocking out any sunlight. Other residents are gathered inside, their eyes filled with sadness. The little girl from across the hall is clinging to her father, a blank stare on her face. Shula grabs the doorjamb as the building is rocked by an explosion. She helps her father onto the couch.

"I'm going to look for him," she states. "Where did he go?" she asks Rachel.

"He said he was going to walk down to the beach with some friends. Oh, I don't know why I let him, but it was quiet this morning and it was so early..." Rachel looks at Shula, pleading with her eyes.

"I'm going," she says.

"Be careful, *motek*," her father says. "I'm sorry I can't go myself." He shakes his head and shivers. Rachel wipes his forehead with a cloth.

"So, Yaakov," their neighbor Ephraim says. "This is how the Arabs welcome us to the neighborhood?"

"The government should have been ready for this. They knew it was going to happen!" Rachel snaps.

"So did the British! And still, they left like they had no more responsibility for this place," he counters.

"We don't have the British anymore! We have to take care of ourselves!" Shula cries. The room quiets. Her father covers his eyes with his arm.

"Go find him," Rachel says.

Shula heads for the spot by the beach where Yisrael and his friends like to sit. How stupid of him to go out today of all days. Typical of a young boy, thinking they were invincible, like running through a field in an electrical storm won't result in being struck by lightning. Nothing can touch me, she imagines him thinking. Well, she knows that isn't true any longer. That's a difference ten years makes.

As she nears the waterfront, she sees the wreckage of a building like her own, but blown apart, the laundry hanging from a line over a nonexistent balcony, the interior of the kitchen exposed for all to see. The sight makes her sick to her stomach. Her city, her beloved Tel Aviv destroyed. What kind of war is this? Attacking women and children, ordinary people who are trying to do their laundry?

She reaches Hayarkon Street, which to her surprise, is filled with people. Passing another bombed-out building, she glimpses the body of a young girl, her blood-covered face covered with a thick layer of dust. She heaves and panic floods her. Searching the crowded promenade for her little brother, she hears the familiar whine of plane engines. Heading north along the coastline are three Egyptian Spitfires. All her senses heighten as the drone of the engines gets louder and closer.

"Shula!" Yisrael and three friends stand in the doorway of a building. Running over, she grabs her brother's arm.

"What are you doing here? What were you thinking?" she yells, unable to contain her frustration and rage. "Are

175

you trying to get yourself killed?" Yisrael pulls his arm from her grip.

"We just wanted to see!" he says. One of his friends pushes his way between them.

"We knew we could run if we had to," he interjects. Pushing deeper into the stairwell, they gather together. The noise of the Spitfires grows so loud it is as if she is sitting at the airfield watching Avraham take off on one of his glider flights. The three planes fly in formation north along the coast. The engine sound recedes, followed by distant explosions. People run, crisscrossing the street, panic on their faces. Smoke rises in the distance.

"Come on, Yisrael," she says pushing him towards the sidewalk. "We are going home."

One month later, Shula practices Chopin's Polonaise-Fantaisie, Op. 61[17], the piece inspired by a Polish lullaby Aunt Leah sang to her when she was little. Stopping to stretch her fingers, she picks up the latest postcard from Avraham. She smiles at her brother's drawing of a crying baby wearing a Star of David shirt, bombs falling all around him. An arrow points to the baby with the text: *State of Israel. Born under fire.* She rereads the rest of his message:

I'm in the Galilee with my platoon. Had a coffee in Nahariyah and ate a cream puff (or two, maybe three...) just for you. Love, Avraham.

Babies, bombs and creampuffs. So Avraham. She tries to pick the stamp off for Yisrael's collection. These Hebrew Post stamps were only printed for a few weeks.

17

All the stamps now say State of Israel.

Hearing voices in the living area, she opens the door to find Danny sitting by her father. Their eyes meet. Dark circles rim his eyes. He looks away, and fidgets with an unlit cigarette in his hand. Her father waves her over.

"Look, Shula. It's Danny. He's come to say hello after all this time." She stands behind her father and remembers their last unpleasant meeting in the café. Danny lifts his hands in retreat.

"Shalom, Shula. I'm not here to fight. Just here to talk to your father for a bit," he says. Yaakov pats his daughter's arm.

"Make us some tea and join us." She smiles, glad to see him sitting up and not prone in bed like he has been for the past forty-eight hours.

A few minutes later she returns with the tea and biscuits. She places the glasses on the table and sits on the couch next to Danny.

"I don't know if you've heard, but they say Begin and the Irgun are going to surrender to Ben-Gurion today," he says.

"It's about time!" Shula says. Her father shushes her.

"Let Danny talk. What did you hear?"

"Ben-Gurion's been calling for the Irgun's surrender for weeks, months even. The great compromiser, that man," Danny continues.

"*That man* will bring an end to this war," Shula says. "Jews shouldn't be fighting other Jews when seven Arab nations are trying to push us into the sea. Enough is enough."

"Well, it seems that they agree with you too," Danny says. "Listen, I won't stay too long. I know you are not well, but I ran into Avraham in Nahariyah last week and he told me about your illness, and, well, like you said, Jews shouldn't be fighting other Jews right now, and you…" Stopping for a moment, he lights a cigarette. She notices his hand trembles. There is a deep scar where his thumb and forefinger meet. "Mr. Dubno, you always treated me well and with a kind of respect I never got at home. I want to thank you." Stubbing out his cigarette, he raises his hand to Yaakov. "All my respect to you," he says and they shake hands. Shula can see the tears well up in her father's eyes. He places his hand on top of Danny's hand.

"It was my honor to have you here in my house," he whispers. "And I wish you all the best in life." He pushes himself up and gives Danny a hug. "Now, if you'll excuse me, my bed is calling."

"Take care, Danny," she says shaking his hand.

"You too," he says.

A few hours later, Shula is on her way to pick up the afternoon papers when her mother stops her at the door. Rachel puts her hand on her daughter's chin and moves her head side to side.

"You look pale. Take a walk and get some sun. The exercise will do you good." She pushes Shula towards the door. With Rachel splitting her time between their own home and her two sisters' houses, Shula doesn't get out much between caring for her sick father and youngest brother. She kisses her mother on the cheek.

"I won't be long," she says.

Heading to Allenby Street, she window-shops at the boutiques lining the street. Most of the stores are closed at this time of day, but Shula enjoys the warmth of the sun and the change of scenery. While she's looking in the window of the bookstore, a man runs by, smashing her on the shoulder as he passes. Shocked by the hit, she grabs her arm. He turns and yells, "They bombed the *Altelena*! The Haganah bombed the Irgun boat!" Shula follows him to where he stands outside a café. He turns towards her, his saucer eyes wide, his round face covered with thick black stubble. "The *Altelena*! Ben-Gurion! He bombed the

Altelena!" Shula tries to step back, but more and more people surround the café and hem her in.

"I saw it! The horror at sea!"

"What did you see?" someone shouts from behind.

"A large boat, *Altelena* inscribed on its side. I could see thick black smoke rising up from it like an angry column of evil spirits!" The man looks around from face to face. "And then I could see people...soldiers...men... jumping off the side into the ocean and trying to swim to shore!" The crowd around her is quiet.

"He did it! Ben-Gurion did it!" A voice from the crowd shouts. The first man looks out into the crowd again, searching each face.

"Jews are killing Jews! Jews are killing Jews in the name of the Jewish State! This is not right! This is not human! Lord!" he yells as he looks up into the sky, his hands gesturing towards the heavens. Then he pushes his way out of the café and hurries down the street. A wave of nausea passes over Shula as she stumbles back. She finds a seat at an empty table and sits, staring off into the distance, trying to make sense of this act. Voices filter around her.

"He had to do it!"

"There wasn't any choice!"

"That Begin doesn't understand anything but force!"

"This is the beginning of the end, I tell you!"

"*Oy gottenu*! Jews killing Jews!"

She looks down at the sidewalk until a feeling of right returns to her body. Did it have to come to this? Is violence the only way men know how to deal with one another? It is something she can't understand, yet hopes it is the right path to take.

One month later, the family gathers around the radio as a ceasefire is announced. Yaakov leans back in his seat, a look of relief on his face.

"That is good news," he says. He is getting weaker

each day and worries constantly about Avraham. There has been no word for several weeks and each one of them yearns to hear something, anything, from him. The ceasefire will give them some relief.

After the announcement, she walks out to the balcony. She looks up and down the street, noticing for the first time how tall the tree across the street has grown in the last ten years. She remembers that she and Avraham were able to touch the top of it when it was first planted. The corner store is shuttered as usual these days. Since the war for their independence started, Mr. Abramowitz and his wife Batya stopped keeping regular hours. Sometimes it was because it was too dangerous, other times because there was not enough food, and still other times, she guessed, they didn't feel like it. Their son, Amit, was killed in battle two months ago and Batya is still in deep mourning. She sits for hours outside the shop on a rickety folding chair rocking back and forth while tears stream down her face, murmuring under her breath. Occasionally, she dabs her eyes with a well-worn rag that she keeps in her dress pocket, twisting it until it is long and rope-like, at which point she shakes it out, flattens it, and starts all over again. After a while, if she is not able to "rejoin the living" as Mr. Abramowitz says, he locks up the store and leads her home. She avoids the store when Batya is there these days. It makes her think about Avraham.

The sound of her own voice shouting her brother's name wakes her the next morning. Her heart is racing and she's covered in sweat but she can't remember the dream. Grabbing her robe, she goes to the kitchen. Her mother stands at the counter crying.

"Eema! What's wrong?" Shula asks, her stomach tightening. Rachel sniffs and wipes her face with a tea towel.

"I don't know what I will do without your father," she says hugging Shula.

"Oh, Eema. Don't talk like that…"

"What's going on?" Yisrael's sleepy voice interrupts them from the doorway. The women break apart and open their circle squeezing him between.

"I'm hungry," his says, his voice muffled by their embrace. Rachel laughs.

"Come, *motek*, let's get you some breakfast," Rachel sniffs.

By mid-morning the house is filled with visitors paying their respects to Yaakov. At one point Dr. Levy comes by and sits at his side for an hour talking about literature and politics and reading to him from books by S. Y. Agnon and Eliezer Ben Yehudah. She notices that her father is less interested in current events these days, unless the news has to do with Avraham. And for now, there is still no word.

"Is it okay if I practice, Abba?" she asks at a quiet point later in the day.

"Nothing would make me happier," he whispers. He closes his eyes and relaxes into his pillow, shooing her towards the piano.

She sits and lifts the key cover. She closes her eyes and tries to relax. She feels her shoulders tightening so she pulls out the Hanon book and turns to exercise sixty[18]. There. That should do it. The more difficult the exercise, the better. She has played these drills over and over, and never tires of practicing them. It is her warm up, her time to get her fingers moving, to focus her attention on the page, to read the music even though her fingers know the notes better than her mind. She moves across the keyboard

---

18

with sharp steady movements, completing the pattern and then moving it up one note, over and over again. Some people complain about these drills, but to her they are relaxing, meditative. There is only the music, no war, no thoughts of death or loss.

Two hours later the house is full again and Shula sits on the couch with Miriam and her baby girl. Her cousin tells her about her husband's recent visit home.

"Zalman got a ride all the way to Tel Aviv to spend eight hours with us. I didn't even know he was coming. He just showed up in his uniform at the front door. You should have seen the look on my mother's face. She didn't know what to think." She laughs while relaying this to Shula.

"So? What did your mother do?"

"What did she do? She cooked!" She exclaims and the cousins laugh. Shula hasn't felt happy all day and it feels good. Relaxing back onto the couch, she hears Yisrael's voice from outside.

"*Chayalim ba'im!* Soldiers are coming!" he shouts as he runs up the stairs to their house and bursts through the door.

"I saw the Jeep, Eema! It's parked on the corner and the soldiers are sitting there looking at papers." He grabs his mother's hand and drags her towards the balcony.

Shula runs over and sees the Jeep parked at the corner. The dreaded army Jeep, the one that carries the soldiers that carry the news. Always bad. Sometimes worse. Anyone home on the street is staring out at the Jeep with them. The soldiers look up and walk towards their building. When they are out of view the family piles back into the living room.

"Maybe they're going to the Shlomovitzes' apartment?" asks Yisrael. Then, the knock at the door. Shula looks at her mother. Miriam gasps. Rachel squares her shoulders, takes a breath and opens the door.

Chapter 11

Tel Aviv, State of Israel

July 1948

Two uniformed soldiers stand at the door. The one on the right is tall with fair skin and light brown hair. His companion is a few inches shorter with olive skin and dark hair. They wear khaki uniforms unbuttoned at the top, rifles slung across their shoulders. Their uniforms do not match, but that isn't unusual; this new army wears castoffs from the British, Australians and Americans. On their heads are those Hittlemacher hats that she was told were donated by an anonymous U.S. haberdasher. They are funny square hats with a brim and a flap down the back to protect the neck from the sun. She remembers seeing Avraham wear one during a parade in early April. He looked so good, so smart, and like these men, casual. *Casual. The new Israeli Army is casual.*

"Is this the Dubno family?" the tall one asks.

"I am Rachel Dubno," Rachel answers. Shula's surprised by how normal her mother's voice sounds. Miriam sniffles behind her. *Damn her. We don't even know why they are here.*

"May we come in?" asks the darker one with the bright green eyes.

"Who's there? What's going on?" Yaakov calls from the bedroom.

"Just some visitors, Yaakov," Rachel replies.

"I see soldiers! What are soldiers doing here?" he says. The two men exchange an uncomfortable look. Rachel looks at Shula.

"Take Yisrael and go help your father out of bed." Slowly, and with one on each side of him, they lead him to the couch. Yaakov sits by Rachel clasping her fingers in his. His forehead shines with a light sweat. Looking up, he smiles at the two visitors.

"Welcome to my home. Something to drink?" The two soldiers shake their heads and thank him.

"We're here about your son Avraham, sir," the tall one says. Miriam stifles another sob. Shula can feel her heart racing.

"We are very sorry to inform you that Avraham Dubno is missing in action. He was caught — " the soldier is cut off by Rachel's sobs. Yaakov leans toward the soldiers.

"Since when?"

"Yesterday, sir," says the tall one.

"Is he dead?" Yaakov asks. Shula hears the urgency in his voice.

"We don't know yet, sir," says the dark one. "We only know that he didn't return with his platoon — " Yaakov groans and leans back into the couch. The intense pain and sorrow in his face reflects her own gut-wrenching fear. This isn't supposed to happen.

"Well, where is he?" Rachel says. "Why can't you get him?"

"Madame, believe me. His comrades, they are doing everything they can to find him — "

"But he may be wounded!" she explodes.

"Rachel!" Yaakov turns towards his wife, gripping her arm. "He could be fine. We have to believe, with God's help, he is fine." Turning to the soldiers he says, "I am a very sick man. It is important that I see my son, you understand."

"*Adoni*, sir, you will know as soon as we have more information. I promise you that," the tall one says. Shula has heard enough. She gets up, goes to her room and slams the door shut. Kicking off her shoes, she feels the smooth tiles under her feet. She flops down on her bed and wills herself to cry. No tears come. She isn't sad, just angry. Angry at the war for taking her brother away from her.

Angry at her father for being so sick. Angry at the soldiers out there for making what was already a hard situation unbearable. Grabbing her pillow, she sticks her face into it and yells as loud as she can. Then she cries, her sobs silent, her shoulders shaking. When her eyes are empty of tears, she falls into a fitful sleep.

In the late afternoon, she wakes. The sun low in the sky. People talk and pots clank in the next room, the sounds of normality, the sounds of her house. Gathering her hair, she twists it into a bun. She wipes her face and neck with a towel. It feels rough and heavy from the lime-rich water. *I'll have to get a new towel soon.*

Joining Miriam out on the porch, she slides a cigarette from the pack. Her cousin draws a wooden match across the side of a matchbox and offers the flame to Shula. Taking a drag of her cigarette she watches as their twin plumes of smoke curl around each other, then drift away.

"Did I miss anything?" she asks.

"No, no. Not a thing. Don't worry. They'll find him," Miriam answers.

"I'll walk over to the Military Administration in the morning and see if I can find out anything else," she says, grinding her cigarette into the ashtray.

"It's unbelievable. Just unbelievable." Miriam lights another cigarette with the one still burning in her hand. Shula looks out over the street and watches as people begin to put up the blackout paper required on all windows these days.

"I'm going in to see how Eema is doing," she says heading back inside.

Rachel is in the kitchen peeling a mound of potatoes. She sniffs when she sees Shula and wipes her eyes with the back of her hand.

"Here," she says handing her daughter a knife. "Help me cut these." Rachel's knuckles are white from holding the knife too tight. She attacks the potatoes like they are some kind of threat.

"How is Abba?"

"He's been sleeping since the soldiers left. Why don't you check on him while I finish?" Rachel says, grabbing the cutting board from underneath Shula's hand and plucking the knife from her fingers. Taken aback at the suddenness of her mother's actions, Shula is too dazed to react.

It is dark inside her parents' room. The heavy window blinds block out most of the light. She reaches down to the table and turns on the bedside lamp. Yaakov lies on his back; his eyes closed, mouth open, his breathing shallow. She takes his hand. It is cool and clammy, not warm and dry like it is supposed to be. She loves her father's hands. His fingers are long like hers, piano-playing fingers, he always says. She starts to tap out a tune, pressing the pads of her fingers against his cool flesh. It can't be that Abba and Avraham will be gone from her life at the same time. It isn't possible. God wouldn't do that to her, to them. She has to believe that. She has to.

She sits there for a long time, lost in her thoughts. Just one year ago, she was on top of the world, well, at least the highest point in, what is now, Israel. And she was so happy. She was on the adventure of a lifetime with Avraham, and not only that, they were planning so many more. And now, a year later, she sits with her dying father, wondering if she will ever see her brother again. Just that thought, that she will never see, hear, or talk to Avraham, makes her shake. She takes in a sharp breath, grits her teeth and straightens her back. *I should go practice. Abba likes to hear me play and it will occupy my mind.*

Back in her room, she sits at the piano, opens her Hanon exercise book and places her hands on the keyboard, but the notes are a blur. Her eyes fill with tears, as she puts her arms on the keyboard and, head down, cries.

In the middle of the night, she wakes. It is pitch black and her room is stifling hot. She turns on her lamp and picks up a book, but doesn't feel like reading. She needs air.

As she tiptoes onto the balcony, the slight breeze and floor tiles cool her. She takes a deep breath and leans over the balcony. While no light escapes from any windows, the white Bauhaus buildings that line Melchett Street glow in the moonlight. She lies down on the balcony floor and watches the stars. No lights in the city means that the stars shine brighter than ever. *Because we may be bombed, we have to turn out the lights, but because we have turned out the lights, we can see the stars. Was this what is meant by a silver lining?* The buildings, the stars, the moon, all give a brilliant silver lining to her otherwise storm-cloud-filled life.

Later that day, Shula and Yisrael walk to Army headquarters. The long line of people look as desperate and sad as she is. After an interminable wait they arrive at the cramped counter.

"No word yet, miss," the officer on duty says. "I'm so sorry." She smiles and takes Yisrael's hand. Each lost in their own thoughts, they walk home in silence. At the corner shop, Yisrael gets an ice pop and Shula a bottle of *Mitz Paz*. She relishes the cold sweet orange juice as it travels down her throat.

As they step out of the store, the metallic rattle of a two-stroke engine grows louder and closer.

"Uncle Yehoshua and Sabbah Dubno! They're here!" Yisrael yells, pointing to Yaakov's younger brother and father pulling up on an old Military Norton motorcycle. Her uncle and grandfather remove their dust-covered goggles in unison.

"Sabbah Dubno!" Shula cries as he gets off the bike. Her father's father is short and wiry, his white goatee neat and trim. Wiping the dirt from his jacket sleeves, he then pulls out a cotton handkerchief and cleans the dust from his black round-rimmed glasses. A knot forms in her stomach and a lump in her throat. She throws her arms around him, to keep him from seeing the tears already forming in her eyes. A cloud of rust-red dust billows from his coat.

"Oh, *motek*, be careful! I am covered in dirt!" He shakes a small mound of rocky sand from his pant cuff. "Look at that," he says, pointing to the pile. "You know, in some places people pay a lot of money for that!"

"Grandpa! It's just dirt!" Yisrael says, a smile replacing the serious pout he's had for the last few days.

"Ah! But no, it's not just dirt." He reaches down and sifts the powdery substance through his fingers. "If you say that the dirt is from the Holy Land, some of those Christians will pay good money for it. I have seen it in shops in London! Little jars of this dust, water and olive oil packaged together with a note saying 'From the Holy Land' and then another note that says '*Two shillings, please!*'" He winks at Shula, and the knot inside her relaxes. Yehoshua removes his helmet and flashes that wide Dubno smile from under his curly red hair.

"Uncle Yehoshua," she says, hugging him.

"Ah, Shula. It's so good to see you, and you!" he says putting an arm around Yisrael.

"We had quite a time getting here," her grandfather says. "Even with the blockade lifted, it still took us an extra two hours. But thank God, we made it," he holds out his arms for his two grandchildren. "I am so grateful to see you my *kinder*. Any news of Avraham?" Shula shakes her head, worried that if she says the words she'll fall apart.

"Rachel!" Sabbah Dubno greets her mother upon entering the apartment. "How is he?" he asks, walking with her to Yaakov's bedside. Shula hesitates by the door.

"He hasn't woken up since the soldiers were here about Avraham yesterday. Abba, I'm so worried." Yaakov sleeps, his breath shallow, his lips slightly apart. Her grandfather takes his hand and brings it to his lips.

"Yaakov, my son. I'm here."

"I knew you would come, Abba," Yaakov whispers. His eyes flutter open. "Yehoshua. I'm glad to see you." The two brothers were carbon copies with different tints, but now Shula's father is a jaundiced ghost of himself.

"You're a good brother," Yehoshua says, kissing him on the forehead.

"So are you, Yehoshua. So are you."

That evening, after dinner is cleared and tea served, Sabbah Dubno sits at the table with Yisrael on his lap. Shula remembers how her grandfather's whiskers tickled the back of her neck when she sat like that at his age.

"Now for a present," he says winking at her and pulling out a small metal box from his pocket. Inside is an array of buttons in all shapes, sizes and colors. He picks out a shiny brass one with a relief of a dog on it. "This particular button is from the Ashlee company. Very nice people. I picked it up in London in February. Do you know how cold it is there in February, my little one?" Yisrael shakes his head.

"Not as cold as Poland, I would guess," interjects Rachel as she set down a plate of honey sesame seed candies.

"No, Rachel, you're right. Not as cold as Poland, but colder than here, that's for sure," he said. "Do you know what happened one day? I was walking down a street in Hackney, after a nice long lunch with Mr. Williams, and you know what? My beard froze!" He laughs and pulls on his short white beard. "Now, this one," he holds up a Kelly-green glass button with a glittery gold swirl thru it, "This is from the island of Murano in Italy where the streets are lined with glass-blowing studios. Do you know, when I go to visit Alfredo Barbini's workshop, I take a water taxi from Venice!" He digs around the colorful pieces and pulls out a large mother of pearl button with two holes. "And this one? Do you know which factory made this beautiful piece?"

"Your factory!" Yisrael says.

"Yes! My humble workshop in Jerusalem makes these beautiful buttons." Shula puts her arm around her grandfather, hugging his shoulder and kissing the top of his head.

"I'm glad you made it, Sabbah," she says.

"How could I not?" he answers. "It would take more than a blockade to keep me from my family. Now, if you'll excuse me," he says. "I'm going to visit with my son for a while." Sabbah Dubno sits by Yaakov's bedside, whispering to him while he sleeps.

"They finally called a ceasefire up north!" Yisrael yells when the news comes over the radio two days later. Shula grabs her purse and races down to military headquarters with renewed hope. *They have to find Avraham now! They have to!* She imagines telling her father that they found Avraham and the news gives him the strength he needs to get well. She wants to do this for him, for them. But after a long wait, the answer is the same. It is still too dangerous up north, even with the ceasefire, and they are unable to locate her brother. She takes her time on the way home, not wanting to hurry back to deliver the bad news. When she tells her father, he turns to the wall and sleeps for the next forty-eight hours.

Two days later, Yaakov wakes and asks about Avraham. His eyes fill with tears when he hears there is still no news.

"I pray for him all the time." Taking Shula's hand, he holds it to his lips, too weak to be able to properly kiss it. He falls back asleep, his breaths shallow. His chest barely moves. She sits with him, compelled to make sure he still breathes, and repeats the prayer she has been reciting for days, *Please, don't let him die. Please, don't let him die.* An hour later, an imperceptible change in the air passes over her and she can tell he is dying. Running into the living room she grabs her mother's arm.

"He's dying, Eema," she says leading Rachel, Yisrael and Sabbah Dubno into the room. Surrounding the bed, they hold hands and watch her father's labored breath.

"It's all right, Yaakov. You can go now," Rachel says kissing her husband's forehead. After a few minutes, even though his chest is moving, Shula knows he is dead.

"He's gone," she says, her voice sounds bewildered, unsure.

"But his chest is still moving," says Yisrael. A moment later though, Yaakov's breathing stops. His lips are parted, his yellowed face skeletal. Tears stream down Yisrael's cheeks. Rachel wraps him in a hug, her tears streaming onto him, the bed sheets, her dress. But Shula can't cry. Her grandfather takes her hand, but she shrugs him off. Leaving the bedside, she slams the door to her room, and throws herself onto her bed. Then she cries and the grief doesn't come quietly. She cannot stop the guttural moans. There is a throbbing pain in her solar plexus. She can't catch her breath. She curls into a fetal position, hugs her knees and rocks. *He's dead, he's dead, he's dead.* She cries until she is spent of energy. Lying there, she stares at the wall but sees nothing, her tears an unstoppable river of pain and sadness. *No! No! Avraham! Where are you? I need you.*

L ater that same day, the undertaker arrives to remove Yaakov's body.

"Good thing he didn't die on a Friday afternoon, Mrs. Dubno," the man says to her mother. "It's always more difficult when these things happen on the Sabbath," he continues, unwrapping a long white cotton sheet. Shula puts her arm around her mother's shoulder and hopes she can be as strong for her as Rachel is for everyone else. The undertaker motions for his assistant to move around to the far side of the bed. Turning to them, he gestures towards the door. "It's better if you are not here," he says. Rachel leaves the room, but Shula stays put.

"I'm staying," she says. The two men look at each other.

"Are you sure? It might be — "

"I can handle it, thank you," she replies straightening her shoulders.

Pulling the sheet off her father they straighten his arms and legs. His skin is waxy, his facial features exaggerated — his high forehead too wide, his nose too sharp. He's in his striped cotton pajamas. *Eema just washed those.*

The assistant lifts her father's legs while the undertaker slips the white sheet beneath the body. He begins to unbutton his shirt, but the undertaker stops him with a look. He nods and finishes wrapping the body in the sheet. *Shalom Abba*, she thinks as the sheet covers his face for the last time. *Goodbye, Father.*

Hoisting her father's body up they move it onto a canvas stretcher. She worries that they will hit his head on the doorjamb or worse than that, drop him, but they maneuver out of the room without incident. Rachel and Sabbah Dubno stand behind Yisrael, their eyes bloodshot from tears. How long will she look at her family and see puffy red eyes? Is this how they will look from now on?

192

She can't imagine a time when she won't feel like bursting into tears.

"We will see you at Nahalat Yitzhak at noon tomorrow," the undertaker says on his way out.

Shula and Yisrael watch from the balcony as the body is loaded onto the horse-drawn cart. Her neighbors across the way watch from their porch. There are no secrets on this street. Looking at the corner store, she sees Batya rocking back and forth in her chair, tears streaming down her face as she watches the cart rumble down Melchett Street.

At the cemetery the next day, the service is mercifully short. Shula flinches when they lower her father's shroud-covered body into the ground. With each handful of earth the mourners throw into the hole, they bury her childhood. Then it is her turn to add to the mounds of soil covering him. It is strange to throw dirt on her father like this, but she reminds herself that this isn't her father any longer. Abba is gone.

They drive back home in her cousin's dusty '41 Ford to begin the *shiva*, the traditional Jewish seven days of mourning. Rachel heads straight for the kitchen but is stopped by her sister Sarah.

"No, no, no, my sister. You didn't let me lift a finger after my Yosef died. You know the rules. You sit, we serve you, and you mourn your loss with your family." Shula and her mother sit on the couch with Yisrael. He shifts around on the hard surface where the cushions have been removed, unable to relax.

"Eema, it's so uncomfortable with no cushions!"

"Come sit here, next to me," Sabbah Dubno says patting the low stool next to him. "You know why we sit low like this during *shiva*?" Yisrael shrugs and his grandfather hugs him close. "Losing someone we love, especially a close family member, is the biggest heartbreak a person can endure in a lifetime. We need to sit and feel

193

our loss, as painful and uncomfortable as that may be. Our family and our community," he points to the siblings, aunts and neighbors preparing the house for *shiva*, "*They* get to take care of *us*. It's a mitzvah to help us heal. So, stay close." Pulling a fresh linen square from his pocket, he pats the lone tear marking a path down the boy's cheek.

An urge to wash the dirt and grime from her face propels Shula towards the bathroom. Standing at the sink, she pats her irritated, red eyes with a wet cloth. The coolness relieves the heat emanating from her face for a moment. When she removes the cloth, her blotchy skin and tired face reflect back at her.

"Now, now, now," her Aunt Sarah says, entering through the open bathroom door. She whips a white sheet over the mirror. Aunt Rivka grabs it from the other side, covering the rest. "No looking in mirrors for one whole week, which believe me, is a blessing at a time like this. But, most importantly, for seven days, it's not about what's out there," she waves her hand towards the covered mirror, "But what's in here." She places her palm over Shula's heart, and kisses her forehead.

"You know what the kabbalists say," Rivka says. Sarah folds her arms across her chest.

"*Nu*? What do they say?"

"They say that evil spirits are attracted to the void left by the dead person's soul. The demons are only visible in mirrors, so we cover the mirrors so the bereft shouldn't be alarmed."

Sarah rolls her eyes.

"The only scary thing to see in a mirror during *shiva* is your own face, my dear."

The family sits around the coffee table while plates of food are placed in front of them: olives, sunflower seeds, pita bread, hummus, *techina*, Arabic salad, watermelon with cubes of cheese, and then later in the evening the hot items are brought out from the kitchen — noodle kugel,

194

savory *burekas*, a thick beef stew from their next-door neighbor. *We Jews, we drown our sorrows in food.*

For days, they sit and eat, sleep and weep. It is cathartic. Shula thinks of nothing else but her father and her family. No music to hear, no newspapers to read, no radio to bring the outside world in. After days in the house, just sitting on the balcony feels like an exciting change of pace. It is healing, this cocoon-like Jewish death ritual. Miriam stops by the military headquarters each day for news of Avraham, but so far there is nothing new. He is still missing and no one can tell them when he will be found.

On the fourth day of *shiva*, Shula leans over the balcony and watches the activity on her street. Mr. Abramowitz sweeps the steps of his shop, and Mrs. Goldman waddles alongside her dog. She can hear the muffled voices from inside and takes a breath of the hot and humid air. A military Jeep pulls up to the building. Inside it, two soldiers sit and collect their paperwork. *Who could they be coming for this time?* They put on their hats. *It couldn't be us. We are still in mourning for Abba and have three more days to go. Can you even sit shiva for two people at once?* Thoughts fly through her head as she watches the soldiers get out of the jeep and head towards her building. A buzzing starts in her ears and her palms sweat. She feels her body and mind separate, like she is watching from high above the street, looking down from the top of the tree to her left. She sees the men move up the walkway, and her legs fuse to the ground. She can't walk or talk or breathe. *They are coming here, but they can't be coming here. No. It just can't be.*

She needs to get into the apartment before the soldiers to warn her mother, but can't. Catching her mother's eye, she tries to convey her panic, but Rachel just cocks her head. The sound of knuckles rapping on the door freezes her. She stares as Miriam heads to the door, knowing that her whole world will change once again when it opens.

It is two different soldiers this time, and later, when she tries to play the moment back in her mind, she can't make out their faces. Were they tall? Short? Dark? Fair? What does it matter at this point? She sees the soldiers take in the room. It is clearly a house in mourning, what with the low boxes surrounding the coffee table, the sheets draped over the mirrors, the food piling up on the kitchen counter. Miriam speaks to the soldiers as her mother sinks onto the couch shaking her head. There is a buzzing in Shula's ears, a narrowing of her vision, a wooziness, and she steadies herself. Then, she can make out the sounds of the traffic rising up from the street below and she is back in her body and enters the apartment.

The soldiers look up at her and introduce themselves. *I wonder why they bother telling us their names. Who wants to know the names of the bearers of bad news?* The soldiers remove their hats and sit down opposite Rachel.

"We are sorry to inform you, that Avraham Dubno was killed — " Rachel's cry stops them. Miriam sobs in the background. Sabbah Dubno moans as Yisrael crawls into his lap. A stone-faced Shula sits on a box on the floor.

"But there's been a ceasefire since last week? How could this be?" Rachel asks.

"He was killed on July 16 and the ceasefire went into effect on July 18, but unfortunately, it was too dangerous to get onto the battlefield until yesterday."

"But yesterday was the twenty-third! That's seven days!" Rachel cries. "What was he doing for seven days? Was he alone? Was he in pain?" Rachel is frantic. Shula thinks of Avraham, lying in a battlefield, wounded and bleeding, for days. It is too much to bear. She speaks up.

"How did he die?" she asks, her voice steady and low. Her mother grasps her hand.

196

60, far slower then she's played in years. She begins her routine and the hypnotic power of the repetition calms her. For a few moments, she feels no pain.

In the first week of August, Rachel moves onto the sofa and rents out her room to a boarder. Mr. Horowitz is a nice enough man, quiet and clean, but they are still getting used to sharing a bathroom and meals with a stranger. Shortly after that, they add another bed to Shula's room that her friend Naomi rents.

With Rachel busy helping her sisters and taking care of their boarders, Shula walks Yisrael to and from school every day. She thought he would balk at his big sister accompanying him, but he doesn't ever complain and seems to welcome their time together. For her, time spent with Yisrael lightens her mood. Being with her youngest brother is a constant reminder of why she has to pull herself out of the darkness. Their family went from five to three, and although the wounds are healing, they are still raw.

"Are you feeling all right?" Miriam says when Shula arrives at her house for dinner on a Friday evening in early October. Shula nods and kisses her on the cheek, then hands her the flowers she picked up on the way over.

"I'm fine," she says and smiles, reassuring her cousin that she won't burst into tears for no apparent reason. That only happens once in a while now and usually when she is by herself. "Shabbat Shalom, Miriam," she adds and takes a cigarette from the box on the coffee table as she heads out to the balcony. She's the first of the guests to arrive, which is a relief. Making conversation is still hard for her, and she can't react to events in real time. The extent of her condition didn't hit her until the day she sat down on a shirt her mother was mending and didn't feel the needle jab into her leg. It was the strangest sensation, as if the signals to her brain were going in slow motion, like her

199

whole body was stuck in molasses and the source of the irritation was so far away, connected and disconnected to her at the same time.

In late October, Shula receives a postcard from Solomon. She runs her fingers over the 1948 Olympic stamp, the first Olympics since 1938 and the beginning of the world war. *The rest of the world is ready to move on, trying to make peace and work together, except in Eretz Yisrael.* It's been five months since the declaration of the State of Israel, and the fighting between the Arabs and Jews continues.

"Dearest Shula, I can't wait to see you in November. I'm sorry that I am not there to give you support during this terrible time of loss and war. I've booked passage and will arrive on November 5th for three weeks. Yours Truly, Solomon."

It's nice to have something to look forward to, she thinks, folding the laundry hanging on the line. She hasn't seen Solomon in four years and is no longer a sixteen-year-old girl, but a twenty-year-old woman. So many life-altering events have occurred since then she isn't sure how she is going to feel about him.

The butterflies in her stomach take flight when she opens her eyes the morning of his arrival. They made plans to meet at Café Tamar, even though she rarely goes there anymore. Since the deaths, she only goes to cafés with her cousin Miriam, who prefers the coffee, and people watching, at the Rowal on Dizengoff. She rushes to get ready and is heading for the door when her mother stops her with a cup of hot coffee and a fresh baked roll.

"What's the rush? Here, have this," she says shoving the items into Shula's hands.

"Eema, I have to go."

"You have five minutes to eat something. Come on." Rachel motions. Shula takes the offering and sits.

"So, today is the day?" Rachel asks. Shula takes a bite of the warm bread and washes it down with the sweet black coffee.

"Yes, Eema. I'm meeting him at Café Tamar."

"Then you can bring him over for dinner."

"Eema! I haven't seen him in four years. If I still like him, I'll think about inviting him over."

"You'll still like him," Rachel says with a smile. "I'll set an extra place."

On the walk over, she finds herself singing "Tzena, Tzena, Tzena," the bubbly melody matching her mood. It takes a moment, but she finally names it. Happiness.

She spots Solomon sitting at the café, his black hair slicked back. He wears a tailored blue double-breasted suit. He is more handsome than she remembers. His eyes find her and her heart flips. She breaks into a wide smile and he shades his eyes as if from a blinding light. She laughs. Just like the first time they met.

He takes her hands in his warm hands. He kisses her lightly on each cheek. She sits when he holds the chair out for her, and positions it once she sits. She can't remember a *Sabra* boy doing that for her, but then again, she can't remember the last time she saw a *Sabra* boy in a suit and tie.

"You are as beautiful as I remember, Shula," he says and her cheeks flame up.

"That's a very nice suit," she replies, embarrassed by her answer.

"Why thank you, although I realize that I am a bit overdressed for this place. I hope you don't mind," he says.

"I don't mind one bit, in fact, I quite like it. It suits you, so to speak." A coffee appears before her and she sips the drink.

"So, what's new?" he says and they laugh together. Yes, she likes this man. Good thing Eema set another place for dinner.

A week later, they walk the promenade along the beach after a performance at the Habima theater. Solomon takes her hand. She looks into his eyes and smiles then looks down at the sidewalk. She likes the feel of his smooth skin against her own and moves toward him. He lifts his arm and puts it over her shoulders, drawing her closer still. She feels a tension in her stomach, not butterflies like she feels onstage, more like hummingbirds whose beating wings are a blur. When they reach the intersection of Hayarkon and Rothschild he stops, pulls her towards him and kisses her on the lips. The explosion in her brain fills her body with an intense euphoria. She reaches her hands around his neck and kisses him back, feeling his mouth melt into her own.

On the morning of November 20, Shula waits for Solomon on the sidewalk outside her apartment building. Though she begged him to tell her where they were going, he refused. At nine o'clock on the dot, he pulls up to her doorstep in a British Army Jeep.

"Come on, Shula! We're going for a ride," he says as she slides into the seat. There are three other passengers in the jeep and she smiles at the woman sitting to her left. She pushes against Solomon. Solomon's friend, Paul, drives while whistling "New York, New York" from *On the Town*[19] as they head south out of the city.

"May I ask where we are going?" she whispers in Solomon's ear.

19

"You may ask, but I won't tell you," he says winking at her. "Don't worry, you'll enjoy it." Shula leans back against the leather seat and hopes that she will. She is not much up for surprises these days.

They drive for hours, first past Jerusalem then south towards the Negev. The conversation centers on the U.N.'s order for Israel to pull out of Be'er Sheva and how the Israeli Army is refusing to budge. There are few other vehicles on the road except an occasional military transport, which kicks up huge clouds of dirt from the unpaved roads. She looks out the window and sees an olive grove by an ancient rock wall and is instantly back in the Nazareth of her youth. She smiles and breathes in the dusty scent of the desert and realizes she misses it.

"Is that Be'er Sheva?" she asks, when she sees a town in the distance.

"Yes, it is," answers Solomon, taking her hand.

"What are we doing here?" she asks, wondering why they have come this far south in a disputed territory.

"Don't worry," the driver says. "We are safe."

They wind their way through the narrow streets of the city stopping outside an ancient amphitheater. The area is filled with Haganah soldiers, both men and women, thousands of them. Some sit scrunched together on the ancient seats, others sit cross-legged on tarps lain over the dusty ground all the way up to the foot of a stage. The tops of the three ancient walls surrounding them are populated with soldiers, most with rifles hanging from their shoulders but a few on alert, guns at the ready. The stage is set for an orchestra with wooden chairs in a semi-circle, each facing a music stand. And in the center of the stage, a piano.

"What's going on here?" she asks as they find a spot along one wall. A soldier waves at her from atop the crumbling façade. Solomon searches the crowd.

"Over there!" he yells. Shula looks across the sea of people to the road. An orchestra moves towards them, each musician carrying an instrument in hand. She can see the string section, the brass and woodwinds, all following the conductor, a handsome young man with a bowtie and dark suit.

"Is that…is that *Bernstein?*" she whispers. Solomon looks at her and smiles.

"I know how much you admire him and well, when Paul told me about this and was able to secure the transport, I just assumed — "

"Leonard Bernstein!" Shula bursts out and cranes her neck for a better view of her newfound idol. Since she was introduced to his music, she is now an authority on the Jewish American composer, conductor and pianist. The crowd parts to let Bernstein through as he leads the Israel Philharmonic Orchestra towards the stage.

"Like Moses parting the sea," says Solomon, and she turns to him and laughs. It is all too much. The crowd is chattering with excitement and she can make out at least half a dozen languages — Hebrew, English, German, Russian, Arabic and Yiddish — a melting pot of Jews from all over coming together for music, all knowing that they are here for a momentous occasion, that their souls will be lifted when the music begins. She wants to absorb every note.

The concert begins with Mozart's Piano Concerto No. 15 in B-flat Major[20], a light and airy piece. She closes her

---

20

eyes as the piano takes over and imagines herself up there performing for the great conductor. The music soars to a crescendo and then trickles down to the original melodious theme. She is in awe of Mr. Bernstein's mastery of the instrument and is intrigued with his interpretation of the slower movements. He closes his eyes and sways. She closes hers, feeling a deep connection to him, the crowd, the music.

Next, he plays Beethoven's First Piano Concerto[21] and her fingers follow every note. She observes tiny nuances that he adds that make her want to learn it all over. Then, the oboe squeals out the first notes of *Rhapsody in Blue*[22], and the crowd roars its approval. Bernstein smiles throwing his head backwards then forwards, his thick dark hair falling onto his forehead. He conducts from the piano, commanding the instrument and the orchestra, not to mention the crowd of worshipful soldiers surrounding him. She is transported by the mournful melodies Gershwin created that soar through the air and echo off the amphitheater walls. What was at one point a place that brought music to the people of this region, today serves its purpose once again.

Shula wraps a green wool blanket around her and snuggles up to Solomon in the back of the Jeep. She is grateful for this gift he gave her. It stirred such passion for Solomon, for music and for her country. Leonard Bernstein, known the world over for his musical genius, risks his life in a war zone, so Israel is heard. Maybe as

---

21

22

Gershwin, a Jew, interpreted the American experience, she could, in her own way, let the world hear what an Israeli sounds like.

The concert replays in her head. The months of sorrow and sadness, of anger, confusion and bitterness, are all swept away. Resting on Solomon's shoulder, she closes her eyes and sleeps.

Early the next morning, the group is back on the road and heading towards Tel Aviv. Two hours into the bumpy ride, Paul slows to a stop.

"What the hell is going on up there?" he asks. Shula looks over his shoulder to see what is causing the slowdown. Hundreds of people are marching down the road heading east. The north/south route is blocked by a U.N. convoy. They stop and Shula follows the men over to the nearest soldier. The road is filled with families, all Arab. Men push carts piled high with boxes and carpets, women balance enormous stacks of wrapped packages on their heads, children lead smaller children or animals by hand or rope. With only the possessions they can carry, they walk east in a great line to nowhere.

"What's this? What's going on?" she asks.

"The Arabs are leaving," answers the U.N. soldier.

She searches the faces in the crowd and her heart jumps. She spots a little boy that looks like her friend Mahmud. She stares at him a moment, searching for the face she knew so well. Then realizes that like her, Mahmud is now an adult.

"But why?" she asks.

"Lots of reasons," the soldier continues. "Some feel it's not safe to live amongst the Jews, others hope that Jordan or Egypt will come to their rescue, others say that maybe they'll come back once the fighting stops," he says, flicking his cigarette onto the ground and crushing it under his boot. "I don't know. Myself? I think the Jews have won this round and maybe the Arabs' time here has come to an end." Shula looks down the endless line of dejected souls, people with families and lives and jobs and homes, all people like her who had experienced inconceivable losses over the past year. She stifles a sob and runs back to the Jeep.

When they reach Tel Aviv, Solomon insists that they take a walk on the beach before heading home.

"You don't want to deprive me of my last Tel Aviv sunset," he teases her, and she allows a detour to the waterfront. As her feet sink into the soft cool sand, she watches the setting sun turn the rows of white buildings opposite them a deep, warm orange. Solomon stops and takes her hands.

"Shula, you know that I care for you, but I need to return to England." He stops for a moment. His hands are hot and sweaty. She shifts her grip in his. "I want you to come with me. I'm starting a good job in my father's company. I'll make a decent salary and we can live a comfortable life. You'll be able to pursue your musical career — it's safe there now."

"Leave Israel?" she asks. He seems surprised by her question.

"I want you to be with me, and my life is in England. I want you to be safe," he replies in a tone that suggests she should agree with him. She drops his hands. She cannot imagine leaving her mother, her family, her city, her country, her home.

"Solomon, I can't leave. Can't you see that? I want to be with you, but my mother needs me, my brother needs me, for God's sake, my country needs me! Do you not understand?" *This doesn't make sense at all.* "I thought you were thinking of coming here, the way you were talking to Paul about business opportunities. Is that not the case?" She looks at him, her eyes searching for the truth she thought she had seen before. Solomon looks down and shakes his head.

"Shula, you are so talented. What are you going to do here?"

"What do you mean? I'm going to be a concert pianist."

"You could do that in England as well. I would support you 100 percent, at least until our children were born." He takes her hand but she pulls away.

"Solomon. I don't plan on having children for a long time. I want to travel the world before becoming a mother."

"How long do you want to wait?"

"I don't know! Five? Ten years?"

"That is quite a long time. I'd be thirty-two before we had our first child."

"It's what I plan to do."

"Oh," he says and they lapse into silence. The waves kiss the shore. The sea shimmers. She breathes in the salty air.

"Shula, I have to be honest with you. I think you will be wasting your talents here. You'd have so many more opportunities in London — "

"Better than playing with Leonard Bernstein? Or Arturo Toscanini? Here, in *Eretz Yisrael*, I will study and play with some of the greatest musicians in the world, who are only here, may I remind you, because the world made it clear that Jews aren't welcome."

"It's not like that anymore, Shula. Europe is different. Things are good for everyone, including the Jews."

"For now, Solomon, for now. The Jews have been saying that about the world for 2,000 years. But do you know what is really different this time?" He shakes his head. "The *Sabras*. Me and my generation. We are not going to be complacent any longer. We are strong, we are smart, and we can fight. Bernstein gets it."

"I get it," he says.

"I'm not sure you do." They continue to walk in silence. The sun has dipped into the water, and she can see the first stars in the darkening sky.

"Shula, I love Israel, I love the Jewish people and I will support this place with all my heart, but," he stops and takes her hands. "My place is with my father and my family. I'm not a 'pioneer.' I'm a simple man who wants to do good in the world in the best way that I can. Helping my father and his business and supporting the state in mind and spirit, I can do. But I'm afraid I can't commit my body to this cause. And you? Haven't you given enough of yourself?" Shula looks into his eyes. This is not meant to be. She will not be leaving her home, her country, her soul.

"I'm sorry Solomon. I can't do what I need to do from another country." Solomon's eyes fill with tears which he quickly sniffs away. Red blotches appear on his cheeks.

"I'm quite disappointed you feel this way, Shula." She tries to hug him, but he is stiff and doesn't respond.

"I'm sorry too," she says and walks away.

Chapter 12

Tel Aviv, State of Israel

December 1948

Once Solomon returns to England, Shula experiences wide mood swings, going from light-hearted and talkative to dark and brooding in an instant. A thick black cloud presses down on her head, filling her with anger and insecurity. Unpredictable and uncontrollable, it causes her to lash out at the smallest things.

In mid-December, Rivka's husband is killed in battle. The family gathers at her aunt's house for the *shiva*. The routine kicks in, sheets cover the mirrors and low crates are borrowed from a nearby farm. Shula picks at a red and blue sticker on the side of the box. *Apples. They used to hold apples.* Rachel cooks and cleans and wipes the tears from everyone's faces. The sum of their losses overwhelms Shula. Only seven months ago her mother and aunts stood listening to the declaration of the State of Israel with their husbands. Now all stood alone, having only each other to hold onto once again.

Following this loss, the boarders and Yisrael become Shula's responsibility once again. After doing her chores, which include laundry, breakfast, lunch, cleaning, she dives into her music. She practices six hours a day, sometimes more. Being social isn't a factor for her any longer. Getting through the week without bursting into tears is her goal. She falls asleep exhausted in the early evening, only to wake again in the middle of the night, wide-eyed, awake.

Then in late December, she opens the front door to find her piano teacher, Isaak Brandt. Smiling, he removes the brown fedora from his head.

"Oh! Mr. Brandt. Did we have a lesson scheduled?" she asks, wondering how she could have forgotten this appointment.

"No, no. No lesson. I received a letter today and I had to come right over to speak with you. May I come in?" he asks.

"Of course," she says showing him inside.

Sitting on the couch, he motions for her to sit across from him. He pulls a thin envelope from his jacket pocket and lays in on the table between them. "So, I received this letter yesterday." *The City of New York Golden Anniversary* the red stamp reads. The postmark is New York, NY, United States of America. "It is from a friend, a colleague of mine. You see, when I was second violin at the Berlin Symphony, he was the principal oboist. Then, as you know, we all had to leave, and when I went to the Yishuv, he decided to go to the United States. Now he works at the prestigious Manhattan School of Music. Have you heard of it?" She shakes her head.

"It's not Juilliard?" she asks. She has heard of Juilliard, and knows that Leonard Bernstein attended Harvard University. "Is it near Harvard?" she asks. Mr. Brandt laughs.

"That, I don't know," he says. "The geography of the cities in the United States is not my area of expertise." He clears his throat. "As I was saying, I think this may be of interest to you." He pulls a thin sheet of paper from the envelope.

"*Dearest Isaak,* — okay, I don't have to bore you with the pleasantries between old friends," he stops and scans the page. "Okay, here — *There is a wealthy Jewish benefactor at our school who would like to extend a full fellowship to a worthy Israeli pianist to study here, at the Manhattan School of Music. The man, who wants to remain anonymous, was referred to me because the school administration told him that I have contacts in Eretz*

Yisrael. So, that is why I am writing to you and other friends in Israel. Is there someone you know who would be worthy of this gift? If so, prepare them, as a representative of this illustrious man will be traveling to Israel this spring to audition candidates. Please, send me a letter with a list of your top students and I'm sure we can help get the first Israeli over here to study with the best in the world. Yours truly, etcetera, etcetera, you don't need to hear any more of this." He puts the letter down in his lap and looks up at Shula. "So, I was thinking of my 'list' when I realized that out of all my students, there was only one person I would suggest," he looks into Shula's eyes. "And that is you." A wave of excitement rises deep inside her. Her heart flutters. *Almost two months now. That's a long time to not feel any hope.*

"Mr. Brandt, I don't know what to say." He holds up his hand.

"Shula, I know how much you and your family have gone through and I don't expect an answer on the spot, or even soon. We have plenty of time before you have to decide if you even want to perform in this competition, let alone make your way to New York," he says. "All I ask is that you think about it. Talk to your mother, your family, and friends. See what they say, but think about what you want in your heart of hearts. You are talented, my dear student, and I know that if you want this, it is yours."

"The *mamzer* Zvika!" Rachel says as Shula helps her with the groceries later that afternoon. "He almost had me buying a bag half-filled with rotten tomatoes. I will never go near that man's stall again. So, how was your day?" Shula pauses for a moment and bites her lip.

"Mr. Brandt stopped by."

"He did? What did he have to say for himself?" Rachel asks as she fills a pot with water. Shula takes a deep breath. She isn't even sure how she feels about this, let alone how to explain it to her mother.

"There's this letter," she says holding up the envelope. "It's from Mr. Brandt's friend in the United States. At a music school in New York — "

"A music school? Which one? Juilliard? Harvard?" interjects Rachel.

"The Manhattan School of Music."

"Hmm. Never heard of it. Go on."

"He says that a wealthy American Jew wants to pay for the first Israeli to study there. He thinks that I should at least audition — " Rachel covers her mouth with her hand and her eyes fill with tears.

"Oy," Rachel says. Shula feels like the featherweight letter is a piece of lead in her hand.

"Oh, Eema, I would never — "

"Let me see that!" Rachel grabs the letter from Shula and marches over to the dining table. She watches as her mother pores over the contents. Tears fall down Rachel's cheeks as she looks up at her daughter and smiles. Leaning over, she kisses her on both cheeks, covering them with her tears. Taking Shula's hands in hers, she looks into her eyes.

"You not only will train for this audition, but you will win it and you will go." Shula looks at her mother in shock.

"Eema. I can't go. It makes no sense."

"You will win and you will go."

"But I want to be here, not thousands of miles away from everyone and everything I love."

"And, when you finish your studies you will come home."

In the weeks that follow, Shula and Mr. Brandt go through piece after piece, searching for the best music to showcase her talents. He suggests various pieces by Beethoven, Bach and Haydn, but she wants Rachmaninoff. His music has pulled her through some dark times, and she relishes the challenge of conquering the wide chord stretches and lightning-fast runs. She has handled enough of his most challenging works to know how well they suit her. She presents her teacher with her choice: Rachmaninoff's Prelude Op. 23 No. 5[23], the piece that Emil Gilels played to uplift the Russian troops in 1942. She hopes it will lift her up as well.

Right from the start she is sure this is the right piece for her. The marching tempo showcases her strength. Attacking the keys, she stretches her fingers to cover the wide chord changes, while the *pianissimo* sections allow her to highlight her lighter touch. The rolling lines of the piece are pure Russian romanticism, of which Rachmaninoff is the master and she a faithful interpreter.

A knock on the door in late February interrupts her practice. She opens the door to find a stranger, his face badly scarred, his right eye a milky white. She takes a step back.

"Shula?" he says and only then does she recognize Avraham's friend Yuval standing before her. Stunned, she is grateful when Rachel steps forward and takes his hand.

"Yuval, how are you? Come in, come in," she says and ushers him towards the couch. She sits next to him and holds his hand.

23

"Make some tea," she says to Shula. "Add some *na'ana*. You like mint?" she asks. Yuval nods and smiles at Shula. Shula realizes that she doesn't know this man. He became friends with Avraham at the Technion University in Haifa, and though she met him a few times when he visited with her brother, she was always so engrossed with her piano, or her own friends, they never interacted much. But she knows enough to see he is devastated.

Yuval stirs some sugar into his cup and Shula watches as the green mint leaves swirl around in the amber liquid. He lifts the glass to his mouth and she can see his hand shaking. Opening his shoulder bag, he pulls out a pack of cigarettes.

"Is it okay?" Glancing up at Rachel, he taps a cigarette on the edge of the coffee table. Running her finger over the raised gold logo of the brass Israel Defense Forces ashtray they received in the mail this week, she opts for the turquoise Pal ceramic ashtray instead. Her mother's eyes fill with sadness as she looks at Yuval's shaking hands. Anxiety rises in Shula's chest. He was in Avraham's platoon, but she has no idea if he was there on the day he was killed. She wants to ask him if he knows how her brother died, if he was killed instantly or not, but she can't ask this broken man.

"I was so sorry to hear about Yaakov. I know Avraham would have been devastated," Yuval says.

"Yes," Rachel replies. "I guess in a way it is a small blessing that neither one knew of the other's death in the end. They both died with some hope." Rachel wipes the corner of her eye. "Where are you living now, Yuval?" she asks. Yuval shrugs his shoulders.

"Here and there. Our house was bombed in the first month of the war, completely destroyed, the whole building. So, I'm staying with an aunt in Petach Tikva...um...I'm not really working right now, it's kind of hard with this arm," he says as he lifts the damaged limb. Rachel *tsk tsks* beside him.

"Yuval, were you with Avraham when he died?" Rachel asks, surprising Shula with her forthrightness. Yuval takes another drag on his cigarette and stubs out the rest in the ashtray. He runs his fingers through his hair, using the better arm. Shula's heartbeat quickens as she waits for his answer.

"I wasn't there when he died, no," Yuval begins. He stops and pushes another cigarette out of the pack. "But later, I saw his body, I mean, him."

"Tell me," she implores, her voice dropping. Taking a long drag of his cigarette, he taps it over the ashtray. Shula watches the ash float down and land in the center of the receptacle.

"It was on July 16 and we were trying to push the Syrians out of Mishmar Yarden way up north in the Galilee. We were ordered to man the lookout at Pardes Houry and Avraham was in charge of our group. There was heavy Syrian fire and then they just attacked, Syrian soldiers running towards us, guns pointing right at us. You could look right into their eyes." He stops and brings the trembling cigarette up to his mouth. "Our comrade Eitan was hit in the leg. He couldn't walk. Avraham ordered us to retreat while he stayed and wrapped Eitan's wound as best he could. Last I saw him, he was holding the boy's hand and waving us away."

"Then what?" Shula asks, leaning forward. "They didn't know he was dead until the twenty-third!" Yuval stubs out the end of his cigarette, crunching it onto itself.

"We tried several times to get to him, but the Syrian fire was too heavy. It was a week before we could get to his body." He stops for a moment and lights another cigarette. Shula looks down at the ashtray. Three cigarette butts. She watches as Yuval blows smoke through his nostrils, then puts his head in his hand. He clears his throat. "They called me in to identify him. I'll never forget how he looked. Charred. Like he had been burned." Rachel covers her mouth and gasps.

"Oy! No!" she cries between gasps. Shula moves over and sits next to her mother. Rachel leans into her daughter's shoulder and cries. "My poor baby! Oh no, no, no," she says over and over, shaking her head. Yuval spills his tea onto the tray. The mint leaves in the glass are now a dark green. *Cooked*, thinks Shula.

"I'm so sorry, Mrs. Dubno. I didn't mean to come and upset you so — "

"No, Yuval, it's good that you came and told us. It is worse not knowing anything, you understand?" she says squeezing his hand. "It's so sad. All of it. It is just so sad," she wipes her eyes. "You know, sometimes I think, will I ever stop crying?" Shula puts her arm around her mother's shoulders and holds her. She isn't sure what she is feeling at the moment. The great sadness that recently lifted pushes onto her again. She is exhausted and sad, but no tears come. She looks up at the "Avraham" spot on the wall, as she now calls it to herself. Then Yuval's voice pulls her back into the room.

"I have something for you. Something Avraham was hoping to give you, well...he wanted you to have this to remember your trip last summer." Yuval reaches into his bag and pulls out a large brown envelope. He pulls a sketchbook from inside and hands it to Shula. She recognizes her brother's handwriting.

A Trip to the Galilee is written across the cover. There is a hand-drawn image of the Lion of Tel Hai statue and two small hikers climbing a hill in the distance. Shula gasps.

"This is about our trip! Last summer! Eema look." Shula holds it out to her mother and together they lean in and flip it open. She smiles when she sees the first page, a sketch of her standing under the clock at the Tel Aviv

Central Bus Station, an annoyed look on her face. She hears her mother laugh as she reads the text.

Eight o'clock already,
And Avraham is late.
"Your Majesty insults us!
Such a thing has never happened!
If he does not appear,
Or peek around the corner
I am taking leave alone
To Kinneret and Ein Vered,
To the upper Hanita!"
Says an excited and angry
Shulamit.

She flips through the pages, each one telling the story of their trip in verse with delicate and expressive sketches. On one page, she is complaining about the sharp rocks at the Sea of Galilee, and later on she is gorging on cream puffs in Naharia. It is touching, funny, and beautiful. She is overwhelmed with conflicting emotions. Happy, sad, and angry, but the tears still don't come. And then she turns to the last page.

There is an image of two people in an embrace, their bodies melded together as one. It is the most loving image she can imagine and she can feel Avraham's arm around her shoulder. Next to it he wrote:

And here we ended our trip
We'll say goodbye and see you later
And do not cry
And dot, dot, dot...
See you soon!
Next year in Italy or the U.S.A.
And once more see you soon!
And dot, dot, dot...
To be continued.

Shula can't stop herself now. She lets out a sob and the tears spill from her eyes. But it isn't the shock she felt when she heard the news last summer. This is a coda replaying the deep sadness that once again opens an enormous hole inside her that has not healed, and maybe never will. She can't imagine ever feeling light or happy again. That emotion is lost to her forever.

A few weeks after Yuval's visit, Shula walks into the apartment to find Yisrael sitting with two friends at the dining table and reading through her *Trip to the Galilee* book.

"See how he drew Shula in her bathing suit?" Yisrael says.

"Oh! My feet hurt! These rocks are so sharp!" his friend says in falsetto.

Shula feels her pulse quicken and the dark cloud covers her head. An unstoppable anger rises in her.

"What the hell do you think you're doing?" she yells, startling the boys. She marches to the table in four long strides and grabs the book from Yisrael's hands.

"This is *my* book. Do you understand me? Don't you ever touch this again!" she snaps, then slams into her bedroom, smashing the door shut. Crying, she stumbles across her room and puts Rachmaninoff's Trio Élégiaque No. 2[24] onto the small Solid State 78 record player. Clutching the book in her arms, she sinks down to the floor. *Isn't it fitting. Rachmaninoff wrote this piece as he mourned Tchaikovsky's death.* The somber melodies match her melancholy. His grief echoing her sorrow.

24

"It's here!" Mr. Brandt shouts when he comes to see her shortly after her twenty-first birthday. He waves the unopened letter back and forth, motioning for Rachel and Yisrael to join them on the couch. "Should I open it?" he asks.

"Yes!" Rachel says. Mr. Brandt opens the envelope. He reads from the whisper thin paper.

"*Dear Isaak*, and so on and so on…hmmm…Ah! Here it is! *My boat will be arriving on March 29, 1949 at the Tel Aviv seaport…* yes, yes, details of the ship's arrival…umm…okay! Here! *Please arrange for your pupils to be ready to perform on April 3 starting at one o'clock p.m. at the Habima Theater. They should enter through the musicians' entrance…*and so on…hmmm." He looks up at Shula and smiles, his eyes sparkle with excitement.

"This is a good thing, Shula," Mr. Brandt says. "We have a date and a goal in sight. Now, the real work begins."

After a week of fulltime practicing, Shula begins to feel the darkness lift. She finds that she once again enjoys spending time with her friends and family and is even able to participate in the conversation. Sometimes, though, a pang of self-doubt will come out of nowhere and she can feel her insides turn to dust, but she is better at pulling herself out of these moments, and music always helps.

The constant practicing is also an excuse not to participate in social events when she doesn't feel like it. Yuval has stopped by several times to visit with her, and each time she begs off to practice. After a few weeks, the visits stop. She hardly notices, so focused is she on her goal. She wants to win not only for her mother, but for her father and Avraham. How proud they would be if she won. More than once she imagines what Avraham would say at the news: "Wow! What a great excuse to visit the U.S.A.!" Hearing his voice in her head, she doubles down in her determination to win.

She goes after her performance outfit with equal vigor. After several frustrating shopping trips with her mother, Rachel gives up.

"You are worse than my sister Leah with the shopping! Nothing is right, nothing is perfect." Her mother wants her to try a French or British design from the Salon Rachel boutique, but Shula wants something Israeli.

"Shula!" comes the cry from the street one afternoon. Shula steps out to the balcony. There is her cousin Miriam, pushing a sleeping Oriah in the stroller, her belly starting to pop out with her second baby.

"What?" Shula says.

"Let's walk to Dizengoff. There's a new dress shop next to the Leica store, you know where I'm talking about?"

"Yes."

"I think they have what you want," she says. "Come on. I told them I would bring you by." She waves at Shula to come join her. "This one is out for at least another hour, maybe more if we keep the stroller moving."

It is a perfect Tel Aviv day, as they make their way over to Dizengoff Street. The air is warm and dry, and above her, a perfectly blue sky. Miriam is prattling on about Oriah's latest developmental milestone and Shula half-listens and half-daydreams about what she might find at this store. Something between East and West, that speaks to a melding of cultures. Indefinable but right on target. *I'll know it when I see it.*

When they arrive at the shop, Shula is a bit disappointed. The place is small, more like a closet that happens to open onto the street. The two women and the stroller stand single file between two glass cabinets filled with embellishments, from buttons, to bows, to pieces of embroidery. A tall well-dressed gentleman greets them. With his slicked back hair and his pencil thin mustache, he has an air of elegance and refinement about him.

"Shalom again," he says to Miriam. "Is this your cousin?" He sticks out his hand to Shula to shake.

"Shulamit Dubno," she says.

"*Enchanté*," he answers in French, and holds his hand up to his chest. "I am Olivier Wolkowicz, formerly of the House of Dior in Paris. My wife Nina is an expert in Yemenite embroidery. Welcome to our shop. Your cousin thinks we may be able to help you in your search."

"I'm looking for a dress for a recital on April 3." The man starts to make notes on a pad with a pencil.

"That gives us about two weeks then? That may limit our choice of embroidery, but it's doable," he says.

"I want something Israeli, you know?" She says, finding it once again hard to articulate exactly what she is searching for.

"Ah, I see what you mean. Maybe something like this?" The proprietor turns to the racks of dresses behind him and flicks through them. Shula looks through the part in the curtain that leads to the backroom and sees a young girl bent over a table cutting a piece of cloth. She leans further forward and catches a glimpse of a Yemenite woman, the colorful embroidery she works on spread across her lap. She turns when she hears Mr. Wolkowicz's voice.

"Pardon? *Mademoiselle*?" He holds up a black chiffon dress. It is styled like one Katharine Hepburn might wear in one of those movies she does with Spencer Tracy. Shula loves the padded shoulders, loose long sleeves falling into cinched cuffs, a wide fabric belt around the waist and flowing mid-length skirt, all trimmed in a delicate Yemenite crisscross embroidery in yellow, red and gold. He hands the dress to Shula. She holds it up to her body and looks in the mirror.

"Would you like to try it on? If you like it we can go back into the workshop and pick out the fabric and embroidery colors." She follows him into the back room and he holds aside a curtain for her to change behind. Shula glances around the workshop and counts six people crowded into the small room. Two women sit at sewing machines pushing fabric through the machines. Sitting on a low stool, a man holds a rope-like hookah hose to his mouth. Looking up, he blows a stream of smoke out through his nostrils. He glances at Shula and nods his head. She lets the curtain drop and changes into the dress.

As she puts it on, she notices the way the fabric feels against her skin. She adjusts the shoulder pads and then reaches her arm behind her to pull up the zipper. At the top, the small metal hook and eye are cool against her neck. She ties the matching wide belt made from the same black chiffon fabric embellished with the identical embroidery. Twirling around, she admires the way the full skirt flows around her legs.

When she exits the dressing room, Miriam claps with delight. Shula laughs and stands in front of the narrow mirror wedged between the display cases. She looks at herself and bursts into a huge smile. This is it. This dress reflects exactly what she wanted to say about herself and her country. She is sophisticated, elegant, *Sabra*.

Chapter 13

Tel Aviv, State of Israel

April 1949

After months of practice, the date of the recital is upon her. She knows the piece inside out, and can play it without error time and time again. She's played it wearing her dress, and if she feels the slightest pull — on her shoulder, across her back — she takes it back for adjustments. Mr. Wolkowicz and his wife never complain about these changes. She is buoyed by the people around her.

What makes her most nervous is not being able to practice on the stage beforehand. She has been in the audience at the Habima Theater many times. She knows how the room sounds from the back of the hall where she usually sat (or stood). But she has never been on the stage as a performer. Mr. Brandt, as always, tries to assuage her anxiety.

"Once you start to play it doesn't matter where you are, right?" he says when she brings up her concerns. "You've played on many stages and there are always a finite number of steps to the piano. You must march out there as if you own the whole place, for once you convince yourself of that, you will convince everyone in the room of that same thing."

The night before the performance, she has no appetite. Her mother invites the family over for dinner to celebrate, but that is the last thing Shula wants or needs. She joins in the dinner, picking at the food but not eating. Then before they have had a chance to finish the tea and sesame seed candies, Shula shuts herself in her room. Leaning against the door, she closes her eyes. She imagines herself in the wings of the theater's stage. Lifting her shoulders, she takes a deep breath and strides over to the piano. She rests her hand on the instrument and makes a small curtsy to the imaginary audience. Then she takes her seat and gathers her thoughts. She places her hands on the keyboard, but doesn't play. Instead, she runs through the routine again. After the third time, she puts on the new dress and shoes. She closes her eyes then walks, feeling the soft chiffon flow back and forth against her legs. The cuffs are secure around her wrists and she notices the cold metal of the hook and eye at the back on her neck. She rehearses this walk a dozen times, each time imagining the stage and the piano lit by a spotlight.

And then there is nothing left to do but sleep.

Shula wakes with a start, her heart pounding. She looks at the clock and sees that it's only six o'clock in the morning and she has plenty of time to get ready. This is the fourth time she's woken up, panicked that she missed her recital. She hears her mother clanking pots in the kitchen and pushes herself out of bed. There is no way she is going to sleep at this point. She puts on her dress and twirls around liking the way she looks in the mirror. She pins her hair back with barrettes, then takes them out, one, two, three times. They keep the hair out of her face, but they make her look too young. She fiddles with them, and decides to keep them in. The fewer distractions, the better.

By ten o'clock she is so nervous she can't stay in the apartment any longer. Mother and daughter walk the short distance to the theater arm in arm. Shula thinks back to the time when she was about eight years old and Avraham was ten. Habima was still under construction and her brother convinced her to sneak into the unfinished theater. They made their way up to the stage where they performed for the stacks of lumber and mounds of stone. She remembers the excitement she felt that day looking out into the cavernous hall. And here she is, about to do just that. *I did it*, she thinks and laughs.

"What is so funny?" Rachel asks.

"I remembered how Avraham and I snuck into the theater when they were building it and performed on the stage, and…"

"And here you are. About to do it for real," Rachel says and squeezes Shula's arm. "Next stop — Carnegie Hall!" She stops and takes Shula's face in her hands. "I am so proud of you my darling, in so many ways. You are very strong," she says. Shula reaches over and puts her arms around her mother.

"I watch you and I see how to be strong and how to be brave and how to carry on. Thank you for everything."

When they arrive at the theater, Mr. Brandt is waiting for them outside. He ushers them in and Shula is lost for a moment as her eyes adjust to the dark hallway. Someone plays Haydn's Piano Sonata in E-flat major, a piece she performed several years ago. She follows Mr. Brandt to the stage left wing. A young man of about her age sits at the piano, his straight brown hair falling over his face, his thick glasses perched low on his nose. *He is good. I need to be better.*

"*Mazal Tov*," Mr. Brandt whispers as the young man reaches the last movement of the piece. Rachel grasps her hand and there are tears in her eyes. She pushes Shula's hair behind her ear.

"You will be great," she says and kisses her on the cheek before following Mr. Brandt into the hall. Shula looks out and sees three men in suits sitting in the front row, clipboards in their laps. Mr. Brandt stops and speaks to the one in the middle. She notices the light shining off his scalp through his thinning hair. He looks at her over his round wire-rimmed glasses and nods. *That must be him. The man who can change my life.* It is a strange thought. That one performance can mean so much. She closes her eyes and thinks of Avraham and her father. She imagines them sitting out there with her mother, proud smiles on their faces. Opening her eyes, she turns her focus onto the place deep inside her that carries the music through her heart to her hands.

Her name is called. The bench now empty, waiting for her. Feeling the butterflies in her stomach start up, she takes a deep breath to calm herself. She smiles at the men, pushes her shoulders back and walks to the piano. Counting each step, she notes the sound her heels make as they clip across the wooden floorboards. Just like she practiced in her room, only this time instead of four steps it takes twelve. She puts her hand on the piano and turns to the half dozen people in the audience. She curtsies and feels the moisture collect between her hand and the wood.

"Name?" The man in the middle asks.

"Shulamit Dubno."

"What will you be playing?"

"Rachmaninoff's Prelude Op. 23 No. 5[25]," she says, and her voice sounds clear and strong. Her heart pounds, the butterflies are whacking their wings inside her, and all her senses are heightened.

"Very good," he says. He shifts in his seat and pulls a handkerchief from his front suit pocket, wiping the sweat off his upper lip. "You may begin when you are ready." Shula curtsies again and turns to the piano. She sits on the bench and adjusts it to her liking. She glances at her mother, then looks back at the piano and closes her eyes. She sits for a moment, hands in her lap, and goes over the first lines of the piece in her head until she feels ready. She

---

25

opens her eyes, places her fingers on the keys, takes a deep breath and begins.

After the first several measures, Shula relaxes into the piece. She still has a sense of excitement inside, but now it is directed towards the piano keys. The music flows out of her. She closes her eyes and her body sways to the melodic lines. When the music speeds up her fingers are a blur. She hits the notes at the right time and tempo, lifting herself off the bench in the process. In just under four minutes it is done, and she can feel herself, and the butterflies, settle back down to earth.

She puts her hands in her lap for a moment, knowing that it was her best performance yet. She stands and pushes the bench back, places her hand on the piano and faces the hall. She gives a quick curtsy and hears her mother's solo applause and yells of 'Brava!' Then the man in the middle clears his throat.

"Very good, Shulamit. Your mother has every reason to be proud. We will be in touch. Thank you," he says, and Shula hesitates for a moment. She looks over at the wings and sees the next talent waiting there. A girl this time, her long, thick hair falling in ringlets around her shoulders. *I shouldn't have worn my hair in barrettes*, she thinks, as she makes her way towards the backstage shadows.

Later that afternoon, the whole family is over at the apartment to celebrate. At first, Shula protested when her mother suggested a post-recital party.

"But what happens if I don't feel like celebrating?" Her mother turned to her, an incredulous look on her face.

"What are you talking about?" she said, to Shula's surprise. "You don't think I haven't been listening to you for these last few months?" Rachel reached over and stroked her daughter's face. "Shulinka, whether or not you win this competition, we all have something to celebrate." She held her arms out to her daughter for a hug. And for the first time in days, Shula reached out to her mother and allowed herself be enveloped in her arms.

When they arrive home from the theater, Yisrael is the first to greet them.

"It happened! Jordan signed the armistice agreement! That's three out of the four Arab nations to agree to stop fighting us." Shula looks up when she hears the whoops of delight coming from the apartments up and down their street. She smiles. Maybe they could have peace one day.

That night Shula eats more than she has in weeks. Her grandfather is here from Jerusalem and plays the 78s he picked up at the flea market in Covent Garden. Sabbah Dubno grabs her hand when the Benny Goodman Orchestra comes on, twirling her around the room. She laughs out loud, for the first time in months. Naomi breaks into their dance and then the whole room is in a circle dancing the *horah*. The shouts of *Am Yisrael Chai! The Nation of Israel Lives!* ring through the room over the sound of stomping feet. Her mother is right, of course, There has been little to celebrate for so long. Just getting to this point is cause for festivity.

"You see!" Sabbah Dubno says as he swings her around. "This is a doubly great day. You have accomplished a great feat and Jordan has promised to put down their weapons. Life is beginning to look up, no?" Shula smiles. Maybe life, or God, is going to give her and her family a break, and let them enjoy some happiness for a change.

For a few days, the post-recital elation stays with her. Sitting with friends at cafés, she claims she is on "vacation" after the long, intense months of preparation. But then she begins to feel at a loss, that her life is in limbo. Within a few weeks the anger returns, the black cloud covering her and darkening her mood for hours on end. She goes back and forth in her head about the competition, sometimes imagining that she won and how she would feel, but pushes those thoughts from her head. How can she leave her mother? How can she leave Yisrael? They need her. The reality of her situation weighs on her until she convinces herself that she never had a chance at winning. The odds are stacked against her.

In the third week of May, Shula sits with Miriam one afternoon during a brief relief from her private torment. She laughs when her cousin regales her with stories from last week's First Independence Day celebrations. They revel in the experience of being able to celebrate with the whole country this time.

"And to think," Miriam says as she takes a sip of her coffee. "Just one year ago we were sitting *shiva* for my father." Oriah crawls over to her mother, and she reaches down to pick her up. "And you!" she says as she kisses her daughter on her cheek. "You were so little! Look how big she is now! Do you believe it? With children, you see how fast time flies." Shula is about to agree with Miriam when a knock on the door interrupts them.

"Hallo! Anyone home?" a male voice calls from outside followed by a *rap-tap-tap* on the door. "I have a Special Delivery for Shulamit Dubno!" Shula looks at Miriam from across the table and their eyes lock.

"Do you think...?" Miriam asks. Shula's heart flips and she pushes back her chair. She bites her lip, and tries to smile.

"Coming!" she announces as she heads for the door, smoothing her skirt and shirt and tucking her hair behind her ear on the way. She feels the butterflies start up and her palms begin to sweat. *Silly*, she thinks, as she wipes them across her skirt. *It's probably not even the letter.* Then she takes a deep breath and opens the door.

A man leans against the doorjamb, a bored look on his face. He wears an old British Postal Service uniform, but the Royal Mail patch now reads Hebrew Post. She notices these little differences lately. Signs of change, she hopes. Good change.

"Hello, I'm Shulamit Dubno," she says. The man holds out a letter and she sees the U.S. airmail stamps in the corner. Her heart flips and she takes the letter from him, holding it with two hands. The man sticks a pad in front of her and holds out a pen.

"Sign here," he says and points to the bottom of the form.

"So, *nu*? Open it already!" Miriam says when Shula returns with the letter. She sits and stares at the envelope. *Should I open it now? Wait for Eema?* Winning or losing will cause huge changes in her life. She gets the brass Pal Bell letter opener and brings it to the table, catching Miriam with the letter in hand. She grabs it back.

"What are you doing?"

"Sorry! Sorry! I was looking at the stamps," Miriam says and leans away, but moves forward when Shula sits down.

"Open it!" she whispers into her ear, and Shula picks up the letter opener and slides the blade through the envelope flap, cutting a clean line across the top. She blows into the slit parting the thin covering, and pulls out two folded pages. She begins to open them, then stops.

"What if they say no?"

"What if they say yes?" Miriam answers back. Shula inhales, then opens the paper as she breathes out. Reading the letter to herself, she wants to know the news before she is required to share it with Miriam and the rest of the world.

"*Dear Miss Dubno, We are pleased to inform you that you have been awarded a full fellowship to the Manhattan School of Music on behalf of an anonymous donor —*" Shula stops and looks over at Miriam, dazed. "I won," she says. Her cousin jumps up from her chair with a loud *whoop* and claps her hands together.

"I knew it! I knew you were going to win!" Miriam hugs her cousin and kisses her on both cheeks. "You did it! You're going to America!" Shula sits there still trying to process this new information. After six months of buildup and anticipation, she has an answer. *I won.* She looks over to the spot on the wall. *I did it, Avraham. We did it.*

"Guess what?" she says to her mother later that afternoon.

"What, *motek*?" Rachel replies, unloading the groceries from her bags. Shula feels a smile creep onto her face.

"A letter came from America — "

"A letter came? *The* letter? What did it say?" Rachel steps towards Shula as she pulls the envelope from behind her back. Her mother grabs it from her, pulling out the sheets. Gasping, she holds her hand to her mouth. "Oy! You won! My baby! You won!" She holds up her arms, her eyes sparkling with tears. Shula feels her own eyes well up. "You did it! Shula! You did it!" Then they are crying and laughing and hugging each other again. "Does it say when you go?" Rachel asks as she scans the paper in her hands. Shula stops and looks at her mother, the realization hitting her hard in the chest. She did it. She won. But can she leave her mother, her brother, her family and friends? Can any of them suffer another loss?

"It says that a packet of information is on its way," Shula answers, pointing to the line on the page. "Eema, are you sure that you want me to leave you and Yisrael — "

"What are you talking about?" Rachel says throwing her hands in the air. "Of course, you are going! After everything we've been through? How can you not go? Don't be silly," she says, and begins to unload the groceries. Shula stands there, her feet welded to the ground. She wants to go more than anything. To be in

New York. The magical city that she and Avraham used to dream about for hours, imagining how they would walk down Fifth Avenue from one end of the island to the other. How they would hear all types of music, see great museums and soak in the culture around them. And to be able to live there and study? It is too good to believe.

Leaving her mother, she shuts the door to her bedroom. She slips off her sandals, and rubs her feet against the cool tiles. Are there tile floors in New York? She lies on her bed and thinks about what she wants. Until she saw her mother, she thought that maybe she could do it. But now she isn't sure.

She hears a tap on her door and Rachel walks in. She sits on the edge of her bed and rubs her back.

"I think you should go to Jerusalem and see Sabbah Dubno. Tell him the good news in person. Talk about it with him. He usually has some good insights, don't you think?" She turns to face her mother and nods. It has been months since she was last in Jerusalem. Yes, a trip will do her good.

A few days later, Shula boards a bus to Jerusalem. She wears a new polka-dot sundress that Miriam found for her. She never asks where her cousin gets half the items she succeeds in procuring, but she always "finds" a lot of things. Shula hands her small rectangular suitcase to the driver and removes her wide-brimmed sun hat as she boards. Finding a seat near the front by a window, she is grateful to have a view of the outside world and the road her father helped build. In the past year, the trickle of migration has turned into a deluge of Jewish refugees from all over the world. Between that and the continually changing borders, who knows what she might see today.

A man plops down onto the seat next to her, and she smiles as he situates himself. He looks to be in his thirties and is dressed in the familiar ATA brand khaki work shirt and shorts, his boots covered with a layer of fine dirt that reminds her of her father's shoes. His sunburned face is sprinkled with light freckles, and his short brown hair is covered with a *kovah tembel*, the standard hat for Israelis these days.

"*Boker Tov,* Good morning," he says.

"*Boker Or*," she replies.

"I hope you don't mind, but I've been traveling since dawn from Be'er Sheva so I will shut my eyes for a while and then we can talk, okay?" She nods and opens her book as the bus pulls out of the terminal.

When they reached the outskirts of Tel Aviv, blockades of barbed wire cause the bus to veer off the route again and again. Hastily built encampments line the roads, creating an endless sea of white canvas tents. Bedraggled refugees stare out from behind metal chain links.

"You ever lived in one of those?" the man sitting next to her says. She turns and looks down at her hands.

"No."

"Ach, you're lucky. You a *Sabra*?" he asks pulling back to look at her. She nods. "I was in one near here for three months. It was a living hell," he says, shaking his head. "It's not enough that I had to leave my home in fear of my life, sleep in tents for months waiting to get on an overcrowded boat filled with people dirtier, hungrier and sicker than me. Then I get here and," the man flings his arm out into the aisle. "And what do they do? They stick me in one of these camps where we are living in conditions worse than the ones we left. Ahh! I'm sorry. I'm emotional right now." The pain on his face and his sudden confession makes her own dilemma small in comparison. He takes out a handkerchief and wipes the corner of his eyes. "I located my brother yesterday on *Who Recognizes? Who Knows?*" he says.

"How wonderful!" She flashes to her mother shushing them each night when the radio show comes on and the endless announcements are made.

"*Aryeh (Leibush) Kantrowitz, now in kibbutz Hazorea, is looking for his mother Fanya, nee Margolin,*" the voice drones on and on. It sounds like most of the country is hoping to find someone they lost.

"Yes, it's wonderful. Wonderful and sad. You see, most of my family is gone. I thought I was the only one left. Out of a family of ten! And now I find I have my brother. It's amazing when it works, that kind of show. I listened every night, but never heard a thing, and yesterday I hear my brother's name and my name and, I tell you, my heart beat so fast I thought I was having a heart attack!" He stops and lets out a chuckle, then sighs and looks at Shula. "It's a very good thing to have hope, you know?" She nods wondering what her hope may be. To go to New York like everyone tells her she should, take a chance and compete on the world stage? And if that is the right thing to do, why does it feel wrong?

Shula arrives at Sabbah Dubno's house on Mekor Chaim Street in the late afternoon. Her Jerusalem family has gathered to celebrate her arrival. He fills his wine glass, clears his throat and stands.

"*Ahem,* may I have your attention, please," he begins. Shula looks around the table. *It must be funny, to see your face reflected back at you through your descendants.* "I would like to make a toast." He turns towards Shula. "To Shulamit Dubno, who has been accepted on a full fellowship to study at the Manhattan School of Music, one of the most prestigious music schools in the Western Hemisphere, I might add." He looks around the table then back at her. "I know you will excel in whatever you wish to do, my dear granddaughter." He holds up his glass and she lifts hers in return and together they say,

"L'Chaim! To Life!"

The next morning Shula and her grandfather leave the house early to walk to the train station for the journey to central Jerusalem. On the way, they pass by Machane Yehuda market. Sabbah Dubno greets every proprietor they pass, from the spice sellers to the vegetable-stall owners. As they pass a favored tomato merchant she hears her name mixed into his sales chant.

"Right now, ladies and gentlemen! To-ma-toes! To-ma-toes! He-llo, Shu-la! A half a kilo! A half a mil! To-ma-toes! To-ma-toes!"

"So, when are you going to New York?" Her grandfather says, linking his arm in her own. She feels herself tighten and her breath gets shallow, but she forces herself to talk. If there is anyone in the world who can help her with this decision it is her grandfather. She wipes her palm on her soft cotton sundress and adjusts her hat.

"Um…that's just it, Sabbah. I'm not sure that I should go right now." Sabbah Dubno stops and looks at her.

"And why do you think that?" he asks. Shula fidgets with her purse, pushing the zipper back and forth, inch by inch.

"I'm worried about Eema." She looks at him with as much seriousness as she can muster. He doesn't laugh like Miriam does when she tries to talk to her about her concerns. No, her grandfather returns a look as serious, if not more so, than hers.

"Your mother is fine, Shula. You and I know that. She has a boarder and will take in another when you are gone. That will be more than enough money for her to live in comfort. Yisrael is a good boy and is almost a bar mitzvah at this point. He doesn't need as much mothering." Shula nods. "So, that's not a problem. What else is worrying you?" She looks at her grandfather and feels the tears well up.

"I'm worried about you, Sabbah."

"What? Why worry about me? I have Yehoshua and his family here. Ruthie comes one day, her brother the next, the mother, they all check on me, *motek*. And besides, I have Mrs. Vlessing next door," he adds with a wink. Shula laughs despite herself at her grandfather's brazenness. "Next? What's the next worry?" Shula hesitates before telling him the final reason.

"Sabbah, I don't think I should leave Israel." At that, her grandfather bursts out laughing.

"What? Don't you understand? I love this country and we have all done so much to help make *Eretz Yisrael* a reality, but getting to this place took so much away from us — your father, Avraham, Yosef, Lev, the list goes on and on and is far too long. It has been hard for you and everyone in this family." He turns to face her and takes her hands in his. He gazes at her fingers and rubs his thumb down her pointer finger. "Long fingers, like your father's. Piano playing hands, he always said." He squeezes her hands again. "We are all of a place but only some of us understand that we are also of the world. You are one of those. One of the *world*. By going to New York, with your beauty, talent, intelligence and poise, you will be one of the best ambassadors for our country. Every day you will show the world what an Israeli can do. *This* will be of real service." He pauses for a moment. "Israel is here," he squeezes her fingers, "And here," he adds poking her chest, "and *here*," he says as he throws his arm out to the sky. "And now, thank God, you can always come home."

"Oh, my God!" Miriam cries as she holds her infant daughter over her shoulder. She reaches over and pulls the brochure from Shula to get a better look. Shula laughs at her cousin as she pores over the photos. "Look! They have a ballroom! And look at this lounge! This is luxurious! Try to get a picture in one of those chairs, okay?" Shula pulls the brochure closer to see.

"Miriam! That's the First-Class lounge! I don't think I'll be sitting there often, if at all."

"Oh, who knows? Maybe you'll meet a nice man onboard who happens to be rich? But you have to promise me something — " Miriam puts her hand on Shula's arm. "You cannot marry anyone who keeps you away from here. You hear me? These girls need their Doda Shula, right?" Shula leans over and hugs her cousin.

"You know I'll be back, Miriam. How could I not?" She reaches over and takes the baby from Miriam's arms. "And how could I stay away from this beautiful baby?" Shula kisses the baby's head and feels a rush of unreality. It scares her to think that the next time she sees this baby she will be running around on her own two feet.

Later that week she spends a whole day standing in lines to get the paperwork for her travel documents. She isn't happy with her photo, her lips don't look right, but there is no time to change it now. It isn't like she will be displaying it on a mantel for all to see, she reminds herself. Even with her disappointment at the photo, being the first one of her friends to get this document makes her a bit of a celebrity. She loves pulling it out to show people, and each time she takes a moment to look at the light green cover while running her finger along the words printed up front: *The State of Israel, Ministry of Immigration,* followed by the French *ÉTAT D'ISRAEL, MINISTÈRE DE L'IMMIGRATION.*

Miriam brings over a copy of the February 1949 issue of *Vogue,* and together they examine each picture. Shula's own wardrobe is paltry and cheap next to the amazing spring looks from designers like Dior and Givenchy. She likes the spring dresses in a photo shoot from Peru, but with clothing rationing in full force now, she will have to make do with what she has in her closet. She spends days agonizing over what clothes to bring. Will she look like a country bumpkin in a gingham print dress? Or is she a sophisticated woman in all black? Can she fit in? Can she compete? Will she look Israeli to Americans? She can't wait to find out.

The night before she leaves, her mother throws a party at the apartment on Melchett Street. The place is crowded with her family, including Sabbah Dubno, her mother, Yisrael, cousin Miriam and her children, her husband Zalman, Aunt Sarah, and her roommate Naomi. Lilach is there, fresh off the bus from her new home on a kibbutz in the south. The table is covered with plates of food: sunflower seeds, olives, pickles, hummus, pita bread, salad, hardboiled eggs, sliced salami and more. For hours, the family sits and talks about the past, about the future, about life and their family. Neighbors and friends stop by to say hello, and then later, good-bye. Shula feels overwhelmed and from moment to moment her mood shifts. One moment, she is elated talking about her upcoming classes, then she catches her mother's eye and she is on the verge of tears.

Her cousins from their farm in Rishpon arrive with eggs smuggled out of their chicken coops.

"You know, the inspector paid us a visit just yesterday — " her cousin Aryeh says.

"Ha! They were going through my store today! It's crazy! They're treating the citizens of this country like criminals," Mr. Abramowitz from the corner store pipes in. Aryeh lifts the flat of eggs out of the box where they'd been concealed.

"Yes, it's hard on everyone right now, but this family has not had a reason to celebrate in a long time, and Shula," he said hugging her, "Rationing be damned. You are worth the risk." Rachel swoops in and kisses her cousin while taking the eggs from him.

"And that's not the only thing we have to celebrate today!" cries Sabbah Dubno. "Ladies and Gentlemen! May I have your attention please!" Shula turns to face her grandfather, who holds his glass of wine up high. "Today, July 20, 1949, is a special day. Not only is our beloved Shulamit going off on a grand adventure tomorrow, a trip that will take her to America, to the hallowed halls of the Manhattan School of Music and a new chapter in her life, but Syria has signed an armistice agreement with Israel." The crowd bursts into applause. A couple of the men whistle in approval, and Shula covers her ears at the harsh sound. "Today marks a new beginning not just for this young talented woman, but for our young country. Yes, peace will come to our land. This is only the beginning." Sabbah Dubno reaches out for Shula and she hugs her grandfather close. Family and friends burst into applause. Shula feels her cheeks flush, then the heat flows through her whole body. The feeling of impending doom has subsided to the point that she can say that she is hopeful. And for the first time in more than a year, Shula is happy.

THE END

ACKNOWLEDGMENTS

Writing this book took many people who encouraged, read, and critiqued the manuscript as I wrote and rewrote again and again. These are some of the people who helped me along the way.

India Hayford found the photos of my mother's Yemenite, Arab and Bedouin dress collection online, secured a grant, and drove out to California from Wyoming (with her dog) to photograph the pieces for an article in *Needle Arts* magazine. She was the first to encourage me to write my mother's story.

Neva Chonin gave me confidence in my writing (you don't know how much that means to me); Marsha Heckman, my friend and surrogate mother, spent countless hours line-reading every page of this book. I am forever grateful for her help in bringing my mother's story to life.

I am also grateful to the Sea Ranch Writing Group with Marsha Heckman and Miki Raver, where the writing began, and to our generous hostess, Susan Pollard; to the women of my writing circle (Pamela Wilding, Cordie Traber, Miki Raver, and Marsha Heckman) who were with me at the inception of this project and supported me through early drafts; the Pelican Inn writing group (Nina Vincent-Pearlman, Kasey Corbit, Sharon Mercer, and Jeb Harrison) who helped me immeasurably with their comments and patience with my rewrites (and also their wine); to Brooke Warner, who helped me take the seemingly disparate bits and pieces of writing and taught me how to shape it into a novel; to Mary Eisenhart, editor extraordinaire, formatting whiz, and a woman of great patience, who gently teased through my final manuscript with a fine-toothed comb; to Megan Brodkey, who so graciously gave it a final edit.

Thanks to my friends and relatives who read pieces and versions of the book and helped with translating documents: Julie Gordon, Bunny Alexandroni, Gitit Banai, Robyn Tal, Tana Coman (extra thanks for the cover art!), Pamela Gentile (extra thanks for the author photo!), and the *Sabras* I interviewed: Ruthie Dubno Shmueli, Esther Herlitz z"l, Dedi Ben Yehudah, Shulamith Eisenstadt, Shoshana Weiner, Rivka Shmueli, and Tiva Hershman.

My husband and son, Wally Brill and David Neiman-Brill, supported me through years of writing in fits and starts, but always believed that I had this book in me. I love you. To my sisters, Rachel Neiman and Becky Neiman: Thank you for sharing this rocky ride with me and supporting me and this project with stories, connections, editing and research.

You never stop missing your mother.

About the author:

Rina Z. Neiman's mother, Shulamit Dubno Neiman, was one of the first generation of modern-day Israelis. Growing up in the suburbs of Boston, Rina watched her mother sing and play the guitar, representing Israel at cultural events in the area. It was her mother who instilled in Rina a deep appreciation for the land and people of Israel.

Rina lives with her husband and son in Marin County, CA. This is her first novel.

Cover photographs from the collection of Shulamit Dubno Neiman.

Cover art by Tana Coman.

Author photo by Pamela Gentile.

"*Shir Haemek*" © Rafael Elias and Acum.

"Shoshana" © Hayim Hefer and Acum.

83535963R00158

Made in the USA
San Bernardino, CA
27 July 2018